M· At Port Maria

*G*eorges *C*arrack

Neville Burton '*Worlds Apart*' Series

Volume 3

Story by Georges Carrack, 1947-

Cover design by Joshua Courtright
Cover art: Square topsail schooner sketch by Henry Culver ("The Book of Old Ships") with permission from Dover Publications; modified for this cover by Joshua Courtright.

Print ISBN: 978-0-9906492-7-4
E-Book ISBN: 978-0-9906492-6-7

The Neville Burton Worlds Apart Series by Georges Carrack:
1. The Glorious First of June
2. A Journal of the Experiment at Jamaica
3. Mutiny at Port Maria
4. The Stillwater Conspiracy
5. The Atlantic Campaign

Available in paperback or e-book on Amazon

Visit our website at www.CarrackBooks.com

v-1.3 (modified Cover)

A Story for

Liane

The author wishes to recognize the efforts of and thank people who were extremely helpful in accomplishing the publication of this book:

- My wife, Carolyn, for her continuous patience and ideas,
- Joshua Courtright for cover design,
- The group of willing "Beta Readers" who provided guidance on the story line,
- All those authors of this genre who have gone before, providing the inspiration and a basic understanding of life on a British warship in the Napoleonic era, and
- The internet and its contributors, without which/whom the original research necessary to complete such a tale would have been enough to stall my effort.

This is a work of fiction. It is historical fiction, however, and many ships, captains, places and time references are set closely within the actual time of their occurrence. The protagonist and his family, friends and most close associates are fictitious. While some character names, ship names and locations that appear in this work may be found in historical documents, the specific incidents and events depicted in the story and the names of all characters, historical or otherwise, are used fictionally. Any resemblance to businesses or companies is also fictional and entirely coincidental.

Table of Contents

Notice to Readers:

Please take note that the reference materials indicated above may be of help to your understanding of this story.

Mutiny At Port Maria

The Neville Burton 'Worlds Apart' Series

Volume 3

1: *Welcome to The Elephant*

Lieutenant Neville Burton did not dally in London, as many might have done, but took the first available coach for England's South Coast after his unavoidable visit to Whitehall. Neither did he stop in Plymouth. By the time he reached the top of *HMS Elephant's* accommodation ladder the dirty little shore boat that had carried him out was already raising its frayed sail for the short return skip across the harbor. Pleased that he had made no gaffe that would earn him the sneers of a score of seamen watching him arrive, he stretched himself upwards and turned aft to salute the colours. The ship's jerk at her anchor cable, unexpected in the mild weather, took his feet out from under him, landing his face near a pair of freshly blacked shoes. He scrambled to his feet to see an officer of similar age grinning at him.

"Welcome to *HMS Elephant*. She does that now and again," the officer said, "Quite strange, really."

The two men exchanged a quick touch of hats and examined each other. A loud clunk behind gave Neville the knowledge that his sea chest had come aboard. "Lieutenant Burton reporting for duty," he said, wondering whether the other's smirk was the sign of a good nature or the enjoyment of another man's distress. His mind began quickly reevaluating his situation, wondering whether this man was simply the officer of the day or his superior, and whether he would enjoy this cruise or if this ignominious beginning foretold more.

"Get that chest below, Arthurs," commanded the officer, also a lieutenant, to a seaman who appeared from some hiding place forward.

To Neville, he asked, "Are you new?" His smile had not vanished, but it had gone sideways. Neville would liken it more to a sneer than a smile. He was an extremely tall man; almost a head taller than Neville, who stood to a fathom himself. On first glance, one might have described him as thin, but that incorrect supposition would be drawn more from proportion than reality. His face had a French look to it, with close-set eyes, a long thin nose, and hair greased to his head and worn shorter than the more common style of the day's British navy. He completed his appearance with an impeccable uniform, including a hat which must have been new, with nary a dent or salt stain on it.

"New? New to *Elephant*? Yes, of course."

"New to the sea. Is this your first ship?"

"First…?" Neville began in an incredulous tone. He didn't know this man's status aboard, but Neville's stumble was not a call to be rude. No lieutenant in the British Navy could be new to the sea. There were prerequisites. Neville noticed the shore boat skipping gaily home across the harbor with its sail ballooned out to leeward. His neck prickled at this officer's tone, but he decided that no first meeting should be a place for an argument. "No, not at all," he said, forcing a polite manner over his annoyance. He could have bragged about his exploits, which might in all probability exceed this fellow's, but some of them he couldn't admit. It wasn't the time or place, at any rate. "I've just been ashore awhile."

"Very well, then. I'm First Lieutenant Aderlay." He emphasized the word 'First', and spoke with a high-born London accent. "You're Burton, you say? I believe you're third, Lord help us. Captain Foley expects his officers will set the example. We shall sail on fifth October to meet the fleet 'round the bend at Torbay." With that, he turned on his heel and walked away. Third Lieutenant Neville Burton, as he apparently would serve, stood blinking in the morning sun. No greeting offered. No handshake. No useful information. *He's a cheery piece of work.*

"They've kept us busy, I'll say that," commented Neville to Fifth Lieutenant Corbatt when a rare moment found them leaning against the gunwale and staring toward town. England lay to the north and east of them like a green blanket with a smudge. The smudge was Plymouth. On this fall day the chill wind, though light, carried a damp edge 'round from the Channel. The sun shone hard and bright, but without much warmth. Neville wondered if he would ever feel warm again. Little of the scene before him should remind him of Jamaica, but somehow it did - simply being at anchor in a bay with a town in the distance, most likely. "I don't see a single shore boat coming at us. It feels like we've emptied the storehouses of Plymouth."

Corbatt, a stout, un-handsome lad in a rumpled uniform, responded, "Me neither, but I don't think Lt. Aderlay approves of taking a minute to think." He turned his head to look at Neville, studying his face closely, observing a few small scars and the surprisingly lifeless bright blue eyes. Probably looking for signs that his minor complaint against the First Lieutenant would not be taken as mutinous, but he asked, "You all right, sir?"

Neville was his superior, if only by date of service. In comparison to the husky, handsome Neville Burton, now wearing a new uniform, the casual observer would probably also assign Corbatt the rank of toad. Neville did not know Corbatt any more than Corbatt knew him, even after two weeks in the same mess. Less maybe, since Neville kept to himself when he could.

Neville shot the man a glance, trying to remember what he had observed of the fifth lieutenant. He'd kept a weary but careful eye on the ship's officers. As fifth of six, with that poetry-spouting senior Marine Lt. who attended their mess, he was often talked over by the senior warrants and the other lieutenants as if he weren't there. Fifth and Sixth got little attention. *They are probably better off than they would be if I talked up in addition to all the others, but I've no need to join in all that babble...* Anyway, none of them had been allowed much time for idle chat over the last few weeks of furious completion where *HMS Elephant* lay to her best bower in Cawsand Bay in the south of England. The loss of Maria had not left him yet; not in a mere month or two.

"What do you mean 'all right?'"

"Don't mean no offense, Sir. You seem uncommon sad." He stopped there.

Neville thoughtlessly sucked on a tooth while pulling his watch from his trouser pocket. He flicked it open and felt his stomach turn as his eyes traveled to the inscription rather than the time: 'Capt. Nev. Burton – With all my love, Maria, 1691'. They had become lost in each other, and yet only these few months later he could not recapture her laugh; the laugh that had captivated one wardroom after the next in Jamaica. If only he could see the twinkle in those eyes, hear that laugh, and feel her strength – the strength that he knew would carry him forward for the rest of his life... He awoke some nights reaching for her hand as he watched her swallowed by the earth itself. In those moments he called her name and felt the building falling upon him; the moment in which he knew he could never reach her – could never touch her again. He stared silently at the engraving for a few seconds.

"It's all right, Lt. Corbatt," he said. "I'll come 'round in time. I've lost a pregnant wife three months ago. A rare beauty, too." He added to that in a harder tone before turning to walk off, "Don't pass it 'round. I don't need sympathy."

"No, Sir," Corbatt said to Neville's back.

Now off watch, Neville retreated to his cabin, considering writing a letter to his mother up north in Bury St. Edmunds. Methodically he retrieved a piece of paper and a quill, but the ink well eluded him. As he had done yesterday, he sat on his cot and reviewed his thoughts. He remembered his conversation in the Royal Navy Office at Whitehall before taking the coach here.

"Are you up to it, Neville?" the tall wiry man, now with a light dusting of white hair at the temples, had inquired of the young officer opposite his expansive desk. He had just given a brief description of an ill-defined mission. "I can't tell you how to accomplish it. On the surface it's simple, but the doing of it is rather sticky, I'm afraid."

"Yes, but only the wearer knows where the shoe pinches," Neville had mumbled to the table. He'd raised his red-eyed face to stare for a few seconds into the eyes of his mentor; then more robustly answered, " 'Where there's a will, there's a way', they say, don't they?" They stood and shook hands. Sir William Mulholland then did something very unusual for the Navy Office: he came around the desk to give Neville a short but tight embrace. Neville had returned the affection and walked out without further words.

The paper lay unmarked when the boatswain's mates piped hands to dinner – the inkwell not found.

When Neville entered the wardroom, his eyes surveyed the scene. The sixth lieutenant, a portly fellow, and one whose name Neville had yet to remember, was seated quietly at his place next to the table's foot. Lt. Darbin of the Marines stood behind his chair licking his lips, his eyes fixed on the decanter of Madeira wine. Neville was earlier than usual, it appeared, being the fourth to enter.

I'm in a strange mood, I am, thought Neville. *Unlike the gunroom on my Experiment, this wardroom has room to walk about when we're all seated, and the fresh air blowing through from the Channel is a damn sight cooler than the stifling heat of Jamaica. I should make more effort to enjoy it.*

Second Lieutenant Goodwyn, a prodigious fellow with mottled red skin and a bulbous nose, was already at the table. He would have started eating, Neville assumed, if it had been within his power to do so. Despite being seated, he was obliged - as were the rest of them - to wait for First Lieutenant Aderlay, and would be required to stand when the man arrived. "Well, Lieutenant Burton," he began in a voice louder than needed in a room containing only four people. "What graces us with your presence at such an early hour? Are you finally hungry?"

Neville shuffled down the row of chairs to his place, and paused there. He looked Goodwyn in the eye and said, "I couldn't find my inkwell."

The conversation, if it could be called such, was cut short by the entrance of Aderlay himself, followed closely by every other member of *HMS Elephant's* wardroom mess.

"We're all here, I see," said Aderlay, running his eyes around the faces looking his way and stopping at the sight of Neville, "Even Lieutenant Burton, for all love. Will you give us the loyal toast, then?"

The wine being passed, poured, stoppered and drunk, Aderlay called immediately for a second toast – this one to their progress rather than the King. "Raise your glass to being completed. Captain Foley has declared that we shall leave this wretched harbor and sail in two days for Torbay."

The noise level of the room increased immediately as the men congratulated each other on the end of a tedious time, and Lt. Darbin jumped to his feet. "I've saved a poem for this moment," he announced, pulling a paper from his tunic.

"If you must, sir, spout on," said Fourth Lt. Kargrave.

> *"We've trained and strained and far much more*
> *Prepared we are now to sail away*
> *Leaving behind the safety of shore*
> *To defend his majesty's kingdom..."*

The poem continued for another three stanzas. His mind drifted off during the recitation, but he made note of his surprise at the patience exhibited by the company - no one interrupted.

"Lieutenant Darbin," offered Kargrave upon pronouncement of the last word, "It may be wondrous fine sentiment, but it does not even rhyme. What kind of a poem is that scratching?" Kargrave's insult caused the room to erupt in raucous laughter. He had early gained status as Aderlay's lickboot, and Neville assumed the first lieutenant encouraged his ungentlemanly behavior. Neville did not join the merriment. He looked down the table to see Aderlay congratulating Kargrave on his cleverness. He also noticed that Second Lieutenant Goodwyn did not join in the laugh, but rather wore a very disturbed look.

Darbin dejectedly plunked himself down in his chair. "It's open rhyme, you ignorant bastards," he bellowed. "You lot don't appreciate poetry beyond your primary school reading slates."

Neville kept his tongue, as he normally did, allowing him the luxury of observing the other members of the mess. They rarely bothered him beyond the occasional request to pass the peas or salt. He had, during these several weeks past, demonstrated his nature as a singular individual. *True*, he reflected, *the loss of Maria had made him what most would describe as morose.* Previously he had been a cheerful, enthusiastic officer. He had used his capabilities to rise to the rank of acting captain on the Jamaica station, commanding his own frigate, the *Experiment*. He had met her, courted her, and loved her there in Jamaica. He felt a solitary tear ooze from his left eye and quickly dabbed it with his cloth. He looked up to see Corbatt looking his way, but ignored it. *Damn.*

Few more incidents of extraordinary nature occurred at this day's mess. Both the doctor beside him and Darbin were quick on the wine. The latter more so today, it seemed - probably due to the rejection of his literary art. The fifth and sixth lieutenants were talking to each other, at least. Fourth Lt. Kargrave, that toady with a sideways smile that rivalled Aderlay's, continued his usual pretense of being Aderlay's equal, even though his official status, as determined by date of service, would always remain below Neville's. Neville thought the man looked an odd assortment of parts. His somewhat asymmetrical face exhibited plump cheeks and a boyish smile below a narrow forehead, deeply furrowed brows, and angry black eyes that Neville couldn't read. *Perhaps he and Aderlay have a common bond in a London heritage*, Neville thought, *their speech is certainly similar. He keeps his uniform similarly straight, as well.*

"Look what we have here," exclaimed Goodwyn when the meal began to arrive. "It's a sumptuous feast indeed. Fresh pork with a mint sauce, fresh country cabbage leaves and... ahhh... venison with sliced apples."

Neville noticed one of his favorites arriving - sand dabs.

"To what do we owe this pleasure?" asked the sixth lieutenant.

"Something I ordered for our little celebration of completion, of course," answered Aderlay.

"With all this," announced Doctor Ladley, who had apparently decided that the event required him to top it the raconteur, "I must treat you all to a description of the time I saved the wife of an Indian rajah. It was in…" he began with a flourish of his hands – one of which still held his wine glass.

As his next, Neville received the major share of flying Madeira in his lap. The table went quiet, and Neville looked up from brushing droplets of the red liquid off his trousers to see all eyes on him. He knew instantly that his history with them as a recluse brought with it their curiosity. Lt. Aderlay would have exploded into cursing rage. Kargrave would more than likely have thrown wine back at the doctor. Darbin would have rushed from the room in ruined dejection despite the rough-and-tumble image the Marines must uphold. Goodwyn, despite his rank, and Fifth Lieutenant Corbatt would undoubtedly have sat timidly before their betters and endured the remainder of the meal silently.

They want a show, Neville thought. *They have no idea what I'll do. I will deny it them.*

"I'll thank you to wax less eloquent with the completion of your anecdote, Doctor," said Neville with a thin smile. "And I hope the rest of your story does not involve wine…

"Lt. Goodwyn, the mint jelly, please," he concluded.

"Remember to change into clean stockings before the ship's crew see you, Lt. Burton," sniped Aderlay. The useless remark turned the table – that had begun to resume its gaiety - quiet once again as Burton and Aderlay stared into each other's eyes.

"I certainly will, Lieutenant Aderlay. I see you have a bit of the doctor's story on your cuff that you might mind, as well… Jelly, please, Lt. Goodwyn."

In the following silence, Goodwyn passed the mint jelly.

2: *Passage to Anger*

HMS **Elephant** and her fleet rolled sleepily at the Kattegat anchorage for Copenhagen, Denmark. Neville, off watch and taking an unusual moment to lie in his bunk, endured the cramped space of his cabin alone with his dark thoughts: *I still can't believe she is gone from me. Only a few months ago we rode in the warm summer rain of Jamaica and planned our wedding. I can see her twinkling brown eyes and dark soft hair, but I am forgetting the warmth of her lips on mine. I must find a way back to Jamaica to find her – and my child. What is it? Boy or girl? What silly rubbish. They're dead.* **Dead!** *That's enough. This useless musing only makes me worse. A bit of chilly Baltic air might clear my head.* He rose and trudged up the main companionway to see Second Lieutenant Thomas Goodwyn at the starboard rail watching the sun set over Sweden.

"I am beginning to think diplomats are lower than the lily-livered Danish Navy, Neville," said Lt. Goodwyn when Neville joined him. "What say you?"

"I'm not sure I take your meaning, Thomas. What have they done to you?"

"They haven't done anything, and that's exactly my point. How many months have we taken in preparation to come here; then loading these diplomat sheep aboard, and then waiting for them to come back from their delicate deliberations? I picture them drinking wine and eating feasts and talking amongst themselves with no expectations of creating a truce, let alone a peace, as long as their deliberations can continue. If we leave it to them, they'll run this year of 1801 into the next with naught to show for it. Rumor has it that there a council of war was held yesterday aboard the *St. George*, and these same bloody diplomats gave out that the Danish Crown Prince is openly hostile to Britain. The damned Danish are not going to withdraw from their Confederation with France and, worse yet, they are strengthening their defenses at Copenhagen."

"I'd heard that last bit."

"Nelson's *St. George* is cleared for action, for all love, but in the meantime we languish here at the Outer Deep. Look, it's March already. Have you been on blockade duty before, Lt. Burton? I think you must have been if you're in this navy. At least on a blockade we have something to do, even if it's to and fro, back and forth."

Neville's friendship with the second lieutenant had increased considerably. True enough, he was always anxious for the next meal. The man might be corpulent to the point of inability to go aloft, but his division functioned well, his decisions seemed almost infallibly appropriate, and his temperament was more to Neville's liking than the pompous Aderlay.

"Oh, no. I'd rather this. I've been on blockade at Toulon and in the Channel, and I'll take this. I expect we'll not be here long, anyway, if your rumor is true."

Able seaman Moorton approached from behind. He seemed a bit ill at ease in the presence of two lieutenants together, and so removed his hat and knuckled his forehead. "Excuse me, Sirs," he said," I don't wish to interrupt, but I've been sent with Captain's Compliments to Lieutenant Burton here and would he please lay aft."

"Thank you Mr. Moorton. He'll go straight off," said Goodwyn. To Neville, he said, "I shan't guess what that's about, but see if you can find out anything about that rumor. Captain Foley is Nelson's chum, sure. He led Nelson's attack at the Nile, you know. He'd know if anyone does."

Neville's stomach pinched as he walked aft and reported to the captain's sentry. Being called to the captain, if you weren't First Lieutenant or Sailing Master or one of those others who had regular business with him, carried with the summons an ominous edge. After being announced and admitted, Neville crossed the room to stand before the great man with his hat under his arm. The spacious room sparkled of polished silverware and brass lamps and smelled of coffee and cigars. Captain Foley sat at a large desk facing the entry. His head remained down and he continued writing. His clerk rose from a seat next to the desk as Neville entered.

Lieutenant Neville Burton made a reasonably impressive young officer. He wasn't one of those who never had a piece of lint on his uniform or a hair out of place, but whenever the situation allowed – such as life on a seventy-four – he kept himself tidy and close-shaven – unrumpled. He kept his light brown hair combed back into a pony tail in the fashion of the day, and tied it with the customary black grosgrain ribbon. Neville had gained the height of six feet as a Midshipman on the frigate *Castor* some years ago and had filled out well. He might be described as 'sturdy' rather than 'stocky', but certainly not 'heavy'. His horrible left-handedness didn't show, of course. Neither did his financial status. He kept a hoard of money in Hoare's Bank on Fleet Street from previous prizes that would astound most captains, but he would never divulge that. Neville also had little in the manner of 'interest' – that critical patronage of some senior officer, royal, or political figure – that he could speak of. His mentor – a family friend at Whitehall – had already done much for his career, although entirely behind the scenes. Even at his young age, Neville had begun learning the advantages of keeping one's self private.

Captain Foley looked up. "Lieutenant Burton, I need to know if there is a problem between you and our first lieutenant."

Neville looked back through startlingly blue eyes, saying, "No, Sir. Certainly not. Why would you ask such a thing?"

"Because what I see does not agree with what he tells me. What I see is the best-prepared division aboard; always in order, top gun performance, and faster than Corbatt's starboard watch on sail handling. Despite what Lt. Aderlay tells me, I have noticed it. On the other hand, you never, ever put up a man for punishment. Why is that, then?"

"I don't believe in using the cat if it's not needed, Sir," said Neville, straightening his back, "Fairness in all things is my view of command. The men will do right by the officers if the officers do right by their men. You just said we are the ship's best division, a compliment for which I thank you. Why would I send up a man who does his best for some petty infraction of a rule?"

"I have no idea where you get such ridiculous notions. Lt. Aderlay has passed on Kargrave's word that you bribe your men to do their duty, Burton. He says you are too soft to punish a man. Do you not believe in the cat as a way to keep your men in line?"

"I just told you I do not, Sir."

"I don't appreciate your tone, lieutenant. Do you accuse your fellow officer of being a liar?"

"I have said no such thing. As to the punishment issue, every man is entitled to his opinion. As to the bribery, he is certainly misinformed, or himself lied to. I am surprised that the first lieutenant would pass forward such a rumor with no proof to it. Has he some stuff he would offer as proof, Sir?"

"If he does, I've not seen it."

"Call my men yourself, Sir, without me present. Ask them."

"I'll do as I wish without your suggestions, Burton. Don't be impertinent. Would that do any good? If Kargrave's accusations were true, your men would lose their allowances without you. They are biased."

"Call the men of another division, then, and ask them. Every man jack aboard knows everything the other knows."

"Thank you, Burton. I'll do that. But that will be the last suggestion you give me without my request. And Burton, Admiral Nelson himself is moving his flag here from the *St. George* tomorrow, so don't you let your division slouch. If a man needs the cat, he needs the cat. Don't be so damn soft."

"I would never, Sir. If I might add, Sir, Kargrave has his ambition, which is fair enough in the service; but I submit that he has a promotion to gain if he can discredit me. I apologize that this disgrace would take any of your time at all, Sir."

"All rubbish. Dismissed"

"Midshipman Bomford's been called to Foley's cabin, Neville," said Goodwyn to Neville as Mr. Wrey - the boatswain - and his mates piped hands to breakfast the next day. "He's Corbatt's, ain't he?"

"He is. The ordinaries are expecting a great merriment at the punishment of a midshipman, but I assume same as you - that Bomford is Captain's choice for a *cheese eater* on the truth of Kargrave's bloody lies."

"Yes. I don't envy him, but he's a good man for it. He usually stays above all that tomfoolery in the Mids' berth, and he's got no favor I know of from either Kargrave or me. I must apologize to you, Thomas. I never should have told you of this. You needn't be in the middle of it."

"Knowing don't put me in the middle, but it's good to know your First Lieutenant's character. I'd prefer one I could trust." He jerked his thumb over his left shoulder. "That was quick. Look there."

Midshipman Bomford emerged shortly from the captain's cabin and began making his way directly for the main hatch. Even from their position at the foremast bitts, they could sense his distress. His face was ashen and he looked about furtively three or four times in fifty paces before disappearing below.

"Whatever the captain said scared him, I'd say. Excuse me Neville. I think I'll go ask him about it."

"I'll be interested to hear what he has to say. I guess I'll go write the letter I've been putting off."

Below, in the dim light of his cabin, Neville found his paper and quill, and this time also his blotter and inkwell. He intended to write home again. He didn't write often, but his mother would worry if no letter came. She would be angry if letters weren't fairly regular, and he had no reason to anger his mother.

HMS Elephant, The Kattegat   *24 March, 1801*

Dear Mum,

We are quiet now, but things may change. I have it direct from Captain Foley that Admiral Nelson himself will move his flag aboard us today. They say he…

A noise in the next cabin distracted him. A rat? He hated the rats. No, not rats – the door of the next cabin scraping across the floor and closing. Neville put his quill down to avoid dripping ink while he listened. Hushed voices followed.

"Ee's told ... men hear nothing of Burton bribing ... division." The voice was Aderlay's and the cabin next door belonged to Kargrave. The cabin walls were canvas, after all. The men certainly would not have met there if they had known Neville was about.

The next quiet voice was indeed Kargrave. "... have him up on charges within the week... show the child ... or two about ... navy works."

Aderlay again: "... it good."

The sound of the door again.

Neville sat quietly for a few minutes, pondering his options. This was not how he wanted the navy to work, although he had known many an instance when it did.

He finished his letter home and went up to find Goodwyn.

The day of Admiral Nelson's arrival, resplendent with marines and sideboys in their best, drummers drumming, boatswains whistling and Neville at attention with the other officers, had come and gone by two when the fleet raised anchors to approach the Danish coast.

"We'll be going in close to Copenhagen to inspect their defenses and replace channel marking buoys they have removed to dissuade us. For that, we'll take the launch and the pinnace with the sailing master in one and the gunner in the other. Lt. Burton, you'll have the launch, and Lt. Goodwyn, the pinnace. Choose yourselves a dozen good men each for departure directly after dinner." Always a terse fellow, Lt. Aderlay's instructions contained no more useful information.

Mr. Wrey had his party ready at the boats when ordered. Lt. Kargrave, Officer of the Watch, was personally standing by to give the order, "Launch the pinnace, Bo'sun."

"Aye, Sir," Wrey said quietly to Kargrave; then turned and bellowed to his crew: "Sway up."

The pinnace rose three feet from its cradle, then five.

A young voice rang out from the deck to larboard: "Hold! Vast hauling!"

"Who countermands my order?" yelled Kargrave. "Is that you Bomford?"

"Aye sir, there's…"

"Gross insubordination! Put that man in irons," screamed Lt. Aderlay, who had been climbing the quarterdeck stair. "Take him away now."

"But the tackle is…" began Midshipman Bomford.

"Now, I said. Take him away now!"

Kargrave reinforced his order: "Marines, do your duty."

The startled men on the lifting cables paused, and at a hand gesture of the boatswain, the pinnace dropped clumsily into its cradle. While both Aderlay and Kargrave were intent on watching Midshipman Bomford being gathered up by the marines and hustled down the main hatch, the boatswain's men swarmed onto the boat, removing and replacing the lifting tackle in moments. The pinnace rose again as ordered.

Aderlay's sideways smile grew larger as Midshipman Bomford disappeared below. Kargrave's equally sinister grin reflected the sentiment.

On punishment day, the event was described again. Due to the activity of the days, Neville had not been able to gain access to

Captain Foley, who now read the charge: "Midshipman Bomford displayed direct insubordination to Lt. Kargrave when he countermanded his order to sway out the pinnace. Do you deny it, Midshipman Bomford?"

"No, but I had good reason. I was under order from my division commander, Lt. Corbatt, to ..."

"Do you have knowledge of this event, Lt. Corbatt?"

"I'm sorry, Sir, I do not. I was forward at the time, but I vouch for Mr. Bomford. He has always been..."

"Enough. Does anyone else speak for Midshipman Bomford?"

"I do," Neville called out.

"What say ye?"

"I say Midshipman Bomford did the right thing. The lifting tackles were broken. May I have a private word on the matter, Captain? I have attempted to see you about this these two days past."

"This is most unusual... but you may. We shall continue with the remaining crimes and deal with this matter on the next punishment day. Return Mr. Bomford to holding."

Immediately following the punishment session, which included one case of stealing rations from the crown, one of insubordination to Mr. Wrey that earned the man twenty lashes, and four counts of drunkenness, three lieutenants stood before their captain in his cabin.

"Whatever you have to say should be said in front of these two, I believe, Lt. Burton. I hope this isn't just an example of your reticence to use the cat. Go ahead."

"This was contrived, Sir. Not the specific event, but the result. I am truly loath to say it, but this was the retribution of Lieutenants Kargrave and Aderlay against Mr. Bomford for his witness to you in my defense."

"This is mutiny," said Aderlay. Kargrave simultaneously uttered, "I protest."

"Hold your tongues," said Captain Foley, holding up his palm to them, "You'll have your chance."

"How do you know what Mr. Bomford said to me, Lt. Burton?"

"I personally heard these two lieutenants conspire four days ago in the cabin next to mine, though they gave no plot for their retribution. They were both looking for any excuse at all to bring Mr. Bomford up on charges and deal with him harshly."

Neville turned to the other lieutenants, "…teach this child how the navy works, didn't you say?"

The two glanced at each other. Kargrave's plump cheeks reddened and his black eyes glimmered.

"As to the tackle, Sir, the entire ship knows, and I am neither the only witness nor the first to hear it the details. Lt. Goodwyn is aware of it all as well. I simply spoke first. Mr. Bomford did the right thing. He noticed a broken tackle block and called out to avast lifting. Had the order been followed, the launch would surely have been dropped and stove in. Neither Lieutenant Kargrave nor Aderlay asked a reason for the halt. The tackle was replaced immediately by Mr. Wrey's men while the lieutenants were watching Mr. Bomford being led away. Both Lt. Goodwyn and Mr.

Wrey will certainly corroborate my story. The tackle was replaced forthwith, as I said."

"There was no broken tackle," interjected Lt. Kargrave.

"Not now, lieutenant.

"Anything more, Lt. Burton?"

Captain Foley glared at the trio, "This is not over," he said after a moment. "I will investigate further, but right now I must see the Admiral over the side, and we will soon sail into battle. I need every good man in action, not stewing in holding – even Bomford. For now, I am sure you have scared the boy silly enough to toe his line, and I order you to see to your duties with the highest professionalism you can muster under the circumstances. Any more tomfoolery will be dealt with harshly. Dismissed."

Neville retreated below, again being off watch. He knew without question that he had made dangerous enemies. *Would the two have me knifed in my sleep? No. That would be too obvious. The captain would smoke that.*

He sat on the edge of his bed. He felt different this day than he did even in the morning.

I have been hiding, skulking, and pandering to my superiors, just like these diplomats in Copenhagen. It has taken this confrontation with Aderlay to bring me to my senses. Maria is gone from me, but it is not her fault she was struck down. How could I blame her? It is my own stupidity that I could even think of blaming her - the one I would love forever. It is me. I am the damnable beast. No, the damn time itself is my curse. I would beat it with a club, stab it with my sword and strangle it with my bare hands if there were anything to touch, but there is nothing. It has taken my Maria and she will never be at my side again. I have this loathsome toad, Aderlay, instead. It's him I should beat.

Neville felt himself grow hotter and could tell that his neck and face were red. He felt a pressure in his forehead. His hands clenched, and his left felt for his sword.

*Aderlay. Now there is something in this world worth beating. And
Kargrave as well. I will hold my tongue for the moment, but if those toads play
this game again they shall feel my wrath regardless of the consequences. What is
that hubbub above, now?*

The sound of the boatswain's pipe, calling for the ship to be
cleared for action, reached his ears. Even as he departed his cabin
for his action station at the main deck larboard guns the carpenter's
crew arrived to remove the officers' cabin screens. On deck, he
found the action seemed less frenetic. Aderlay had his stopwatch
on the procedure as directed by Captain Foley, but no attack by
another ship appeared imminent. It looked to be more of a drill,
although the ship would remain in this condition until a battle
began or the drill ended.

Neville had time to find Lt. Goodwyn standing by the
mainmast bitts. "What's this about, then, Thomas?"

"Not quite yet, Neville," he answered. Immediately the
sideboys and marines were called to pipe the side for Admiral
Nelson.

Immediately following Nelson's departure aboard the lugger
Skylark, Neville sought Goodwyn to ask, "Where's he going,
Thomas?" The small ship was already gaining speed toward shore.

"For a final reconnaissance of the enemy's defenses with some
of the other captains, as I understand it," Goodwyn answered, "and
then he'll go aboard the frigate *Amazon.* You see her waiting there,"
he said, pointing a chubby digit across the water. "It's 'hurry up and
wait' as always, you see. I must assume Nelson's expecting things to
happen quickly on his return, though, since he's had Captain Foley
clear us for action before he left."

"On that other thing, Thomas… Do you have an idea what's
just happened in the captain's cabin?"

"I've an idea, and I thank you for calling out. I must admit to a failure of character. I don't know if I would suffer the wrath of Aderlay very well."

"You'll be called about the tackle, I'm sure, as will Mr. Wrey. It's not your worry, but I don't know if the captain will stand behind his first lieutenant regardless of the evidence. In the meantime I have made enemies."

"**T**he wind is fair for us to approach the harbor," announced Sailing Master Shepps to nobody in particular. Neville and several other officers were gathered haphazardly on the quarterdeck to view the activity. In the early morning two days later, a chilly light wind blew from the southwest as a weak sun rise over the rocky coast of Sweden.

First Lt. Aderlay continued to keep his distance from Neville, which suited Neville just fine. Captain Foley had yet to pronounce a verdict on his deliberations.

"It's a sticky wicket we have here, I think," said Lt. Goodwyn to Neville. "The Swedes over there could shoot at us, and we might be in their range, since we've kept to their side away from the Danes. And their fleet – over there, I think that's them," he said, pointing to several anchored ships at several leagues distance near the Swedish coast. "They might come down on us, and there's that rumor of a Russian squadron just over in the Baltic, too."

"Aye, I agree that's them, but I see no activity there, and any Russians must be too far away to join in if we go at it soon. Admiral Parker's fleet between them and us should keep those swords in their sheaths, anyway. We were too far out for the guns of Kronborg to reach us as we passed by, so it'll be Trekroner and the Danish fleet. I think it will just be us going at the Danes since those insipid diplomats couldn't accomplish anything. I expect we'll hear the call to raise anchor any time now. It's time to get into it, Thomas. I, for one, will be happy to hear the guns. I am tired of sitting about."

"You seem agitated today, Neville."

"I am. Whatever it is, I think it's time for anger; time to stand up and fight." *I know what it is,* he thought. *It's that moronic Aderlay – not Maria. I can't beat him, but I can beat the Danes. I will get my relief somehow.*

Nelson himself appeared on deck with Captain Foley an hour and a half later.

"Call to action stations, Mr. Wren," yelled Aderlay moments later. "Heave the anchor short."

"Really, Neville? Today? Maundy Thursday?"

"Fine by me. Let's get at it."

Quiet changed to noisy efficiency. *How is it the first sound is always the stomping of the marines' boots?* Neville wondered. The slapping of hundreds of calloused bare feet and tramping at the capstan soon accompanied the marines' stomping. Men were swarming up the ratlines. Gun crews were organizing by their cannons and boys were sanding the decks. The clattering of marine sharpshooters taking their muskets into the tops added strange metallic sounds to the mix.

In what seemed only a minute or so Neville had moved to his station by the upper deck larboard forward guns.

"Straight up and down, Sir," Sixth Lieutenant Busby yelled from forward.

Neville knew the plan. *Elephant* would be last in line to sail up the channel inside middle ground and anchor opposite her Danish counterpart. Neville's anxiety increased. His hand fidgeted; his left repeatedly lifted his sword out of its scabbard an inch and dropped it back in. Not that he expected to use it for anything other than a signal. They should not be closing to board.

"This will be a very strange battle," Goodwyn had said. "There is no sea room here between the mud of middle ground and the Danish ships anchored off the strand. No strategy to gain the weather gage. No sudden tacking to rake the enemy from astern. Unless something unexpected happens, once we are in place it will be a cruel competition of cannon against cannon. We might get close enough for the marines in the tops to be effective, but otherwise, we'll just hammer at each other with the great guns."

HMS Amazon led the raising of anchors in the Outer Deep. *Agamemnon* and *Polyphemus* followed *Amazon's* intention to sail directly into the Royal Channel toward the Trekroner Fortress guarding Copenhagen's harbor.

Goodwyn crossed the deck to where Neville stood watching the movement.

"Raise anchor," cried Wren from the quarterdeck. Tramping at the capstan resumed, and sailing orders were bellowed. "See to the fore tops'l, Lt. Corbatt. Lively, there."

Isis, Glatton and *Ardent* had their anchors up, as did *Bellona* and *Russell.* Captain Riou's *Amazon* and a group of smaller ships of the squadron were among the forward group, but the position of any vessel less than a ship of the line was irrelevant. As long as Riou got his marines in to the shore to attack the fortress after the ships of the line had bombarded it, his duty would be served.

"What do you see there, Neville? It looks to me that *Agamemnon* is aground. She has not weathered the turn into the Royal Passage, has she?"

"I think not. Her sails are full, and there should be movement, but it appears there isn't any. See there: *Polyphemus* passes her now."

"So she does, and is taking fire." They heard the low thumping of cannon before clouds of white smoke erupted from the Trekroner fortifications, a shore battery on Amag Island to the left of Trekroner, a Danish ship they couldn't identify, and *HMS Polyphemus*.

"*Ardent* and *Glatton* are around the mud, and *Isis* has made the turn as well, Thomas, you see?" queried Neville.

"As long as the wind carries the smoke toward shore I can. All three have passed *Polyphemus*. That must be her station. She is anchored now, I believe. Neither *Russell* nor *Bellona* is moving, and that is surely not where they are intended to be. They're stuck on Middle Ground, you think?"

Elephant had sailed almost to gun range and would soon make the turn into the channel. "We had better be ready at stations, Neville," Goodwyn yelled over the noise of cannon fire from the others already engaged, "We're about to come under fire."

"Run out larboard!" screamed Aderlay.

Neville's time slowed to a crawl. His rage at the world took command of his soul, and he fought his guns as if the devil stood behind him. He descended into a world of smoke and noise – cannon fire and crashing timbers and screams of pain and death. *Elephant* anchored in approximately the center of Nelson's division between *Ganges* and *Glatton* and almost opposite the 60-gun *Dennebroge*. The cannon fire became furious; some ships sat at less than 50 yards from their opposites. Neville paced quickly back and forth behind his gun crews, avoiding fallen tackle and shards of wood while screaming exhortations at his men to work at their fastest.

He happened a glance at the quarterdeck where Captain Foley and Admiral Nelson stood. *What on earth?* wondered Neville. *Nelson is blind in his right eye. Why is he holding his glass to it? He's looking… aha, I see it now. Admiral Parker's flying number 39: 'leave off action'. Nelson's not having it. Hoorah.*

"Again, men. Boy! Get that rammer in there. Now!" he screamed, and hacked the rail with his sword.

"Gunboat!" he yelled, first at nobody. Because he had hacked at the rail and looked shoreward, he had seen it. Then he turned aft and, spying Lt. Kargrave descending the quarterdeck stair, he yelled again, "Kargrave Do you see it? The gunboat. A Danish gunboat in the water there, maneuvering to fire upon us! Are you blind, man?" *Or deaf, gormless, or a coward?*

"Do something! Get forward and have Lt. Busby put a foredeck gun on them! The swivel gun should do!"

Lt. Kargrave stood stupidly staring at Neville, not moving. *Isn't he supposed to be commanding the guns below? Where is the first lieutenant? Where is Aderlay? There, by the mainmast… doing what?*

Neville came to the realization that Aderlay was not being particularly useful, either. Although he had his sword out, as if to command a battery of guns, it was down at his side. Moreover, he was leaning against the mainmast on the side opposite the enemy. *Just taking a breather or sheltering? Hiding?* At that moment, Aderlay looked Neville's way. The two met eyes, and Neville knew. And he knew that Aderlay knew it. The man was hiding from the battle.

Already flushed from exertion, Neville felt his skin prickle red. A musket lay at his feet. From a dead marine? He seized it, checked its charge, and swung its barrel up past Aderlay. Slowly past Aderlay – the man's eyes went round - and then toward the gunboat. The boat was close enough to be within musket range, but Neville would never know if he hit anything. He stood up high above the rail and flung the weapon at it – no more than a gesture of rage.

No time for this twaddle. I must see to the gunboat, if no one else will! He beckoned Kargrave to come to him. To his surprise, Kargrave did so, stumbling stupidly twice over fallen rigging and slipping on blood. Over the tumult, Neville yelled, "Go forward to Busby. Point out the gunboat and have him aim the bow chaser there! The swivel gun, too. Do you understand me?"

"Aye. Gunboat. Bow chaser," said Kargrave, apparently without much perception.

Neville turned Kargrave by the shoulders and pushed him forward, "Get on!

"Second gun, there. What are you looking at? See to your gun!" Neville yelled, his attention now returned to his division.

An even more horrible explosion forward shuddered the ship. The gunboat had fired, and its huge 32-pound ball had carved a large jagged furrow in the foredeck, removed a big piece of the rail with it, and created a great curved gash in the base of the foremast. The foremast held. A blue-jacketed man was thrown aft and toppled over the foredeck railing into the waist an instant before the gunboat disappeared into splinters. The boat's crew – or parts of them – went into the water. The remainder of the boat, with its extremely heavy gun, sank at once like a rock.

That must have been Kargrave, but he couldn't even have got there yet. Busby must have seen the gunboat. I sent Kargrave to the wrong place at the wrong time. Is it my fault he's dead? He was a useless lickboot, in my opinion, but I didn't wish him dead.

Several Danish ships came loose of their moorings and began drifting with the wind and current between the Danish and British lines. Some were afire and had their colours down. For those he paused. Others came into the sights of his guns with their flags abroad, and those he showed no mercy. Neville's division fired their guns five times to the four of any other and by 2 in the afternoon they could not be stood by for the heat. His men were loyal to his commands despite his extreme behavior.

A huge explosion occurred aboard the *Dennebroge* and she soon began to list.

"Cease your fire, Lt. Burton," said Lt. Goodwyn. "She's done. You can see the men going in the water."

"Not 'till she's under," responded Neville. He turned to his guns and yelled, "Fire!"

"No, Neville. Stop. That's an order now!" yelled Goodwyn back at him. The two stood nose to nose and glared at each other.

"You're right, Thomas," said Neville, cooling surprisingly fast. "We have done our job…

"Stand down, men. Good work! I'll see you an extra tot for it!" His order brought a cheer.

By some means during the fighting that Neville had not cared to comprehend, several Danish captains had surrendered and been brought aboard. Some British captain whom Neville did not know left the ship soon after. Rumor had it that this captain had carried an offer from Admiral Nelson for a negotiated cease-fire. Sporadic cannon continued, however, between a few of the forward ships, the shore battery on Amag Island and the Trekroner fortress. White smoke told the tale of who was firing, but it was too far away to involve *Elephant*.

The noise of bombardment slowly died away and the focus of *Elephant's* crew turned to caring for the injured, setting the dead aside for burial, and ship repair. Shortly past noon, when the Trekroner fortress ceased firing, a Danish officer came aboard and stayed for about half an hour. Very soon after he left the captain's clerk appeared in front of Neville: "Captain's compliments, Sir, and all officers are to lay aft."

"They have surrendered to us," Captain Foley announced once they gathered. "That's the end of it, except for the Admiral concluding his negotiations and us cleaning up this mess and getting our ships afloat again. We've ourselves gone aground in this wretched mud, if you haven't noticed. It will be tomorrow before we have the butcher's bill from belowdecks, but I can tell you that we lost Lieutenant Kargrave. Cooper will put him in spirits for the passage home. We also lost Captain Riou of the Amazon and a great deal of his marines.

"As a side note, Tsar Paul of Russia was murdered by his court on twenty-fourth March. He is replaced by his son, whom I am told hates the French, so we are hoping that this damned French coalition with Holland will fall apart. We've done well here, and we've not lost a single British ship. We have taken eighteen or nineteen Danish ships, though. That's all I have now. Have your reports to me by noon tomorrow. Dismissed; except you, Lt. Burton. Please stay a moment."

The officers, to a man nearly exhausted, trudged out the captain's door. Neville, as tired as ever he could remember, waited without moving, but suddenly far more awake. This would not be a good time to have a conversation with the Captain of the Fleet. Neville began to sweat despite the chill air and he knew his cheeks were reddening. *Could this be the result of a complaint from Aderlay about the musket?*

"Come with me," said the captain, and exited his cabin.

Neville followed Foley to Admiral Nelson's quarters where they were admitted without challenge. Neville's anxiety increased as he neared the great man's desk. Nelson raised his head from his papers when he sensed their arrival.

"This is your man, Sir," said Foley. *I stand in front of cannons and the enemy's muskets and wave my sword without fear,* thought Neville, *yet I tremble before a single man.*

"So it is. What is your given name, Lt. Burton?" asked the admiral as he stood.

"Neville, Sir."

"From where?"

"Bury St. Edmunds, Suffolk, Sir."

"Suffolk, eh? My mother came from Suffolk. I'm a Norfolk man myself."

"Yes, Sir."

"I would shake your hand, Lieutenant Neville Burton, but I have only the left arm, as you know. You can't imagine what it's like to be left-handed."

Had he not been so tired and nervous, Neville certainly wouldn't have taken the liberty to offer anything not asked, but he said, "Oh, I can sir. I'm terrible left-handed myself. But I understand, Sir, and I am humbled by your compliment. To what do I owe such an honor?"

"To what? Your actions in the face of the enemy. I observed your zeal, your ferocity, your leadership. Your division is close to the best I've seen. I commend you for it. I believe Captain Foley will put a letter in your file."

"Thank you, Sir," he said, feeling the anxiety draining from him like water from a bucket. He knuckled his forehead to the Admiral.

"Thank you, Sir," said Captain Foley to Nelson.

To Neville, Foley said, "You are dismissed, Lieutenant."

Neville left the cabin; Admiral Nelson departed in his barge shortly thereafter, for negotiations with the Crown Prince of Denmark.

3: *A Short Encounter*

Only two days hence, a very similar scene repeated. Neville stood with Goodwyn at the larboard rail taking a breather and watching boat after boat rowing or sailing to and from the great city of Copenhagen. Again, the captain's clerk appeared in front of Neville: "Captain's compliments, Sir, and will you visit him in his cabin?"

"I wish you luck, Neville," said Goodwyn. "He's probably finally got back to 'the other thing'."

"Aye. Be sure to bring me something in the brig tomorrow," said Neville, trying to steel himself with a bit of wry humor.

He found First Lieutenant Aderlay in Captain Foley's cabin. Neither man looked the least bit amused.

"This will be short, Lt. Burton," Foley began. "As much as I hate to say it, I have put a letter of reprimand in my first lieutenant's file regarding the incident with Lt. Kargrave, may he rest in peace, and Midshipman Bomford. For Lt. Kargrave's part, I would have had him sent down if not for his connections, but it is moot now. You'll not speak of this, and I won't have my officers slinging words at each other, so the two of you step up now and shake hands."

When Foley had seen them do as he ordered, he continued, "I could not afford to make this judgment before the battle. All officers were needed, but now it's over. I expect the same continued loyalty and ardent and lasting exertion from the both of you, and, Lt. Burton, I will never hear you top it virtuous to my First Lieutenant Aderlay or the situation will reverse faster than you can say 'set ashore without pay'.

"We are finished, and I have the pusser's reports to review. Both of you – out."

Outside the cabin door, they turned opposite directions. Neville pulled a great breath and exhaled slowly.

"We have orders that I may make public," announced Lt. Aderlay to the assembled wardroom before dinner two weeks later. "First, you have seen the Admiral's goings and comings over the last week. I can announce that an armistice of fourteen days has been negotiated. With that confidence, our next duty will be to defend against a Swedish fleet which is rumored to be coming out. We set sail for the Baltic the day after tomorrow with seventeen sail of the line. That's the news for what it's worth, and you can tell it to anyone you want. Let's have the toast, shall we?"

It could be worse, thought Neville, remembering his time aboard the frigate *Stag* when she patrolled there back in 1795 and -6. *But it's a cold place.*

They returned to Copenhagen in three weeks. No Swede threat materialized, and the Russians were presumed to be set in the ice in the Gulf of Finland.

"I, for one, am glad to be back here out of the Baltic," said Corbatt to Neville as they approached the sandbanks of Copenhagen. "I think the cold has sunk into my very bones."

"I already hear we're not done with the Baltic, Lt. Corbatt, but it's almost summer. The ice will melt, ha, ha. But I'm glad to be here for a while, as well. We can send our letters home, and there's sure to be some come in. Here's the packet now, of all things. See it there?"

"Why going back?" Corbatt asked with a displeased look on his face.

"Nelson's in charge of it all now, as you've heard... or he soon will be. Something about going after the Russians at Tallinn because Admiral Parker refused to go. I would think such refusal would not go well for Parker. Even admirals have somebody to answer to."

On the sixth of May, Nelson hoisted his flag over *HMS St. George* as Commander-in-Chief. He immediately took the fleet to Tallinn at the mouth of the Gulf of Finland.

"There's naught here either, Neville," commented Goodwyn upon their arrival, "The Russians are just like the Swedish fleet."

"We came because we were led to believe the Russians were caught in the ice, you remember, but as we can see, there's no ice. The Russians have gone off to join the rest of theirs at St. Petersburg or somewhere, I suppose. Nelson's going into Talinn, though. More negotiating, I'd wager."

Three days later Nelson had completed his deliberations ashore and the fleet had set sail for their return to Copenhagen. Dinner the first evening at sea was slightly more spirited than it had been for the last month. After recovering from the exertions of battle and an odd grief at the loss of Lt. Kargrave from their table, the two back-to-back voyages into the Baltic had brought mostly un-satisfied anxiety. The future now held a prospect of some peace and possibly even movement to warmer climes.

Dinner being done, Aderlay motioned for Neville to wait. "Lt. Burton," he said, "Captain Foley requests you to stop in for breakfast."

"Why?"

"We'll discover that at two bells of the forenoon watch, I'm sure."

"Come!" yelled Aderlay when the captain's sentry announced Neville.

"Good morning, gentlemen," said Foley to the two lieutenants. "I shall first say that I hope to enjoy our breakfast. Please take seats there."

They passed pleasantries and Neville sat quietly while Foley and Aderlay had a short conversation about the condition of the ship's boats. The senior pair asked Neville's opinion when the talk turned to the toast and kippers but, for a while, they divulged no reason as to why he had been invited.

Finally, Captain Foley leaned over to Neville and said, "I am rather sorry to pronounce this order, but you are being transferred off this ship."

Aderlay said nothing, and did not appear to be at all surprised. If anything, he might have been stifling a smile.

After an uncomfortable short pause, Neville decided that although he had not actually been asked to speak, he would be allowed the obvious question: "Where to, Sir?"

"An unusual assignment, I must admit," said Foley. "I am loath to lose you, although we are all aware of the tension between you two lieutenants; such a thing is not good aboard any ship…"

And certainly not on his.

"Lt. Aderlay made the request for your transfer to another ship in the fleet…"

Aderlay winced, as if he had hoped the fact would never be known. *The weasel's afraid of me,* thought Neville. *He has a right to be, but he doesn't know me very well. I wouldn't bother with him at all if my career were at stake.*

"…and it was approved," continued Foley, "but then a very unusual thing happened… the transfer was rescinded and new orders arrived from the Navy Office – carried by the advice boat that just came yesterday - appointing you 'liaison to the Americans on the situation at the Barbary Coast'."

I smell Sir William Mulholland here. It moves me closer…

"You are to go aboard the *U.S.S. Boston,* presently somewhere in the vicinity of Algiers. Such orders being quite unusual, and since the fleet will sail soon to join the blockade at Toulon, Admiral Nelson himself was advised. He sends you his best wishes and a request that you might copy him with your reports."

"But…" began Aderlay. A glare from Foley silenced him.

"It would be my honor, Sir, and I shall certainly do so," said Neville. "When is this transfer to take place?"

"You are to leave on the first packet we can hail in Copenhagen. There is little of significance in your remaining aboard the *Elephant.*"

The little packet they found was a joy to be aboard. The experience of sailing a three-masted lugger was new for Neville and he found it a great amusement. *Lark* sailed like the wind. They quickly passed back through the Skagerrak, North Sea and English Channel, and the ship proved large enough to take the abuse of the Bay of Biscay. She was at times surprisingly tender, nonetheless, heeling quickly to a puff of wind that would scarcely be noticed by a seventy-four. As a supernumerary, Neville had no official function. He was welcomed as a volunteer officer of the deck whenever he wanted, however, as it gave the officers a bit more time asleep. Ushant and Finisterre fell behind, and in a scant three weeks, the great rock at Gibraltar loomed before them. They fell against a foul wind in the gut that persisted for three days. Despite the lugger's ability to claw upwind, another four days passed before they sighted a small Swedish fleet off the coast of Tripoli.

"What's this, Lieutenant Burton?" asked *Lark*'s commander.

"My briefing says the Americans are blockading the Tripoli harbor together with them – the Swedes. After what I heard in Copenhagen, I find that odd, but here in the Med 'the enemy of my enemy must be my friend', I suppose."

Lark carefully approached *Boston,* a thirty-two-gun, three-masted frigate, wishing to present no threatening intentions. Once at an appropriate distance, she backed sails, swayed out her boat, and rowed Neville across.

"Ahoy, *Boston,"* called *Lark's* coxswain.

"Who goes?"

"British Liaison officer Lieutenant Burton."

Boston cried out nothing further while *Lark's* boat rowed close and threw out her painter to a waiting seaman in the main chains. It remained quiet, except for the slapping of wavelets and the occasional thumping of the boat against *Boston's* hull.

An American officer appeared above and leaned out over the rail. "Come aboard, Lieutenant. Will you send a message back to your ship asking them to wait until we decide if we'll have you remain?"

"Aye, Sir…"

"We heard, Lieutenant," said the coxswain.

Neville climbed up the side of *Boston*. *Lark's* coxswain ordered, "Shove off. Out oars. Make way all."

Neville decided the usual custom should apply. He turned aft and saluted the stars and stripes, then the officer who had received him. "Lieutenant Burton reporting for duty, sir."

"We'll see," said the officer in a not-unfriendly tone. Neville took him to be the first lieutenant. "Captain McNeill's waiting."

McNeill and Neville got along from the beginning. It came out that McNeill's heritage was Irish, and his personality similar to that of Captain Troubridge, with whom Neville had served for two years on the frigate *Castor* some years before. McNeill had received a communiqué regarding the liaison experiment but it left Neville's involvement to his discretion. He could have sent Neville back the moment he stepped aboard ship.

"We have much to discuss about your assignment," said McNeill. "I'm not really sure what the point is, but our continued friendship with Britain is important to President Jefferson, and I know you have great concerns about this part of the world – as do we."

"I must admit my orders are sketchy as well, Sir. I've had only the slightest of briefing on the subject, and I'm a career navy officer, not a diplomat, but I'm sure we can work something out."

"Waters," yelled the captain. When the man appeared, McNeill said, "Go up top and tell that little boat to heave this man's chest aboard and shove off. We'll keep him."

"How do you see it, Sir… this job of mine?"

"It looks a one-way proposition to me. You send out reports to Britain, and that's it. I can't imagine what Britain would send us, unless she can help in some way with negotiations with these blackguards ashore here. I must ask to see your reports before you send them. We can't be giving out American secrets, can we?"

"No, Sir, I understand. In the meantime, I have a request. May I be counted as one of your officers for the purpose of standing watches? I would imagine it would be worse than boring if I don't do something of the sort. I'm quite familiar with a thirty-two-gun frigate – English or Dutch-built."

"Certainly. We'd be glad of the help. I appreciate your not taking a diplomat's attitude. We have a cabin available, surprisingly enough. Lt. Smith died of an unfortunate accident just last week and I have not rearranged the officers' duties. Rather lax, I know, but there is not much stirring here. Settle in and lay aft for dinner. We'll make it an event and I'll make introductions."

At dinner in McNeill's cabin – he had invited the gunroom – McNeill introduced Neville and informed his officers that Neville had volunteered to stand in for Lt. Smith. He then began with a short account of the American situation: "I don't know how much history you are aware of, so I'll start at the beginning. These Barbary Pirates," he said, "have been extorting money and taking sailors off European shipping for generations – perhaps a million Europeans sold as slaves! The United States has not been protected by France since the Treaty of Alliance expired in 1783, so they are at us now, too. We have been paying a million dollars a year either for the return of our sailors or for tribute. Now, President Jefferson has had Congress raise six frigates as a navy. We are here to stop the piracy and end the tribute payments. We have authorization to destroy or capture any Tripolitan ships we find on the water."

"What about the others – those from Algiers?"

"Oh, not just Algiers. There is also Tunis. They also ask tribute. We are officially at war with Tripoli, however. The silly Pasha there declared war by cutting down our flagpole at the embassy. Here we are together with the Swedes – the four you've seen - attempting a blockade. We fought an action in the harbor just last month against six Tripolitan gunboats. One we forced ashore; and we made some damage to their forts."

"If I might add, Captain," interjected First Lieutenant Martin, "The Swedish ships are not much help. They are big cumbersome things that sail like pigs - and the Tripolitan craft are quite swift. They still come and go."

"He's right, I'm afraid," said McNeill, "although it means we are not completely alone. I doubt our effectiveness here because of it, but we will blockade until called off."

In another two days Neville began to remember the details and procedures of a frigate – and learning a few of the peculiarities of an American one – when the lookout called, "Sail, Ho."

Mid-afternoon found Neville on watch, but not alone. He did not expect the Americans to give him command of their ship without close supervision for some time. "Where away?" he called.

"Straight north, Sir. Brig, maybe."

"Keep an eye, Fennick," cried Lt. Glover, who had been standing in conversation with Neville.

"What do you suppose, Lt. Glover? Tripolitans coming home?"

"Deck, there. Three sail. Two small ones with the brig."

"With a prize, maybe?" said Glover. "Mr. Lowe, run down and ask the captain to come take a look."

"No 'compliments of the officer on watch' and 'if you please'?"

"Mr. Lowe knows what to say," said Glover. "We don't keep sticks up our arses like you Brits."

"Oh, thank you so very much." *I'll put that in my box of American tricks.*

McNeill appeared on the quarterdeck, and Glover went off to tend something at the mainmast.

The northern coast of Africa straight south of Sicily – where Tripoli is situated – is a long line of inhospitable cliffs of stone or sand, with harbors a rarity. Blockading Tripoli might have reminded Neville of blockading Toulon except that even less of interest presented itself ashore. There were no picturesque towns or visible shoreside activity. The small waves were short and uncomfortable. The distances were short. No other ports were nearby.

"Two small sail and one large," said McNeill, snapping his pocket glass shut, "smells to me of two Tripolitan corsairs and a merchant prize...

"Lt. Glover - or, I'm sorry - Lt. Burton, signal the Swedes to intercept, and that we intend to do the same."

"We have a nor-east breeze here, Lt. Burton; on-shore. There are rocks close in. Take care."

"Aye, Sir. Do we signal the Swedes? *Can* we signal the Swedes? Do we share the signal book?"

"We have made arrangements for the basics, yes. I doubt there is much need for secrecy, though. These Berbers are an ignorant lot. With this breeze, we can go straight at 'em. Signal the Swedes to back us up if we don't intercept."

"You have a signals officer?"

"We did. The duty fell to Lt. Smith. Lt. Glover will take over. He was third, as you are acting now, but I doubt you Brits and us Americans have the same signals – and it is not in my purview to teach you ours. Signals mid is the boy there, Mr. Stiles, and he's heard us. Here he comes with it now."

"I'm impressed."

"We're not just a bunch from the back woods, you know."

"I meant no such thing, Sir. Shall we cross in an hour?"

"If they do not turn; see, there they go now off to the east. They'll run with the wind to some other dirty little hole in the desert."

"The distance between the two little ones and the big one is increasing. They are leaving their prize behind. It is probably not fast enough to keep up. They'll leave their prize crew to us, and we'll find the ship's crew gone or dead. This is our best point of sail. Let's see if we can cut the blighters off…"

"Bo'sun, clear for action – take stations. That's starboard guns to you once we're into it, Lt. Burton… Let's get all the fore-and-aft sails we've got on her as well. I think we have a chance.

"Sailing Master Royce, let's catch her."

Royce stepped enthusiastically over next to the helmsman. "Bear off two points to larboard," he called immediately. *Boston* began to accelerate.

"Breeze is up a bit, which should favor us. Call me when we are close enough to tell if we might win or lose her. I'm going down."

Neville went off duty in fifteen minutes. He made his way to the captain's cabin and requested entrance. "I'm sorry if I am being an annoyance, Sir. I have a question, but it could wait."

"Come ahead. I find I am quite impatient waiting up there while we close on some enemy ship. And it's hot, anyway. There is always some paper I can push around down here. What is it?"

"My question is about your relationship with the French. Well, I mean the US of A, not yours personally. I am afraid I am not well versed in the politics. We British have been at war with them forever, it seems, but my understanding is that they are quite the allies with the United States."

"Well, they were," said McNeill, emphasizing the last word. "They were critical to winning our independence from you twenty years ago. But lately – the last few years, you know, after they chopped off King Louis's head – things have been… strained. They put an embargo on our goods, but no war is yet declared as far as we know. Our big frigate, the *Constellation*…"

"I've heard of her."

"Yes, as you should. Back in ninety-nine she had two run-ins with French ships. She didn't lose."

"Would you expect hostility if you, say, put in to a French port for supplies?"

"That's an odd question. I wouldn't expect hostility unless there has been some new argy-bargy we haven't heard of. However, I would not expect to get much in the way of supplies, either. I doubt I'd bother to go."

"Thank you, Sir, for the edification."

Neville returned to his cabin and began writing a letter. He heard the captain being called up about a half hour later, stowed his paper, and went topside to watch the action unfold. He heard the belch of a chase gun on the foredeck just when he stepped on deck. The splash of a wave passing the bow washed half the smoke from the air.

Lt. Glover crossed the deck and met him as he leaned on the starboard for a good look. "I thought I had only been below for a few minutes," said Neville, "but I see we have ready passed the prize and are now taking pot-shots at the slower of the corsairs."

"Yes, Lt. Burton. The other was a lugger and is quite gone. She has probably only an hour to harbor, but I think we've run this'n to ground. We can't take long to play with her, though. When that lugger gets to port she'll probably bring her friends back out looking for us."

"I think I'll go see what the captain has in mind."

"Ah, Lt. Burton," said Captain McNeill. "I think we have her. What do you think she'll do?"

First Lt. Martin yelled "Run out starboard." The rumble of moving cannon momentarily shook the ship.

"I am more interested in how you intend to proceed, Sir. Lt. Glover seems to think we can't remain in this area for long. Nevertheless, since you've asked, I would expect her to suddenly double back to weather and broadside us. She has the weather gage unless she's poorly handled. I would expect it at any minute, so excuse me; I'll go to my guns."

Neville returned to stand behind his battery. Lt. Glover returned. "Am I wrong, James, or are there an unusual large number of men on that ship?"

"Aye, there are; a great number for a ten-gun packet, even for Berbers."

"The captain seems quite sure of himself, but I'd like to take a bit more caution against her actions. Will you command my number four gun personally? I'll load the rest with round shot for the broadside that I am certain we will have to throw soon, but I think their move will be to turn, broadside, and then crash alongside and board. If you load number four with canister and withhold fire until those men are about to jump at us, it may make all the difference. Or, wait. I'll have the guns loaded as I said if you would go give my fears to the captain – or Lieutenant Martin. We need to pass out the weapons and string the boarding nets as well. It would be better you suggest it than me. You outrank me, even if I were American."

"You are today, it seems," said Glover with a grin. He trotted aft.

The rattle and clash of cutlasses being handed out and the shouting as nets being rigged was under way before Neville had gun four reloaded. Before Glover returned, Neville heard another shot fired from the chaser, followed by cheering. *We hit something. Now they know they won't get away. They'll turn in moments.* "Ready, men. It'll be soon," he yelled. "Gun four: hold fire! On the uproll, gunners. On the uproll!"

Lt. Glover returned to stand behind gun four. He stuck his head out the gunport to get a better look, and immediately jerked it back in, slamming it against the sill. Now on his knees and holding his head, he managed to yell, "They're turning!"

Over the rail, Neville could see the pretty packet going up into the wind. Then she tacked neatly to starboard and continued around until she pointed on a reverse parallel course to *Boston*. Both ships held their fire. *Boston* could have come up on the wind to cross the pirate's path, but the action would almost assuredly mean a collision costly to both. *Boston* had the advantage of firepower, though, and stayed to her plan. The packet began firing her small guns as soon as *Boston* closed within her range but did not fire high to cripple her opponent. There was no question she intended to board.

"As she bears," yelled Neville. The two ships closed rapidly, the smaller one now backing sails to stop alongside. Boston's first gun fired, and the packet's bowsprit drooped a yard or more. Second gun, third gun, and a pause. Neville could see thirty men jump to the rail, most with a cutlass in one hand, a dagger in the mouth, and either a grapple rope or another dagger in the other hand. The fifth gun fired directly into the side of the smaller vessel.

"Fire!" yelled Lt. Glover. Most of the men on the packet's rail disappeared. Another twenty came up and ten went down to the sound of swivel guns. Three grapples were successfully thrown, but two of the three throwers were dropped by musket fire from marines in the tops.

Guns six through fourteen fired almost at the same time, point blank into the packet's side. The smaller ship was too short, however, for guns one and two to have a target after the packet slid by, and they remained silent.

"She's afire," someone yelled. "Cut loose! Shove off!"

Cutting loose was not needed. The one grappling line holding the ships together parted with a sound almost as loud as a swivel gun. The quarterdeck swivel gun fired again, at another small group of pirates gathering to leap aboard *Boston*. Those who survived threw their weapons down and tried to leap anyway, apparently preferring whatever treatment they would get at the hands of the Americans to the treatment they would get in the sea.

The sadly beaten packet, littered with bodies and rigging, was being dragged quickly away by the breeze in her remaining mizzen.

"Sharks!" another voice shrieked. "There's a dozen of them!" Neville had seen several, and the amount of blood pouring into the sea would probably draw hundreds.

The fire increased, and a pair of men jumped overboard. "Look at those poor buggers," said Glover, still rubbing his head. A small patch of foaming water indicated where the two had landed. A dozen more pirates stood at the rails looking into the water, but none dared jump.

"Fall off to larboard," yelled Lt. Martin, and as *Boston* began to respond, the fire on the packet began to spread even faster.

"Let's go get that brig," Glover said nonchalantly to Neville.

"We may not have to, James. It's hard to tell from this distance, but it looks as though the brig saw no alternative but to make a run for Tripoli harbor. With us out of the way they only had to avoid those sluggardly Swedes. She'll be in that crowd of sail there."

They continued a close watch over the next two hours, but as they came nearer, the situation became clear.

"The Swedes have managed to capture the brig, Sir. She's grappled onto one there," said Martin to McNeill while pointing to starboard.

"Can you tell whose she is, Lt. Martin?" asked Neville.

Martin raised his glass again. "Her colors are down, but she looks quite French. I don't know the situation between the French and Swedes, but I suspect she'll never make it back to France. We can only pray that a few of her crew were allowed to live and are aboard."

"Back to the humdrum of blockade, then, I suppose."

Neville retreated below as *USS Boston* carved a graceful turn past the harbor. *I must write a letter to Sir William, and I should write a letter home,* he thought, and lay down on his cot. *It's funny; I don't feel the anger I had before the battle at Denmark. I am most disappointed with myself. I can't get the thoughts out. I should have done something different in Jamaica. Maria didn't have to die. If only I had been more careful in my good-byes, she wouldn't have come down to the fort. If she had stayed home, she would never have been involved. I could have seen what would happen with the carriage. I should have grabbed her hand. I couldn't reach it after she fell out...*

It was a struggle to write, but he forced himself to do it.

4: *The Run From Toulon*

"**L**ook, will you. An advice boat arrives," Lt. Martin commented to Neville, "Thank the Lord for his wondrous ways. It boggles the mind that in this day and age it takes two weeks to get a return letter from your station at Gibraltar," he said, laying emphasis on the word 'your' and all the while drumming his fingers rapidly on the larboard rail.

"Even more if it goes on to England, Sir. I sent something a month ago and have seen nothing at all."

A sleek American schooner of about sixty feet bore down on them from the northwest. After the lookout assured himself she wasn't an enemy, he hollered his news down to the quarterdeck. A few officers gathered to watch the event of the day. At about a half cable distant, the schooner set her nose into the wind, brailed up her main and dropped a boat over the side.

"Lively, there, Andrews! Fetch the bag and take it to Captain's cabin. Pass my regards to the Master and ask if he would join me for a cup."

An hour after the schooner had gone there were several letters passed out from McNeill's cabin, and the lucky recipients retreated to any secluded spot they could find to read. Neville had the Lion's share at four – all from Bury St. Edmunds, according to the postmarks. There were two each from his mother and sister. *It would be heaven if I could have one from Maria… a letter from the beyond.*

He determined to open them all at once and then put them in order by date before reading. Neville did not need to read the contents of the second letter, however, in order to determine that neither his sister nor his mother had written it.

What this? Turning it to the signature, he instantly understood. *It's from Sir William. He's had mother address it, as he suspects any official communication to me might be read by suspicious Americans. None of my personal mail appears to have been opened, though. It's not in code. He knows I could take no cipher book with me from Elephant, but he's hid his meaning well.*

> *"…in response to your letter of 18th last: Your proposed solution to the activity I suggested when we last met seems reasonable, but take care in your travels. Don't forget that your attendance at the affair at the good doctor's is not to be ignored. I am pleased to learn that your transfer to Boston might be helpful. I will trust to your promptness. You know how Uncle Georges is with the un-punctual. Regards, Your trusting Godfather, W'm M."*

Neville took his time reading the other letters from home. Satisfied that the news was all good – except possibly one scratchy bit from his sister about his brother-in-law Gage in the army – he went in search of Captain McNeill.

"If I might have a moment, Sir?"

"Certainly. I am encouraged by both my personal and official mails. Would you care for a whiskey?"

"Perhaps you'd like to hear me out first, Sir."

"It sounds serious. Go ahead."

"I am not entirely what I seem to be… I am the liaison to Britain, yes, but although I cannot admit to more, I find myself in need of a favor. I understand your relationship with the French is complicated. As strange as this may sound, I have some unfinished personal business ashore in Toulon – from back in '93 when I visited there on blockade and the city had been briefly given over to the British. As a British officer, I cannot…"

"Maybe you'd best not continue. A girl, then?"

"Oh, no Sir," said Neville, chuckling. "There could never be anyone above my Maria in Jamaica."

"Jamaica… you hadn't mentioned."

Neville looked at the deck. "No, Sir. I'm sorry. She died…" *And all my fault.*

USS **Boston's** jolly boat took him to shore at a spot well out of range of Toulon's guns. McNeill would take no chances that hostilities had increased between France and the United States.

"Just there, Mr. Jensen, set me on the wharf near that group of soldiers. There's a ladder there, see it? I might as well go straight at them. They will be after me like hounds on the fox the moment I step ashore, so there is no sense in trying to avoid them. Pull the boat away the second I set foot on the ladder. I can't be ordered back aboard a boat I can't reach."

The tide being in, his ascent to the pier required but three steps of the slimy ladder. At the top, he stood still, feeling the firmness of land, while the soldiers ambled toward him. Their lack of enthusiasm was obvious. They were between him and the shore, assuring no need for the exertion of hurry, but he could see a shift in the way they held their muskets. He could hear the boat behind him pulling away. Being unarmed, he held his hands away from his body, trusting they would understand he came in peace. He wore an outfit donated by various officers, and had taken time to carefully tailor it to fit him better. Blue trousers, white stockings and shirt, and a black velvet long coat. They had even found him a black bow tie of the current American business fashion.

He moved toward them until close enough that one motioned him to stop. The one who seemed to be in charge – possibly a corporal from an insignia on his sleeve – asked him – in French, "State your name and your business."

Neville understood clearly, but he wanted very much to appear ignorant of all but a fraction of their language. He had listened carefully aboard the *Boston*, and now responded to them with as practiced a flat American intonation as he could manage, "I am American, gentlemen - from Virginia. Not British, you know – the United States of America. I hope to have business here," he blustered on. "Can you direct me to the harbor commander?" He repeated the request in his poorest French. It would be logical for him to have learned at least that much before stepping ashore. "*Où est le commandant?*" He pronounced every word slowly and as badly as he could himself stand.

Neville had no intention of going to see the commander, but he wanted to make a reasonable request. He had hoped any soldiers he met would be disinterested in hand-holding some foreigner who asked for their superiors and would not want to involve themselves. Considerable pointing and hand-waving followed, and a lot of directions that sounded more to him as if they wanted to get him lost than to help him. He paid close attention and walked away as directed.

The harbor doesn't seem to have changed much since '93. The same big stone buildings. I hope it is the same in town. Once he knew the soldiers could no longer see him behind a building, he ignored their instructions and began walking along the first street parallel to the harbor.

I must hope to see something I recognize. Yes, just there. The boulangerie. It is the same, and I will never forget it. It was the first such bread I ever tasted. Here I turn to the right.

He did remember the address he sought - 143 Rue Roche. His last visit had been a very big point in his young life as a midshipman of the *HMS Castor*.

It had not occurred to him before now just exactly why he was chosen for this mission. There were probably not more than a handful of Englishman alive who spoke French and could find the destination he sought without extensive directions. Quite simply, he'd been here before. He had come into Toulon with the *Castor's* surgeon, one Dr. Mills, for the purpose of carrying some things away from Badeau's offices. Furthermore, if he were to arrive at M. Dr. Badeau's office and find someone there, he also knew M. Dr. Badeau, as well as the next most likely person he would encounter, the spy Georges Cadoudal. He had met Badeau aboard the *Angelique* when it was captured by *Castor*, and he'd met Cadoudal here in Toulon and again on his second ship, the *Sans Pareil*.

He walked for a time, inquiring for directions as he passed old men and women. This time he did not hesitate here to use his best French. *Here it is, at last. I see his sign is up now.* Above the door hung the white sign with gold letters that he had found covered with dust in the foyer on his last visit: **M. *Badeau – Docteur Medical*.** *The city is in peace now, with no fear of soldiers searching for medical supplies, I suppose.*

He turned the door handle. It opened. *That's good. Maybe one of them is here.* He trudged up the stairs and opened the door to the waiting room at the top. Nobody here, and it's quiet as the morgue.

The office? He tapped timidly at the door. Nothing. Why am I so timid? He opened the door and went in. Nobody. *It's been painted green. What about the inner office? If there is anyone there, it must be Georges or M. Badeau.*

He tapped on the inner door, but this time immediately opened it, calling out, "Georges?" He kept to the charade: "Uncle Georges? Monsieur Docteur Badeau?"

An unlocked door, but nobody here? His skin prickled and he felt the little hairs on the back of his neck stand up. *What now? Here for nothing?*

He turned to the desk and sat in the creaky wooden chair. The desk, littered with papers and envelopes, didn't look like it had been searched, but it did look messier than he would have expected from the doctor – *as though somebody left in a hurry?* He pawed though the letters and papers. *Nothing noteworthy... In the drawer?*

The desk drawer squeaked as it opened. There were more letters and papers there. *Nothing here, either... ahaa – this one addressed to the "Reverend N. Burton of Boston." It's not sealed... it may have been opened carefully?*

The envelope held a single note:

"Neville, I'm quite sorry to inform you that the event is cancelled. Several uninvited guests of an unpleasant nature will surely appear if you open the doors. I recommend you depart for home immediately. I've left you some travel documents in the credenza."

He's telling me this place is being watched! Neville felt his pulse quicken. He remembered *Captain McNeill's words: "You can have no assistance from us, aside from taking you to shore and collecting you. I'll see you in three days behind the little island in the bay by Bandol to the west, here."* He had looked at the chart, which also showed a road on shore which led there from Toulon. The distance was only about 10 miles.

Neville stood slowly and walked closer to the window. *No activity outside…*

A quick search in the credenza drawer produced a sheaf of papers. *There are a dozen letters, either encrypted or irrelevant. This one is in English– a proposal for a meeting between an M. Stillwater and a man – Citizen Sysson - in the French government. I'll take the lot. Maybe Mulholland can make something of it. The rest of the credenza is just books. I'd best not dawdle, though.*

He looked again out the window – down the street both ways. An officer of some sort was approaching purposefully from the east.

Neville closed the desk drawer and left the offices. At the foot of the stairs, he opened the outer door as casually as he could – not jerking it open as if to run or peeking out carefully – just open, exit, close and leave.

The officer waved. *To me? I won't wait to see.* His eye caught the movement of a door opening two buildings down on the opposite side of the street. An alley formed the corner of the building at 143 Rue Roche. He went there. He found it quite clean, other than a group of trash bins, an old baby buggy without its wheels, and several stacks of roof tiles. Nothing looked at all like a weapon. He jogged past the office building and a house behind it to the next street.

At the Av. Des Roses, he turned left. Nobody following him had turned into the alley behind him yet, but he would take no chance. He also decided to double back in the hope they would take some time to discover his cleverness. Two buildings to the left he turned left again, back toward the Rue Roche. When he reached that street, he peeked his head out to watch for activity. He noticed the movement of a man in a dark blue uniform turn down the alley by Badeau's office, but nothing else.

He crossed the street at a fast walk and down the alley opposite. This alley was quite narrow.

Oh, he thought, *this is a mistake. The second man came from this building. No stopping now, though - on through to the next street.* Whistles began to sound from behind him. They were enough to urge him into a trot. Only about five yards on, a door popped open in front of him – so close he could not avoid it, and he slammed into it at a full trot. The collision threw a diminutive police officer on the other side sprawling onto the pavement. The two stared wide-eyed at each other for only a moment before the man yelled, "Here! He's here." He reached for something in his pocket. *It can't be a pistol. A whistle, perhaps? I need a club!* Neville grabbed a stout stick from a pile of firewood opposite the door. The officer raised his small wooden whistle to his lips, but Neville's club smashed him in the hand before it made any sound. It flew to the pavement in two pieces.

The little policeman changed his attitude; he dropped the enterprise of being an alarm-sounder and became the fighter. His baton came out as a naval officer would draw his sword, and he took the stance of a trained boxer. Neville couldn't help but notice. *This is better. I'd rather fight him than have him delay me while calling help.*

He swung, but Neville parried the baton with his stick. The noise of it echoed loudly down the alley. *I can't stay long,* thought Neville. *He has already cried out once.* Neville saw him draw back, and he took the opportunity to strike for the knee. The gendarme went down with only a whimper. *I see,* thought Neville; *as a small man, he has learned to play tough and not show his pain. That's good – no bloody noise.* He rolled away before Neville could strike again. He leaped up again quickly, but unsteadily, and swung for Neville's head. Again, Neville parried, but the blow glanced the baton downward, where is struck Neville's upper left arm. Becoming desperate, Neville gave a final swing for his opponent's head, and this time his club was not blocked. The policeman went down to stay.

"I'm really sorry for that, but you'll be fine in a few days and have a story to tell," Neville said out loud. "I'll take your baton, though."

Neville's strategy of taking a jagged and disorganized path through the streets and alleys seemed to be working. The sound of whistles grew louder and more threatening for a few blocks; but then suddenly became less as his hunters took a wrong turn and ran off in the opposite direction. After half an hour, he began to think they had given up on him. He couldn't hear them, and they had no idea where he planned to go, after all. *They would probably expect me to go to the harbor, so I will circuit around it. My best route would be just up above, in the hills. I could see the Sea and maybe use the masts in the harbor to help guide me. Farther to the west, I can come back down. My path must cross the Toulon Road from Bandol somewhere before I would reach the Sea. The whole thing is only about ten miles.*

He found a walking path leading up and off to the west, which served well. Another half hour of walking brought him to a stream in an area where the houses were far fewer. The warmth of the day forced him to remove his jacket, and he wished he had worn boots instead of these 'gentleman's shoes'. He splashed the welcome water on his face, drank deeply, and sat on a flat rock to review his situation: *It shouldn't be a problem – I have three days: this is one, one to hide out, and one to find a little boat at the beach. I'll need to find some food and a place to hide and sleep, though. Ow. What's this pain in my left arm? Oh, yes, it's where that fellow's baton struck me.* He removed his jacket, rolled back his sleeve, and looked at his arm. A red welt was rising about four inches above the elbow. He felt it, and could tell it was swollen, but there was no black and blue bruise yet. It certainly wasn't broken.

Neville continued following the stream as long as it went southwest, skirting the hills so he could keep the masts of the harbor in view. The stream began to drop down toward the sea, but not toward the harbor, and he couldn't see the masts any longer.

The stream must cross the road somewhere; there is no question it will flow to the sea.

Beyond the streets of Toulon, he came to a good road, paved with gravel and lined with trees. *I see it curves to the left just beyond that inn. I'll ask there for directions to be sure, and maybe have a bite to eat.*

As he walked closer to the curve, just before stepping out from a hedge, he caught sight of a road blockade in front of the inn.

Those are soldiers, and they are stopping wagons. I must assume they are they searching for me, so I need to take myself back to the woods or a field to hide somewhere and wait for dark. So much for the idea of getting something to eat at the inn. It's probably just as well - the collection of French money the American sailors took up for me isn't much, anyway.

Neville decided to cross the road by following the stream under its small bridge and short-cut across its curve by making his way through the woods opposite the inn. He would move several yards away from the road and wait on the bank until dark, making as little movement as he could in the meantime. As dusk came on the traffic on the road decreased to nil and the guard became obviously very lax – *exactly the opposite of what they should have done.* A sliver of paraselene waning moon and patchy clouds suggested possible rain in a day or so.

The darkness – with enough moonlight to provide some visibility – signaled his time to move. He put the dark coat back on and slunk along slowly from one clump of vegetation to the next, working his way into the woods until he could no longer see the lights of the inn or hear the revelry. The blockade was clearly an adventure to the police in this rural area. *I'm lucky, I see. This is a middle-aged forest without much brush in it, and the locals have carted away dead branches for their fires. I still need to watch for rocks, stumps, and holes.* On his first forward movement, a holly branch scratched his face. He kept to the bank of the stream, and progress became easier, until the stream came to another crossing of the road. Finding the bridge here to be much lower to the water, he decided he would not pass under the road, but cross it like a proper human. It was dark, after all. He stepped out onto the road. Dry leaves and other detritus of the forest clung to his trouser legs, so he leaned down to brush them away.

"Bonsoir, mon ami. Où vas-tu? (Good evening, my friend. Where are you going?)" The voice came from the dark. It was so unexpected that Neville, already on edge, recoiled severely. His hand went to the baton while he peered desperately into the blackness. Where, though? The other side of the road? Yes, there he was, urinating on a large tree.

Neville said no more than, "Bonsoir." He wondered which direction to run.

The man continued, "I'm on my way home, too. We could walk together, yes? I had the most wonderful quiche for dinner…"

This man's drunk. Even if I did want to travel his way, I doubt I would want to listen to him. His slurred speech is difficult to understand, and I suspect he'll talk my ear off.

"The red wine is most delicious, too. Did you have some? They make it right there. Did you see the barmaid who brings it? Haar, haar, haar, yes?"

"I didn't go to the inn," answered Neville, beginning to wonder how to extricate himself from this encounter.

"Didn't go…?" the man seemed incapable of understanding. "Then why are you here?"

"I'm going the other way."

"To Toulon? Well, then you must stop at the inn. Did I tell you they make their own red wine?"

"Yes, you did. I must be on my way. It's late."

"Are you from around here? You don't sound like you're from around here. Are you that man the police are looking for? You're not a fisherman from Bandol." The man was still slurring his words badly, but Neville began to worry that he had become more alert than when the two had first met.

"Yes. Yes, of course. I am from Martigues, on the other side of Marseille." He was pleased to remember the name of at least one town on the chart. *Why would the police look for me?* "Excuse me. I really must take my toilet. I am going into the woods just there. Do you mind?"

"No, no. I am sorry to make you wait. I just used that big tree, there." He almost fell when he turned to point at it. "I'll wait for you here."

Neville moved into the woods on the other side of the road. *I've crossed the road now. I can disappear into the woods and leave the besotted twit behind.* He moved carefully into the trees, slowly so his movements were hard to see; until he could no longer see the man on the road. Then he began walking as fast as he could across the uneven forest floor in the dark.

"Are you alright?" he heard the man yell. "Are you finished? Come and walk with me!"

That cursed drunk. He will probably tell someone in the morning.

He continued walking, using what he could see of the moon as a guide. If the drunk was still calling out, he had moved far enough away that he couldn't hear him. The wood was not large, and he soon came to the edge of a field. He was surprised to see that the night was nearing an end; the eastern sky has a purple tinge, even through the heavier cloud cover.

The treed hedgerows are my best option. I should avoid standing in open spaces. At the end of the hedgerow, he dared a walk across a wheat field. *I could just lie down in the wheat for cover if I see any movement or lights.* He passed through more hedgerows into a second field and then a third where the smell of fresh-cut hay surrounded him. At the far end stood a small farmhouse with a shed, and not too far beyond was another odd structure. *It's a haystack. Back in England, Mr. Wagstaff makes his look like little barns. This one is round and maybe fifteen feet tall, but I'm sure that's what it is. I could hide in it. I can see a pig and chickens, too. I expect the farmer's vegetable crop is in.* His stomach grumbled.

Neville crossed the field quickly – he couldn't hide in the wheat stubble here – to the side of the haystack opposite the farmhouse. It took only minutes to burrow a hole into the side big enough to curl up in and gather some straw back around his 'door'. *I'll stay here a day. I should be able to steal something to eat tonight. This farmer doesn't appear to have a dog. It's stuffy in here, but I'm sure I can sleep. I'll use my coat for a bed and my jacket for something of a pillow.*

When he awoke several hours later, he heard voices in the distance. It seemed distant, at least, but it's difficult to tell when one is inside a haystack. He certainly could not determine any direction. Men talking, for sure. More than two men… different voices; not excited. Maybe by the house? Could it be a search party? *How well did I pull the straw up behind me? What did I do with the straw I had to take out to make a hole?* He didn't remember, and became increasingly nervous as the voices began to move. He could tell the direction changed. A door banged. The shed door, probably. They were searching!

His pursuers didn't search long, however. The farmyard returned to quiet, followed by the sounds of animals being fed. Then, even that went quiet, He could tell it was daylight; he wasn't buried so deeply that light didn't filter in, and it became quite warm. After some immeasurable time it began to cool and grow darker. He dug his way out.

There was no moon yet, but the stars shone through gaps in the clouds – a good time for a foray into the farmyard. He decided to try the shed before annoying the chickens. As he expected, no lock hung on the hasp. This sort of farmer probably could not afford one. The door creaked open. *I wish I could leave it open for a little more light, but it faces the house, and I see there is still a candle there.* Inside, he tripped over the upper edge of a barrel that was almost fully buried in the ground. Only three inches of it protruded from the earth. Another. Three of them. *I hope...* He pried off the first lid, mostly by feel. Inside it, he felt... *Yes! Sawdust and...* the sweet smell of fresh onions greeted his nose. *Onions!* His first big bite delighted his senses. *What's in the next?* Potatoes, they were, and carrots in the third. *A feast! A feast of freshness beyond what I eat aboard ship.* He filled his pockets, again being glad of the coat, although not for the warmth. It was a beautiful evening, despite the threat of rain.

Before I go, I should try for an egg. The door creaked open and shut again as he left the shed. *I'm sure I saw a chicken roost to the left.* Keeping one eye on the farmhouse, he began to creep toward the roost, but as luck would have it, he stepped on the leg of a sleeping pig. Excited pig squeals and grunts aroused the chickens, and that activity aroused the rooster, who flew at him as only an annoyed rooster can do – crowing and flapping enough to raise the dead.

Neville pulled out the police club to fend off the rooster just as the farmhouse door crashed open and a small old man came out yelling: "Je vous recevrai cette fois, vous le renard stupide! (I'll get you this time, you stupid fox!)" The old man carried a sword; its wide blade appeared razor sharp, even in the thin light.

The sight of Neville swinging at the rooster brought him up short, and for a second he just stared. Then he slashed at Neville. Little old farmers are seldom swordsmen, however, and with a simple parry with the police club and a hard smack, the sword finished its battle in the dirt with Neville's foot on it.

"Ne criez pas s'il vous plaît! Je ne vous ferai pas du mal (Please don't call out! I won't harm you.)," said Neville.

The little man refrained from yelling, but despite being half dressed in his work trousers and half with his nightshirt, he stood to his full height of about five feet. He had an old, but defiant, face, tired and gray, with a grizzled beard, bad teeth, a small moustache, and greasy medium-length hair. "Que voulez-vous? (What do you want?)" he demanded. The conversation continued in French.

"Is it just you here? Are you alone?"

"Yes, only me." The response carried a very sad tone.

"I only want some food. I have taken some vegetables, and I had hoped for an egg."

"You are the one they are looking for, aren't you?" the farmer asked.

"I'm sure you know by my speech that I am not French. I am also not British. I am an American," Neville lied, assuming the farmer would never know. "From Boston," he added - *shamelessly.*

The moon arose. It had waned slightly since the previous night, and although difficult to tell for sure in the dim moonlight, Neville thought he saw a brightening of the man's face — a glimmer of... something. "May I take an egg?" he asked.

"Why is an American here?" the farmer asked.

Neville had expected the question to be asked on his trip ashore, so he had practiced the answer for anyone not current on international politics: "I came ashore from a ship on medical business a month past, when relations between our countries were not so strained as now. Your new government is now not so pleased with the United States, and we are being gathered up. They are looking for us." His answer, although not a particularly astute one, did not elicit a retort from the farmer. "Why do you have the sword?"

The old man hesitated, but then apparently decided he would cooperate. "For the wheat. I cut it with the sword. It has a fine blade, and it stays sharp."

Neville picked it up. It looked to be a French navy blade – a very fine one with a gilded hilt – much better than his own. "But why? How do you come to have it?"

This time the man noticeably slumped. "It belonged to my son. Guy was in the navy. He is dead now – killed in a battle with the Spaniards. My younger son was in the navy, too. He brought Guy's sword home to me before he left."

"Left? Where is he?"

"I should not say."

"Not say? Why not?"

"Oh, I suppose I might say to an American. It would make no difference… He was in the navy, as I said, and he went to the wars in America – to help them – you, yes?"

"Yes. You French were of great help to us. Your King Louis was a friend."

"But this new one, pfft," he said, and spat on the ground. "He would kill all our sons for his glory."

"So your son…?"

"Antoine. He did not come home."

"Also dead?"

"No," said the man, looking up into the moonlight. *There is pleasure in his face this time*, thought Neville, *I am sure of it*. "He is alive. He lives in Boston with his American wife. I get letters sometimes, but I know other times they don't let them come to me. They are always opened. They call him a deserter…

"You may have an egg, but for it I ask a favor. If you take me to Boston, I will help you with everything. I can leave. I would leave what little I have here to nobody. I want to see my grandson. You must tell me about Boston, but first – where are you going?"

"To Bandol. A ship will come there for me tomorrow." *But I know nothing about Boston that is not about the ship of the same name. I suppose I could describe Norfolk. He'd never know.*

"It is nothing. This is the road to Bandol," he said, waving his hand to the east. "You can take me, then?"

His help would be worth it... "You will be put to work aboard ship for your food, and it is not easy work. I heard voices today. You say they are looking for me?"

"Yes, they are searching. There were two men each from the police and the army."

"Just getting to the ship will be dangerous, then. I know there are blockades on the roads."

"Oh..." Neville could see him putting two & two together, but he reached his conclusion. "No matter, we can take my farm lanes to the stream and then the fishing trails. It is only about eleven kilometers. I am Louis."

Neville could see his excitement rising. He held out his hand.

Neville shook it. "Thomas," he said, thinking 'Neville' might sound particularly British.

"We can go in the morning and take my old fishing poles. I have no horse. You may stay in the shed tonight. Eat all you like," he said with a crooked smile. "I am sorry, but I use the other room in the house for storage now."

"Your wife?"

"She is there," he said nodding to a small white wooden cross shimmering in the moonlight at the far side of the yard. "She is the only thing I will be sorry to leave, but she would understand."

When morning came, it was cooler. A light intermittent drizzle would decrease the chance of policemen wandering about simply to enjoy the day. They walked Louis' indicated path along his muddy farm lanes to a hedgerow. Neville carried two fishing poles and his police baton in a bundle. Louis carried his sword, wrapped in cloth, with one wrap of leather to prevent the cloth from being cut. He had tied his pack of belongings to the sword hilt, and he slung the sword over his shoulder like a typical carrying pole.

Beyond the trees, a narrow footpath wandered along one bank of a slow-running stream. Another half hour of walking the bank brought them to a clearing where fishing boats littered the beach. A large tree stood at their end of the curved strand, up by the edge of a pasture.

"We'll wait here under the tree," said Neville. "At least we'll have some shelter if the rain increases. I thank you again for the carrots. Who's this, now?"

A man approached from the far end of the strand. He was the only other person about, and there was no question they were coming to him. He didn't look like an official policeman, but he wore a ragged coat that might have been a police jacket at some point in its distant past, and he did have a new police baton in his belt.

"Hold up, there, hey!" the 'beach guard' called.

Neville leaned over to Louis and said, "We should wait patiently so we don't alarm him. Tell him I am visiting the area. It is probably better if you speak, but say as little as you can."

"Bonjour," Louis said when the man came close.

"I know you, don't I?" said the guard to Louis. "From a farm about ten kilometers from here, yes?"

"Yes."

"Why are you here, and who is this?" He stared at Neville.

"He is a friend from Marseille, come to visit with me and my family. Some live here in Bandol."

"You don't look French to me," said the guard, "and we are looking for a dangerous foreigner. How did you get here, and why do you carry a police baton with your fishing poles?"

"He came…" began Louis.

"Not you, him. I asked him."

"I came from Marseille out on a wagon, but then I walked very much of…"

"You are not French, I can tell from your speech. You come with me now." He reached into his jacket pocket and pulled out his whistle. Neville had expected something of the sort, and quickly reached out and swatted the whistle out of the guard's hand. It dangled on its lanyard from a jacket button.

While the guard tried to recapture the whistle, Neville dropped the fishing poles and yanked his baton from the bundle. At that, the guard pulled his own baton and the two squared off for a fight. They swung and parried a few times; Neville got in a few hard thumps to the guard's body. The guard swung wildly next, and his blow landed exactly where the Toulon policeman's blow had struck Neville's upper arm. With a moan, Neville dropped his baton. The guard made the mistake of hesitating before his next blow, and that

pause was all Louis needed to throw a handful of sand in his face –
and for Neville to pick up his baton with his right hand and strike
the surprised and blinded guard down.

"Thank you, Louis. Find something to tie him with. Quickly,
before he wakes."

The guard was soon tied behind the tree with some dirty little
ropes Louis found in the closest fishing boat. He was still woozy,
and blood trickled slowly from a lump on his forehead.

"Oh, look, Louis, here she comes now. Do you see her masts
and bowsprit beyond the island, there?"

USS Boston ghosted slowly toward the little bay, her damp sails
hanging limp and scarcely drawing at all. She would undoubtedly
anchor well offshore rather than risk being caught in the bay if an
onshore breeze arose – and one could never predict the breezes in
this sort of weather. In the deep quiet they heard the sound of
Boston's anchor splashing and her cable running out the hawse,
even though they were almost a half mile off.

"How do we get to the ship?" asked Louis.

"I had in mind to steal a small boat from a fisherman. Not
more."

"Oh, no…" Louis said, obviously horrified at the thought, "I
could never. These boats are their livelihood. However, if we have
no alternative, I can ask my wife's brother here in Bandol to give us
a ride out. He is a fisherman, not a political man. He would help
me, I am sure, but this guard will be a problem."

Louis left the sword and his small sack containing everything
left of his life in France and walked off down the strand. When he
returned, the drizzle had become continuous and increased to a
light rain. With no breeze, it fell vertically; softly. Neville had
enjoyed his rest in this very scenic cove in the dry space under the

tree. The guard had remained quiet. There had been nobody to whom he could cry for help.

Louis returned alone. "He says he cannot, but we may 'steal' his boat, if we must. There will be no one going out to fish in the rain. He will wait until it stops and then go to his place on the beach and cry 'thief'. If we don't take it too far out, the current here will take it to the corner of the bay over there." Louis said, pointing to a rocky spit. "He told me to tie a rock to a long line as an anchor and it will stop in the shallows. He will have it back by nightfall. They all look out for each other."

"All right, Louis, get in," Neville said when they had dragged the boat into the water. "Put those oars in place while I get your pack." He walked back to the tree to fetch it.

Halfway there he noticed two more men walking towards him. They were still a hundred yards or more away. One yelled to him, "Arête, Monsieur. Have you seen our friend? A guard…"

The guard behind the tree began yelling, "Stop him! This is the man. Here! Here!"

The two began running, one toward Neville and one toward the boat. Neville snatched up the pack and ran for the boat. He was closer than his adversaries were, however, and reached it first. He threw the pack in, shoved the boat free of the sand, and jumped in.

"Louis…what? The oars…?"

"I don't know how oars go. I'm a farmer, not a fisherman."

The guard was fast approaching. Neville installed one oar, and then used it to turn the boat toward open water. He had just clipped the second oar in place when the guard arrived. The water didn't stop the guard, who waded in after his fugitives. It was more than waist deep on him when he grabbed the boat's transom. Neville had taken only one stroke, but he knew he could not drag a man through the water from the back of a rowboat.

"Ha, ha! I have caught you," the guard jeered.

"Not today, friend," said Louis. "I am sorry for this, but I must find my son." He whacked the guard's fingers with Neville's baton – first one hand and then the other. They left him howling in the water and struggling for shore.

While Neville rowed hard for open water, he could see the three guards working to move another fishing boat into the water to give chase. It wasn't going very quickly. One man's hands were damaged – possibly with a broken finger or two – and one surely had an excruciating headache. By the time they succeeded, Neville was halfway to the island, and very glad of the cooling rain. It was all he could do to overpower the ache in his left arm.

5: *Boadicea*

Captain McNeill and Lieutenant Martin watched Neville approach from the deck of the USS Boston.

"Why do you suppose he's rowing like a madman, Captain?" asked Martin?

"I'm wondering the same thing, Lieutenant. And who does he have with him? He didn't say anything about bringing a passenger, did he?"

"No, but there's the answer to his mad rowing. He's being chased, Captain. You see the other little boat coming 'round from behind the island?"

"How soon can we leave this place, Lieutenant? There may be more behind that one."

"No wind, Sir, in this rain."

"Can we warp out? Where does the tide stand?"

"Tide is almost out, Sir. It's not very great here, so I suppose we could go now by using the boats, if need be."

"Make it so, Lieutenant. I do not wish to be caught here with the anchor down if we have a little army following our friend."

Boston had heaved her anchor short by the time the exhausted Neville banged alongside. He and Louis clambered up the short ladder hanging from the main chains and stepped on deck. The tumult of launching *Boston's* boats was already under way.

"Let the boat drift, Louis. The guards will surely return it." Louis threw the painter in the water.

As soon as Neville and Louis were aboard, the anchor cable began coming up, accompanied by the tramping of feet and thumping of the capstan pawls. Louis gawked about the ship with his jaw hanging open.

"Anchor's aweigh, Cap'n," called some seaman forward.

After the customary salutes and welcome, McNeill asked, "Lieutenant Burton, how many are chasing you?"

"I believe it's only the one little boat, Sir. I don't think they are armed with anything more than clubs, either, but I'll give them credit for trying up to the last." Their pursuers were only a cable away by then.

"Lieutenant Martin," said Neville, "I'm sorry for this inconvenience."

"Don't think a thing of it, Neville," he replied. "We need to give the men something to do on such a dreary day. As to coming here, I think we are all enjoying a bit of drizzle instead of the incessant heat and dust of Africa. There's no shore leave in such a place, but the men look longingly to land, regardless. A bit of exercise in the boats will be a good thing."

"Shall I command a boat?"

"There's no need. The midshipmen need a little amusement, too. Go below, and take your visitor with you. It is my preference to deny I ever saw you when these characters arrive alongside – and it looks as if they will come all the way here."

Fifteen minutes later, the two boats that had been launched and filled with men had pulled the slack out of their tow cables. They began rowing with gusto then, and *Boston* swung slowly but easily to follow.

The beach guards arrived and yelled for attention, "Arête, arête! (Halt, halt!)" They began an extended tirade that brought other *Bostons,* who temporarily had no duty, over to join Martin in staring down at them, pantomiming their injuries and pointing at injured hands and head.

"I think they are trying to say the Lieutenant Burton has got the best of them, and they'd like him given over," said one.

"I'm sure of it," said Miller, "but I don't speak a word of French beyond 'no' or 'oui, oui'." He yelled back in English, "I have no idea what you're trying to tell me, gentlemen. Perhaps you could have Napoleon send President Jefferson a letter. Please keep clear of the cables." He waved his hand to indicate they should stay out from under *Boston's* bow.

Another half hour of rowing moved the ship at least a mile offshore. The beach guards had given up and gone; with only the one guard having the health to row, and towing the second fishing boat, they left at a much slower pace than they had come out. The rain had stopped by the time *Boston's* towboats were called back alongside, and a very light breeze had arisen.

"Heave the boats up, Bo'sun.

"Sailing Master, let's make something of this breeze," Martin called across to Mr. Royce, who had been waiting by the wheel expecting orders.

"The breeze is almost dead onshore, Lieutenant. We've warped out a good mile, but we must still clear that point there," Royce answered, pointing forward.

"I see it. Fore-and-aft sails only, for now, then. I've seen you get us out of worse."

Royce grinned ear to ear: "Aye, Sir."

"I was more than pleased to see your ship arrive here in the bay," said Neville to Captain McNeill. "Did you have any confrontation with the French?"

"No, none. You may thank your lucky stars that it has been quite peaceful. We could not, in good conscience, have delayed very long in the face of their disapproval, and I would not have risked provoking some international incident by refusing to leave. This little altercation of yours was too close for comfort. What happened ashore… any trouble?"

"I am afraid I overstayed my welcome, but no mischief other than a young policeman who will be awake now with a lump on his head, and those two in the boat."

"You certainly do have some strange ways…"

"By the by, Lieutenant Burton, one of your packets passed offshore where we waited, and they've dropped this letter for you. I would like to know how they knew where to find us." He gave Neville a curious look.

"I…I don't know, Sir." Neville didn't offer anything more.

"You might read it directly," said McNeill. "It looks quite official."

Neville stepped out of the captain's cabin and tore open the red Admiralty seal. He saw nothing peculiar about the contents. It contained orders for nothing more than simply to return to 'normal" British duty. Only the arrival of a letter to a foreign ship in an unexpected location was surprising enough to suspect some urgency, so he decided to request another audience with Captain McNeill. The sentry allowed him back in.

"I'm sorry for the inconvenience," Neville said, "but after reading this letter, I must ask another favor."

"After this, I'm not sure how inclined I am to grant it. Go ahead, though. What is it?"

"Set me ashore at Gibraltar, if you could manage it. I assume you must return to Tripoli, but Gibraltar is not far to the west..."

"Far enough. I'm sorry, but this diversion has been about all I can afford. We will be sailing for Tripoli. Perhaps we will encounter one of yours on passage thither."

"Thank you, Sir. I know I should not hope for more." Neville left the cabin, thinking he should try to find a way to help decrease the stress he had placed upon the *USS Boston*. He was also reminded, by the orders he had just received, of Sir William Mulholland's frequently stated adage, "Don't worry, something will usually present itself."

Noon of the fourth day south of France brought a clear sky and a breeze that shifted from onshore Sardinia to offshore, as often happens near a coast. *USS Boston* had just cleared the southern cape of Sardinia and entered the open waters beyond the island, making a healthy four knots on a south-southeasterly course for the desert shores of Africa, when the lookout called, "Sail ho!"

"Where away, Mr. Alberg?" yelled Martin back up the mast.

"Four points to larboard, Sir. Westbound. Can't tell much yet, but she looks English – and small."

"She's alone?"

"Aye, Sir, alone."

"This may be your ride home, Neville," said Martin. "She's 'English, small, and alone' sounds like a packet or advice boat heading to Gibraltar from Malta or some such, wouldn't you think?"

"I would, indeed, and we've seen her in time to cross her way. Would you impose upon the Captain to prepare a signal to speak her?"

The little brig *Stork* made no attempt to avoid an American vessel. She was, indeed, what they had suspected: a packet returning to Gibraltar. By the beginning of the second dog watch they had spoken, enjoyed a glass of American whiskey with the packet's commander, one Lieutenant Archibald Mewes, transferred Neville and his sea chest from *Boston* to *Stork*, and set sail, each to his own purpose. Neville waved his good-byes to *Boston,* feeling a strange absence from a ship that wasn't even of his own navy. His wave was returned from the waist by a solitary small man: Louis.

Commander Archibald Mewes, a thin man of average height with cat-like reflexes, proved to be an affable, talkative fellow. "You can't know it, of course, if you've never commanded a small ship like this one," he said on the second morning, "but it can be an 'orribly lonely life." He turned to face Neville for emphasis just as a typically square Mediterranean wave smacked the bow. Coffee spewed vertically from his tankard, missing the man's face but leaving a brown stain down the left leg of his white trousers. "Oh, damn, that's hot! I'll take the rod to that Cammack fellow – my steward – if he does this again."

"I might join you. I think I've burnt my lip, Sir."

"And you can stow that 'sir' stuff between us in private, Neville; it's my point exactly. No peer to talk to; not even an educated underling in this lot. Left to my own thoughts all day, I am. I'm quite pleased to have you aboard, even if it'll be a short passage."

"Thank you, Sssss… Archibald, but I do understand. I had command of a small frigate a few years back, and although there are officers and midshipmen, the conversation is just not…"

"You? A frigate? What are you, twenty and four, or so? You must tell me the whole story, and how you came to be aboard an American ship in the Med, as well. I'd guess you've had an interesting life." Archibald now stared at Neville in apparent disbelief. "Back and forth I sail. Back and forth. No action. No glory."

Damn, I've put my foot in it now. Neville noisily slurped the top film of coffee off his steaming tankard to gather his wits. *None of this is something I'm allowed to divulge. Quick, Burton, make yourself a simple story.* "Hot, yes. I think I'll put this aside for a minute or two." *I'll start with the present.* "I have been on special assignment. Do you know what a 'special assignment' is?"

"Don't take me for simple, Neville. Of course I do. It's some exercise in support of one's country that doesn't fit in any normal description of duty, where they need someone of substance to see through. Someone trustworthy, above reproach, and all that. Only a day now, and I see that in you."

"I am greatly flattered by your words, Archibald, but it may also mean something a bit different. Have you ever served on a man-o-war?"

"Not since I sat for lieutenant, no."

"I was third on *Elephant*, a seventy-four, at the Battle of Copenhagen. A packet commander has probably heard all the news and the rumor, as well, yes?"

"My, you have seen some action, then."

"Yes, well the battle was about all the action my first lieutenant could stand. We got off on the wrong foot from the start, and he did not carry himself well in the battle. He knew I'd seen it. His embarrassment resulted in a 'special assignment' for me, even though I never mentioned his cowardice to anyone. He somehow got me transferred to be liaison to the Americans on the North African coast. The duty wasn't bad," *and I won't tell him about the little detour at Toulon*, "but not very exciting. As far as the first lieutenant was concerned, though, the main purpose of the 'special assignment' was getting rid of me."

Archibald sipped at his coffee again, and then pronounced it cool enough to drink. "Hmmm," he said. "How did he get you transferred? It sounds like something that should have come from the Admiralty."

"He's well connected, I suppose."

"It's always that, isn't it? I can only hope my own connections will pay out some day."

"How's that, Commander Mewes? What are your connections, if I may be so bold as to inquire of a peer?"

He looked around, presumably to be sure nobody was close enough to hear his words. "You must keep this on the hush-hush. It's not something I can spread around. We packets carry all manner of things, you know. Not cargo, like barrels of gunpowder or beef or water, but often, officers on the way to new stations, orders for commodores and admirals, or experimental weapons and the like. There's a man in Whitehall who's found me trustworthy and above reproach and all, like I said before…bloody Whitehall itself, mind you! He sends me on my own special assignments from time to time." He looked furtively about, enhancing the cat analogy, and continued in a low voice, "I think this might be one now. I can't see any other reason for being despatched on precisely the date I departed, only to be sent to Gibraltar. I can't say what I'll find in Gibraltar, either."

"Ahhh." *So there it is. I can imagine who we're talking about.* "Who is this fellow, Archibald?"

"Oh, I mustn't divulge that, tut, tut. He's high up in the bureaucracy of 'we don't know a thing' though, I'm sure of it."

"Have you met him?"

"I did once, aye. He wanted to size me up, I suppose. Tall, thin fellow; all legs, he was. Not what I expected."

"Hmmm. Where did you meet him?"

"You know the Navy Office front portico, yea? He's in a big yellow building to the left of it. Not like the Navy Office at all. All quiet and serious; not many people about. Marine guard don't let you breathe right, even."

"Room 4, then?"

Archibald's eyes snapped onto Neville's. "How could you possibly know such a thing?" he demanded.

"I didn't, but I do now. I've just solved your puzzle for you."

"Puzzle? Ah, yes. You couldn't know unless…"

"You've smoked it, Archibald; unless your special assignment is me. This should be easy for both of us. I must add that I am very pleased to meet you. I might say 'honored' to meet you, Sir," using the last word seriously. "I should like to run off and write a few letters now, though. We can pick this up tomorrow morning, maybe, with a plate of collops and some cooler coffee." *I won't mention the frigate again, either.*

"Is there something wrong with your left arm, by the way? I notice you guard it carefully, and don't use it much."

"You've a sharp eye, Archibald. Yes, but it should be temporary. I was struck by a loose boom."

Archibald simply nodded. Neville left for his cubbyhole below.

The meeting suggested for the next morning didn't happen. The weather went sour in the middle of the night, and by morning, a full-on African Sirocco was blowing hard on the larboard beam. The gritty, hot winds out of desert carried surprising moisture, and by evening, clouds were forming to threaten rain. The event caused *Stork* to deviate north of west and disrupted the casual flow of life they had been enjoying aboard. Commander Mewes was taking personal care to ensure the ship's sails were properly set, the helmsmen did not stray from their course, and a dozen other small details that keep a ship safe at sea. As he had commented, the life of a single-officer ship can be a solitary one.

The Sirocco blew itself out in two days, but not before depositing grit all about the ship and then washing it off with a torrential rain.

"This has not been my most pleasant passage, Neville," Archibald grumbled on the morning of day five. "Where is a nice Levanter now to see us in to Gibraltar? We were forced far enough to the north that we have to crawl our way back to our original course."

"Good morning, Archibald. How's the coffee today?"

"I apologize, good sir. We mustn't forget our pleasantries. The coffee's not too hot today. Which reminds me; you were going to tell me another story – about a frigate, I believe."

Forsooth, I had hoped he would forget it. "I was, wasn't I… what's that there?"

"Land, ho!" cried the lookout, as if he had just been reminded to see to his duty. Neville was already pointing to the west-southwest.

"My lookout needs a good scolding," said Archibald. "That's the great rock itself, and we can see it from the deck."

"Lookout, can you not see Spain to the starboard?" Mewes yelled up.

The lookout's response wasn't immediate, "Yes, Sir, I can."

"Methinks he is no longer a lookout, Lt. Burton. What would you say?"

"I'd agree." He gave the short answer in hopes of a change of subject.

"In the morning, then, if this breeze holds, we should be nearing the harbor at Gibraltar," Mewes announced to the wind. "As much as I'd like to hear your story, I believe I must go below and begin preparing my reports for the station commander. Even if he's never seen me before, he'll expect every little detail of my travels."

"**W**hat's that, there, Lieutenant Burton?" queried Archibald on arriving on deck in the early light of the next new day. *Stork* waited only for Mewes' arrival on deck and his order to tack over before she would enter the harbor and drop anchor among the fleet.

"I've been studying it for the last fifteen minutes," said Neville. "I'm about convinced it's my old ship, the *Venerable*. It appears she's been hammered hard, though. There's only a jury mainmast, no foretopmast, and a dozen other mismatched bits. The rigging is all ahoo, and I can see at least two holes in her topsides. I would suppose there's been a great battle somewhere."

"Either that or a terrible storm in the Atlantic, but I'd wager on the battle. Storms shouldn't poke holes in the topsides. There are other damaged ships about, as well. We'll know soon enough. I must report in as soon as we anchor, and the station will be a-buzz with the news and the rumors, I'm sure."

Four hours later *Stork* anchored, Mewes had been into town, made his reports, and had begun his return trip in the little jolly boat that served for his gig. Neville watched as the sails fluttered lazily by the mole, then filled weakly on a course for *Stork*. Gibraltar was host to a beautiful day with a comfortable temperature, slight breeze, and puffy white clouds in a blue sky. The rock itself sufficed to give comfort to any Englishman there. It soon appeared that the breeze wasn't good enough for Commander Mewes, however. The little boat had come only half way to its home ship when the sail came down and the oars came out. *Stork's* crew began rowing in apparent haste.

Neville bit his tongue while the ship's boatswain set about preparations to receive his captain. It was obvious to him that Archibald had news and would want to be aboard quickly. The boatswain did manage to assemble four marines and begin his piping in the nick of time. Commander Mewes seemed scarcely to notice the slackness of behavior, jumping out of the boat at the same instant Midshipman Rawson caught the painter. He pounced on deck and headed immediately for the companion to go below.

"Heave short, Mr. Wrenhouse," he called over his shoulder to the boatswain.

"Come with me Neville," he said. "Quick, now. Lively." He pounced down the stairs.

Below, in his cabin, he said to Neville. "We're leaving right away, if you didn't smoke it. No provisions, no water, no shore leave. We go."

"What did you find out, Sir?"

Archibald looked up at him wearing an annoyed expression.

"Sorry, Archibald. What's your situation?"

"We weren't wrong with our guess about a battle. On the sixth of July, Admiral Saumarez attacked a French force in the Bay of Algeciras. They were beaten away due to the shoals; *Hannibal* surrendered. The French escaped and sailed to the harbor at Cadiz, where Saumarez chased them. Another battle ensued on the twelfth, wherein the French were beaten back into the harbor, but considerable damage was done, as you have seen by *Venerable*, and considerable loss of life."

"So why do we rush away?"

"Because of you, my friend. My orders, as it says in this letter I've received, are to see you to England. The fleet here is now quite short of officers, and will take any who wander in. They didn't see these orders, and I didn't report your presence aboard, but they know I'm here. It is unlikely they would press a packet commander, and I wasn't told to stay, but I wasn't told I couldn't leave, either. I don't need them to come out here and find you lying about, or I won't complete my 'special assignment', will I? That's the long and short of it. Let's go up and see if we're hove short."

Archibald sprung out the door and up the steps as quickly as any proper housecat would do, and began shouting orders to his boatswain before Neville reached the bottom stair.

"Weigh anchor, then, Mr. Wrenhouse," Neville heard Archibald say. He then yelled upward, "Loose foretops'l!"

Stork swung slowly in the light breeze, pointed her nose south into the Gibraltar Gut, and began accumulating momentum as she left the shelter of the mountain behind. Neville noticed that a small launch heading for the spot where they'd been anchored had now turned about for a return trip to the mole. He kept it to himself.

"Everything she'll hold, Mr. Jason," ordered Commander Archibald Mewes to his Second Sailing Master. "Course north by west for Cabo Farol." He was not about to sail leisurely eastward from Gibraltar and then turn north when comfortably offshore. "Let's put as much water under our keel as possible as quickly as we can." *Stork* raced north-west before a fair wind in a low mounding sea. A cloud-free azure sky accompanied their return to blue water.

"Are we not rather close in to the enemy's coast for your comfort, Archibald?" asked Neville.

"Nay, my friend. My destination is London, and I am taking you there in great haste. Our fleet should have any ship of size trapped in Cadiz or some other miserable little hole. Some unrated thing may be loose to hunt for small fry like us, but I'll wager that in the unlikely event we encounter one, we will prove ourselves faster. Once we weather Cabo Farol of Portugal, we'll not be worrying about Spain. The most likely hindrance between here and there is our own blockade."

"True enough. We may be stopped more than once to show our papers – and maybe even be called to carry packets or people – not that those would slow us."

"Sail, ho!" cried the man up the mast.

"We may have cursed ourselves with talk of an uninteresting sail home, Neville.

"Where away, lookout?"

"Larboard bow, Sir. Two points free."

"Whose, and what course?"

"Can't tell yet, Sir."

"Give us a shout when you can."

"We'll crack on without a change until we know more, Neville. Shall we hunt up some more coffee?"

A mere half hour later, the situation had changed considerably. The sail was now identified as a French sloop of war – probably the one type of ship other than a lugger that had a chance of catching them. She was crossing their course and upwind – that is to say, she had the weather gage – and the weather now offered *Stork* no favors. A stronger breeze was in her favor, but the growing waves were not.

"What are your orders, Sir?" Second Sailing Master Jason inquired. His meaning was clear enough. A concerned expression on his face implied that he expected some spar to carry away soon if sail were not reduced.

"No chance of reaching the blockade fleet at Cadiz, then," Archibald said – more of a mumble to himself than a comment to Neville. Mewes' usual practices did not include the confidence of anyone else aboard, let alone asking for opinions.

"I think there are three options," said Neville, "if you'd have my opinion."

"We certainly don't have much time. She's cutting us off from Cadiz, to be sure, so we'll be on our own…but go ahead."

"The first two, of which I'm sure you are well aware, we have little time for – either turn to the west and run or turn tail for Gibraltar. The third might be more fun. How many guns do we carry? I see only four."

"For a packet we're well-armed. Six four-pounders!" Archibald bragged.

"Still no match for her, then, I'd say. Four-pounders might bounce off a sturdy sloop of war. She probably carries eight 6-

pounders, too. A direct action would probably see us captured. Well, here's my thought, anyway. Admiral Duncan used the idea before the Battle of Camperdown back in ninety-seven: We raise the flag for 'enemy', and then several others, one after the other, and we go straight at her. She'll have to decide quite soon whether she wants to be chased by the whole squadron behind us or keep on and fight."

"What squadron behind us?" blurted Archibald. His head jerked 'round like the cat who hears the mouse. "They're not chasing us for leaving Gibraltar without permission are they? Nobody… Oh! Ho, ho. It's a bluff; a ruse. There's not even a fishing boat behind us. Ho, ho, ho. I like it, though. But if he doesn't run? Or if he does?"

If she's unsure and waits until she would see the signals, she would be close, indeed, and theoretically vulnerable. She must turn tail soon, then, or risk the possibility of capture herself. If she comes on, then we have the first two options, but she'll be closer. If this wind continues to rise, she will have the advantage of her size as the sea grows higher."

"Hmm," said Archibald. It's…"

Six bells of the afternoon watch were rung a short five feet away.

"…Six bells. If she comes at us, we could run east and play all sorts of tricks after dark. The clouds are gathering quickly. It may be a dirty night. She wouldn't catch us before dark."

"I agree with your assessment."

"Ease sheets a bit, then, Mr. Jason," Archibald said, "Spill the wind. You heard our plan. We don't want the sails going to shreds or bits to begin blowing off the ship, do we? We must look as though we are still interested in chasing her, but we don't want to get there too soon."

Mewes continued, now to the only midshipman aboard, "Mr. Rawson, raise the signal 'enemy'. Give it two minutes, and then raise the signal 'acknowledge' and leave it up for three minutes. Then take it down and raise 'course west'. After that, raise some other signal of your choosing every two minutes, alternating with the 'acknowledge' signal. Understood?"

"Aye Sir," the boy said without any convincing enthusiasm. A pudgy, dull-looking fellow with stringy hair and particularly dirty sleeves, his very movements lacked excitement.

Neville's understanding of Archibald's obvious loneliness increased as the commander mumbled to him, "Let's see if he can manage that. It should keep him busy a while, at the least."

Archibald noticed Neville's look, and added, "If ever we see England's shores, I shall set him off. He's not much of wit, I'm afraid. I can't imagine he would pass for lieutenant.

"Mr. Wrenhouse," he added, "Clear for action and pipe the men to their stations, if you please."

"There she goes, Commander," said Mr. Jason just twenty minutes later. "She fell for it. She appears to be turning back to the northwest, where she came from."

"That's good, ain't it, Neville? I thought she might just slide off to the west to see if she could see our squadron, and then come chase after us when she didn't."

"I worried the same, Archibald, but she would have left us leading the chase to Cadiz, if she had done. She'll be gone soon, I suspect. There is no reason for her to stick around and check on us again in the morning. We'll be into our Cadiz blockade fleet by noon, if tonight's weather isn't too bad."

"Ah, yes. We'll be stopped by them, won't we? Out of the fire into the frying pan, I suppose."

"Yes, but better that than being captured by a French sloop of war."

"British!" the lookout called down just at the close of dinner. *Stork* was now seven days north of Cadiz and beginning her crossing of the Bay of Biscay. They had been stopped and questioned in Cadiz, as they expected, loaded with several packets and one sick carpenter's mate, and sent on their way. The weather had cleared, but left them clawing their way north into an unfavorable northerly offshore breeze, close in to the Portuguese shore.

"I am more than pleased to be shot of those annoying Portuguese fishermen, I tell you, Neville!" Archibald grumbled.

"They do operate strangely, I'll admit," replied Neville. "There seemed to be no pattern to their schedules, so they gave us the opportunity to run them down day or night. They've never heard of carrying any sort of light, it appears, even with a heavy cloud or new moon."

Better the smoother sea in close to shore, though. A sea of more than six feet slows *Stork* horribly. You can feel it now we've cleared Finisterre."

"Three frigates and a brig, I think, Commander!" yelled the lookout.

"The one ahead is the *Boadicea*, Commander, or I'm a plate of peas," said Jason to Mewes. "Captain Keats. I served aboard her two years."

"What do we do, Commander?" Neville queried. "Speak or avoid?"

"I'd rather avoid, but it would be rude not to speak, if not downright suspicious. They might chase us if we ignore them."

Stork worked her way closer to the small squadron for an hour before she was close enough to let fly her sheets for a conversation. The rough day ensured there would be no extended communication, but Mewes would try his best.

"Ahoy, *Boadicea*," cried Commander Mewes through his speaking trumpet. Neville stood alongside to provide assist in understanding, if it were needed.

"You know us? Who be ye?"

"Aye, Sir. We've a man served aboard your ship. We are his Royal British Majesty's Ship *Stork*, packet to London. Seven days out of Cadiz."

"[unintelligible]... six days out of Tor Bay. Who is there beside you?"

"Lieutenant on orders to London."

"A supernumerary?"

"Aye. On orders, I say."

"...suspend...him across," ordered the *Boadicea's* captain.

"Did you hear, Neville? Did he say to send you across?"

"I think he did, Archibald. Ask him to repeat it."

"Please repeat your last, Captain," Mewes yelled across the waves.

"Send him over to *Boadicea*. He's mine for now."

"I have orders to transport him, Sir."

"...give you a note to... temporary... immediately! We ... our boat."

"I can scarce understand a word with this wind in my ear, Archibald, I'm sorry. I think he means to take me, though. Yes, look. Their launch is being swayed out. We'd best play along. Don't worry about London. I don't believe I'm on any tight schedule to return."

"Makes me look the fool, though, don't it?"

"It will pass. If you must report to Room 4, please be sure to tell him I'm well and will be back soon."

Boadicea's launch, itself almost a third the length of *Stork*, banged hard against *Stork's* hull at the main chains.

"Mind your boat, you lubbers," screamed Wrenhouse at the coxswain. The next wave drove it hard against the hull again, sending splinters form the launch's gunwale across *Stork's* deck.

"There, you idiot," yelled Wrenhouse, "that'll give you something to do back aboard."

"The repair will go to Mr. Chips, won't it, Mr. Boatswain?" said the coxswain arrogantly.

" 'Vast your caterwauling, Mr. Wrenhouse," ordered Mewes. "Mr. Midshipman, are you in charge?" The boy in uniform nodded, but was obviously interested in staying clear of the argument. "Where's the note?"

"Aye, Sir. Here 'tis, Sir." He stood to fish the note from his inner pocket and hand it up, but fell hard against the gunwale when the launch thumped *Stork* again. The coxswain handed up the note.

"Stand off a minute, Coxswain, or come aboard and get ready to paint.

"Throw him his painter, Mr. Rawson, and shove him off."

"What have we got here, Commander?" Neville queried.

"His note states that if he has the right to repatriate English sailors from American ships, he certainly has the right to collect inactive sailors – officers or otherwise – from British ships. As to you, he claims to be in great need, and the assignment will be as temporary as the two of you can agree upon. Nevertheless, this is an order, not a request and, for me, I may take this note to report the transaction at home; and would I please carry his packet which the midshipman has with him. It's signed 'Captain Charles Rowley'. I thought Mr. Jason said 'Keats'."

"We serve at the command of the King – and the Admiralty. His note's a load of codswallow, ain't it? He must have had the first part already written in the hope of crossing some unfortunate ship like yours."

"I'd agree, but it doesn't much change things. He sounds a fair bloke, at least, if he's willing to negotiate terms with you."

"Aye, Commander Mewes," Neville said. "It has been a pleasure sailing with you. We'll meet again one day, I'm sure of it. Can you have them scurry my sea chest up here. I've left without it before, and it's most awkward."

Neville noticed the *Boadicea's* coxswain being far more careful at his own ship than he was at the side of *Stork*. His boat approached cautiously and the painter thrown early to waiting hands in the main chains before the launch ever touched the big ship's side.

Neville swung himself easily up the familiar side of a thirty-eight gun frigate and landed lightly on the deck. After saluting the colours, he turned to meet a sharp-looking lieutenant of average height and build. They touched their hats to each other, and the man said, "Please follow me to the captain's cabin. It's Captain Rowley."

"I saw the note."

"Lieutenant Stutters, First, at your service, Lieutenant…?"

"Burton. Neville Burton."

Conversation ceased until they were standing in front of the captain's desk. The cabin, although neat, clean, and smelling of cherry-flavored tobacco, was the usual cramped space for a frigate. Through the gallery windows, he caught a glimpse of *Stork's* receding sails.

"Lieutenant Burton, reporting as ordered, Captain." Holding his hat, he touched his forehead. "Here are my orders."

A moment passed while the captain read the orders. "These orders are interesting, to be sure, but there is nothing here compelling me to return you to the packet. Your service date, please."

"Third October, 1789, Sir."

Captain Rowley looked beyond Neville to First Lieutenant Stutters and raised his eyebrows.

"Third, I believe, Sir," said Stutters.

"We were ordered to sail from Tor Bay whether we had a full complement or not, Lt. Burton. This ship should have three lieutenants. You have served at sea, have you not?"

"Aye, Sir." Since the usual etiquette for a lieutenant is never to speak to a captain without being asked a direct question, Neville remained quiet after his response. Captain Rowley said nothing, but continued to stare at Neville, who realized after a moment that the captain expected a verbal resume.

"Oh, sorry, Sir," he began, "Midshipman in *Castor*, frigate of thirty-two guns – 1792 until May of 1794. *Sans Pereil*, eighty-gun ship of the line – June, 1794 to the Battle of Groin in June of 1795; Prize crew of the *Formidable* and then Prize Commander of *Spy*, who was then the French *Espion…*"

"That will do, Lieutenant Burton. I think I have the picture. An 'active career' they might say."

Thank the Lord. I could hardly tell him I have experience as a frigate captain. He'd never believe it.

"As I began," continued Rowley, "we set sail with only two of the three lieutenants we are supposed to have. The other ships are one short each, so I could hardly take one from them. You know what being short a lieutenant means, then?"

"Aye, Sir." *Extra watch duty, double the guns to fight…*

"My orders direct me to annoy the navy and merchant vessels of France's allies, which, of course, means Spain. We must deny France access to Spain's ports. We have been sent, therefore, to the nasty northern coast of Galicia, to find any such things with sails we can destroy or take as prizes. Our targets include Corunna, which is only a day away, Bilbao, Santander, and Gijon, specifically. Have you been involved in 'cutting out'?"

Again, I cannot give details. "Aye, Sir. I led a party to take a French frigate on the south of…"

"A frigate? My God! You'll do nicely, I believe. The rest will meet you at supper. Lt. Stutters will confirm your standing and fill you in." Rowley made a motion with his hand something like brushing crumbs off a napkin.

"Aye, Sir," said Neville.

6: *A Coruña*

"**O**ur schooner sent her boats in last night while we were on our offshore patrol," began Captain Rowley shortly after breakfast two days later. "There is a ship which appears to be pierced for 20 guns at anchor here," he said, sticking a pin in a chart of the harbor while the fleet's officers looked on. "She has the look of a new Spanish Navy ship. They report her as the *Neptune*. There are two at the quay: a gunboat armed with a long thirty-two pounder, and what appears to be a packet ship, the *Reyno* something-or-other. There is also a French sixteen-gun corvette or similar farther down, but close enough that the four make a reasonably accessible group worth our effort. The French thing appears to be manned, but they weren't sure about the *Neptune*. There are otherwise three other merchant vessels at anchor in the harbor, but they are over there," he said, pointing a gnarled finger at the other side of the harbor chart.

"Yes, Lieutenant Morely?" he queried of the squadrons' marine commander who had begun an odd shuffling in the middle of the assembly, "What have you?"

"Question, Sir."

"Go ahead."

"Thank you, Sir. There is the fort and there is a semaphore on a great stone box on the west shore. Will we be called upon to remove them from action?"

"Not this time, Lieutenant Morely. We are ordered to 'annoy the enemy', but our time in the harbor is very limited. There will probably be some stars shining through this partial overcast, but a small moon will rise by midnight, if you remember. There may then be enough light for the fort to shoot at us. This isn't England, gentlemen," the captain continued, looking around the cabin. "These cursed dagos stay up all hours to eat. That means we have between whenever they go to their beds – maybe six bells – and the rise of the moon, at eight bells. No marine action, then. This is an in-and-out thing. A marine landing would take too much time. If our timing is not perfect, you might alert the fort and their ships. If you're late, we would be in danger of leaving you ashore as we run from the fort's bombardment."

"We'll take a barge and launch from each frigate, plus the schooner's launch. Be sure to designate eight men to row the gunboat into position where it can be towed by another – the packet, I expect – or it will have to be rowed out here.

"This all brings us to the question of who is in charge of what," he said.

Captain Griffith of *Diamond* chimed in, "I suggest my Lieutenant Kelley to hunt the French sixteen-gun corvette. He speaks French like the very frogs. They should let him climb right aboard, ha, ha."

"Good. Lieutenant Kelley, you are so assigned. With that in mind," said Rowley, "do we have anyone who speaks Spanish?"

The officers looked 'round at each other, but no positive response came.

"I can speak some," volunteered Neville at length. "I'm quite rusty," *to say the least; the Spanish I learned is an 'undred years old. I might not be understood at all.* "They may think me foreign, but not likely Catalonian or English; or I could call out in French.

Rowley stared at him for a moment, and then asked, "Will your arm hinder you?"

Neville was startled. He'd not mentioned the arm injury to anyone, and tried hard not to let it be noticed.

"Not if I don't have to row, Sir," answered Neville.

"We'll use your Spanish, whatever is it, on the *Neptune*, then," said Rowley after another moment's thought. "Take a jolly boat and make up a party that looks to be from shore on some inspection or something."

"At seven bells of the evening…?"

"I said 'make something up', Lieutenant," snapped Rowley, " Just get aboard. You'll have two of our barges behind you."

"Good enough, Sir," said Neville.

"*Fisgard*, your boats go to the quay, then, and bring out that *Reyno* and the gunboat. I expect there will be no crew aboard a gunboat at night, unless they leave a guard, and no merchant carries a large company."

"Aye, aye, Sir," said some voice in the back.

"We're settled, I say," declared Rowley. "All boats alongside *Boadicea* at four bells of the evening watch."

T ension grew throughout the day. Tempers were shorter than usual, as men were chosen to man the boats. While it might be an honor to be chosen, the honor accompanied the knowledge that something could go wrong. Something usually did go wrong. It did not always mean disaster, but it might mean injury or the captain's wrath after an unsuccessful attempt. This mission looked to be easy, but such optimism always proved to be a bad way to look at it. The fort might get some advance warning, or they might just get a lucky shot. The ships they sought to cut out might be fully manned for training or some other unexpected reason.

The marines were visibly offended, conducting an extra morning drill at center deck, tramping heavily in response to stridently-shouted commands. Dinner came and went, and grog was served out. The boats were checked carefully and small stuff found to silence the oarlocks.

"Is there some illness I am not aware of, Doctor?" asked Neville during the officers' dinner.

"If there is, I'm not aware of it, either. Why do you ask?"

"All the coughing; do you not hear it?"

"I have," said the second lieutenant. "I find it most annoying. It seems every man who comes to ask me something begins by coughing in my face."

"I have nobody in sick bay for such a thing," mused the doctor, "but I've felt a scratchy throat most of today, myself. I think it's this bloody offshore wind."

"You've got it, doctor," said Marine Lieutenant Morely. "It is. It carries a terrible fine grit."

"The wind in the Bay of Biscay is normally East – or even north of it, and carries no such thing as grit. Salt, maybe, but no grit," said First Lieutenant Stutters, "but this east-west coast has bent the wind south of east, it seems."

"Lieutenant Stutters," said Neville, "I am concerned that if we take an 'undred coughing men into the harbor at night, we just might not come back with an 'undred; and nary a boat, as well."

The gunroom quieted, and for a moment, the others stared at Neville.

"Do you propose to tell the captain we mustn't go because the men cough?" queried Stutters.

"Ho, ho! I'd like to watch you tell 'im," laughed Morely. The others joined in rudely.

"Of course not, gentlemen. Since I take it I am asked to speak, I propose something the men would all like much better: Every man in the boats must wear a damp neckcloth up over his nose, and we send every one off with a mouthful of rum to sooth his throat."

"Jolly good," said Morely, "now I really want to go!"

"Quite good, Lieutenant Burton. Quite good. Pass word of it to all our boatmen, and I'll have a note sent to the other ships to do the same."

Weapons were passed out to the boat crews during the first dog watch, allowing the men to check them carefully while it the light still lingered. Muskets and cutlasses were then stacked in readiness. Supper came and went, and grog served out.

The bells were rung for last dog watch. They sky grew slightly more overcast, covering even more stars, and the night went dark, indeed. The fresh breeze held. It would be on their bows for the row in, as would the retreating tide. The mouth of the harbor was wide, however, so despite the eight foot tide, the effect on rowing boats was expected to be minor. The schooner's boats reported no great difficulty just two days earlier, at least.

"They're all here, Captain," reported Stutters upon the chime of four bells at *Boadicea*'s binnacle.

"Wave *Diamond's* boats off," said Rowley.

Fifty-two oars dipped into the inky-black water of the Bay of Biscay just southwest of the harbor entrance to A Coruña. A few oars clattered against the other waiting boats, with the expected resulting growls of the voices of angry coxswains. The noise soon died away, however, and only a few flashes of water off the blades of wet oars gave any evidence of three boats departing in a single line.

"Our turn now, Lt. Burton," said *Fisgard's* designated leader. "Shall we?"

"I'll be out before you," said Neville. "Put a bottle of claret on it?"

"I will, indeed." The two shook hands and climbed down into their boats.

Neville, having slightly farther to row to reach his objective at anchor, shoved off first. "No cocked muskets," he announced. "Follow me in one line, and break off a cable short of Neptune as we discussed. 'Quiet's' the word, if you want to come home tonight."

The three boats rowed quietly in the darkness for fifteen minutes; then twenty, before they opened the harbor.

Seawater, as warm this time of year as the Bay of Biscay would ever get, gurgled along the sides of the boats. An occasional wave threw spray over the first three rows of oarsmen, but they were probably pleased to have a little relief from the effort of rowing. Once into the harbor mouth, they were assailed by the smells of land: fish on the beach, cooking fires and Spanish spiced food, and the odors of cattle. The clouds, which had been streaming steadily to the west, broke clear for a moment. Neville gasped. The fort could be seen, and each of the ships they had come to capture, basked in the light of thousands of stars. The harbor became so clear that Neville noticed a sentry walking his rounds on the fort's parapet above. Only a moment it was, and then gone again, jerked back into darkness. Neville blew out his breath slowly, realizing that this phenomenon they had just experienced could happen again, and at the worst possible moment. *For now, though, remain calm.*

Sounds from shore joined the smells. A rooster crowed, and somewhere some dogs were having an argument with harbor seals. A fisherman in the blackness to his left began rapping on the side of his rough canoe in an attempt to herd fish into his net. Although Neville's mind screamed at him to urge his men to row harder, his instincts told him to leave things as they were, resist the urge to use his voice at all, and remain as quiet as mice.

As planned, the three rowing boats approached *Neptune* from head on, expecting a sentry perched on the bow to be very unlikely. Neville, in his jolly boat, began a long swing shoreward, so as to appear to any observer that he had approached from the quay. Before leaving *Boadicea*, he had taken the time to choose the six most "Spanish-looking" fellows he could find – the swarthiest, darkest-skinned and least English-looking in appearance. These were the crew of the jolly boat. Stealth was their plan, with surprise still the best weapon he had.

So far, things were going well. He neither saw nor heard any activity aboard *Neptune*. No tiny dots of light gave evidence of sentries smoking at their posts. They were a half cable away and no one had called out to them. "It is unlikely we will encounter an armed force. Just like us, they would not issue the weapons until a battle is expected. There may be a few armed guards, and we must be wary of swivel guns, but I think not more. Hold your English muskets so you hide the locks," Neville reminded his men. "Our jolly boat is risky enough.

"Ship starboard oars," he commanded at a near whisper. They had rowed upstream of *Neptune*, and the tide would take them the rest of the way to her side now. The jolly boat slid quietly down the ship to her main chains, where four strong arms, no longer rowing, clamped hard ahold of the small warship.

Neville stood, knowing his two larger boats would already be hiding under *Neptune's* bows, and rapped on the gunwale with his sword hilt. "¡Hola!" he shouted, "¡Hola! Necessito hablar con su capitán! (I need to speak to your captain!)"

A man appeared from the dark aft; the probable sentry. He walked quickly, almost at a trot. His hand was on a pistol at his belt, but he had not drawn it; probably because Neville had spoken Spanish.

"¿Qué haces aquí ?(Why are you here?)" He demanded.

"Me quedo con lo de aqui (I'll take it from here), Sr. Bravo," said another voice arriving from forward. To Neville, he said, "¿Cuál es tu respuesta, por favor? (What is your answer, please)?"

The conversation continued in Spanish: "Your captain, please," demanded Neville again. He paused a moment, but decided to add, "I am from the fort above." He included a small wave of his hand toward shore.

This second man, who wore an officer's uniform, by this time stood directly above the jolly boat. He hesitated, looking down into the dark. Not much more than Neville's face and some outline of a boat with men in it could have been discerned. "The captain's not here. I am the first officer. You must deal with me."

"Not here? He is required to be here. I am coming up. Step aside." Without waiting for approval, Neville grabbed the closest stay and swung himself up onto the low deck. There he found himself facing three more men who had gathered, apparently out of curiosity, to view the unusual activity. The only ones armed, not counting the short knives they all wore in their belts, were the officer, with his sword, and the sentry, with his pistol.

Neville did not wait for further objections by the Spanish officer. "I must see your papers," he said.

"I object, you cannot…"

"Come up!" he commanded his men in the jolly boat. He spoke in Spanish, but the wag of his hand made his intention obvious. The four who were armed immediately began to climb up.

The sentry began to interrupt the two officers' confrontation: "Lieutenant Gutierrez, They are not…"

"Enough, Mr. Apellido. I know they're not supposed to be here. Call the watch!"

"¡Halt, Mr. Apellido!" said Neville, quickly drawing the short sword he had worn for this action. He swung it to the first officer's neck and calmly said, "or your Lieutenant is dead, and you will be next." His arm screamed at him.

Four English muskets rose to point at the small Spanish 'greeting party'.

"¡No mueve! (Nobody move!)" commanded Neville. The clicking of muskets being cocked echoed loudly about the small ship. The man with the pistol was now staring down the barrel of one of them. His jaw moved, but no sound came from his mouth.

With his free hand, Neville cautiously withdrew the officer's sword from its scabbard.

"Push your pistol over there," he said to the sentry. "All of you lie down along the rail – over there."

"Mr. Raney, watch over them while the rest of us see to the swivel guns. You two go aft. You, come with me."

The moment they could see the forward swivel gun, unmanned on a pedestal, Neville slapped his two swords together four times – two pairs of two strikes. Englishmen began to swarm over the bulwarks forward from the _Boadicea's_ boats. The kept their noise relatively quiet, however, owing to the task at hand – no bellowing and hallooing as they would have done in a conventional battle. Their clattering of cutlasses and muskets was still not loud enough to drown out the sound of small arms fire beginning a few cables farther down the harbor.

Mr. Ebenezer, who had earlier been introduced as the boatswain's mate who would be in charge of sailing the ship out, appeared in front of Neville. He said nothing.

"Heave short, Mr. Ebenezer," said Neville, "There's a bottle of claret waiting for me."

"Aye, Sir."

Two more lieutenants appeared amongst the small crowd of Spaniards being herded into the center of the ship. They were yelling their condemnation of the British action and exhorting their men to resist. "Mr. Lazard," Neville yelled to a marine corporal he recognized, "Get them all sitting, except those two noisy things. Heave them over the side. It's not too far for them to swim."

"Thank you, Sir," answered a grinning Lazard.

No sound emanated from the quay. A larger gun fired – somewhere in the direction of the French navy corvette – but the small arms fire from the same direction was decreasing. Two splashes and a shout told Neville the ship had been freed of the objectionable Spanish officers.

Mr. Ebenezer appeared again, "Straight up and down, Sir. Sounds like they're having trouble over there, don't it?"

"It does. Get us out of here before the moon comes up and the fort decides to get involved."

"Aye, aye, Sir.

The cry from forward, "Anchor's aweigh!" might as well have been "Run for cover!" The clouds replayed their clearing-away trick. Moon, stars, and billowing new white topsails all conspired to display *Neptune's* exact location to any casual observer in the fort – or anywhere else in the harbor, for that matter. Neville could see the packet and the gunboat still at the quay. The gunboat appeared to be drawn up behind the packet, however, so progress was being made. Further down the harbor, he could also see *Diamond's* three boats pulling hard for open water. The light continued. A cannon fired ... *from the corvette?* Neville saw a plume of water erupt a half cable from *Diamond's* second fleeing boat.

The fort had surely been alerted by the skirmish at the corvette. Maybe they had even seen something the previous time the clouds cleared and been waiting.

"Main topsail, Mr. Ebenezer!" ordered Neville.

A cannon fired on the hillside, its red tongue clearly visible before the dark hulk of fort behind it. Still the light held. The fort would be able to judge the correction needed to hit something. *Neptune* moved faster; the harbor's little wavelets began to gossip down her sides, and Neville could hear a gurgle from behind. *I'll beat the packet out, at least,* he thought, *if there's anything left of us.*

A large splash a cable short and forward leaped into the moonlight. *Shite!*

The packet's fore and main topsails dropped simultaneously, showing another pretty white target for the fort. Neville watched in calm curiosity while the little ship, with the gunboat tied behind, began to draw away from the quay.

The lights went out again as another cannon at the fort fired. Clouds covered the moon and stars as before. *Thank God!* Neville thought, a split second before a ball from the fort tore away the fore topmast. *Thank the Lord they didn't have time to heat the shot. The fort won't have seen it, though.* Someone forward screamed. *They won't know if they were right. They can't be sure where to shoot next. The main topsail is still drawing.*

"Chop it free, Mr. Ebenezer. We haven't many men to sail the ship. The rest are still herding the Spanish below!"

Another cannon fired. Neville listened for the splash, but never heard a thing. *Whatever they guessed, it was wrong.* His pounding heart began to slow. *We should be clear. Even if the moon comes out again, we should be out of range.*

"**R**epulsed, damn it!" cursed Lieutenant Kelley of *Diamond*. "That frog ship was fully manned! Sentries at all corners! We scarcely bumped the hull when they began shouting and firing. We fired back to keep their heads down and began to row like madmen. Then they fired their swivel gun at us, but – ho, ho, they had it loaded as a signal gun. We were lucky it didn't hit a man, though. The wad by itself tore an 'ole in our launch's gunwale. Then, when we were almost away, the cursed moon came out! Bloody hell!"

"We saw the ball hit the water, Lieutenant Kelley," said Neville. "Damn close to your second boat, it was."

"I thought I'd have that bottle of claret when your fore topmast went by the boards, Burton, but the gunboat is a heavy thing to tow," chimed in *Fisgard's* lieutenant.

"Never in life," said Neville. "We had one man down in the tangle of rigging, and another lost a finger – by the ball from the fort, we think."

"Lost a finger? Ho, ho!" roared Captain Seymour of *Fisgard*. "We've taken three of their ships and they've shot off a finger? Ha, ha, ho!"

"If that's the last of your enjoyment of this escapade, gentlemen," said Captain Rowley, "I have a final announcement:

"Lt. Burton, I am appointing you Prize Commander of this little flotilla. You all know I don't need to give my reasons, but here they are: one, your performance in action was exemplary; two, you have the Spanish language necessary to control these ships while taking as few Englishmen as possible from our squadron; three, you already have orders to go to London; and four, we did not have you when we set sail, so although we may miss you, we will simply be back where we were when we began this voyage. I will have your orders for this writ fair by morning, and you may be on your way by noon, after we sort out the rest of the prize crew. If you can do anything to have a few officers and our prize crew sent over to us when you get to the Navy Office, we would appreciate it."

7: *England*

After the usual harangue associated with passing off *Neptune, Reyno Duno*, and the gunboat to the prize court authorities in Plymouth, Neville sought out a Royal Mails coach to London. He marveled at the progress in transportation while, at the same time, he grumbled about the priority system for its use that required him to wait three days before boarding. As he had told Lt. Mewes on *Stork*, however, he had no schedule to keep.

Even in early September, London seemed chilly to Neville – after Jamaica and then the north coast of Africa - and even the south of France. The Bay of Biscay had done some chilling of his outlook, however. It had rained and the street puddles in the morning sun twinkled like a thousand little mirrors. A typical Englishman might consider it a cheerful morning. The cold breeze must have been from the North Sea, though. Unlike many of those around him who were clearly enjoying the weather, Neville wore a scarf tight up 'round his neck.

"Neville, my boy. It's jolly good to see you," said Sir William Mulholland. "Not only are you home safe, but you've done another remarkable thing." The two met in Mulholland's office at Whitehall – Room 4. Neville was always surprised to see Sir William when he sat. Over a fathom in height while standing, the man looked like he must only be five feet tall when he sat. *All legs*, Neville reminded himself. He looked well, but older, although it had been less than a year since they had seen each other. He had been a friend to Neville's father, too, before the latter went missing in a navy battle off St. Vincent when Neville was less than two. Not many understood the connection between Sir William and the navy, either. His guise was a 'senior bureaucrat', one of which Whitehall had many. Neville had stumbled into his circle – or possibly had been guided in by Sir William himself – through orders from the Admiralty – whose source was not always clear.

"It's good to see you, too, Sir. Just to be home in England is a joy… though it's cold here."

"Nonsense. It's a beautiful English summer day out there. How did you get off the *Boston*?"

"*Boston*? You're a story behind, Sir. I would have thought you'd heard some part of it from Commander Mewes by now. After being chased out of Toulon and we got back aboard *Boston*, I asked Captain McNeill if he might take me to Gibraltar. He was more understanding of the nature of my visit by then, but he refused… said he needed to report back on station at Tripoli."

"We?" queried Sir William.

"I thought I told you in my letter. A little old French farmer – Louis – helped me with some food and acted as guide for a few miles in exchange for a ride to the city of Boston to see his son. *USS Boston* took him aboard as a landsman, and they're due back to the United Sates next month, I believe. Louis will be a bit of a sailor by then, I should think."

"Oh, yes. I didn't pay a lot of attention to that part, sorry. You sound as if you were fond of him."

"I was a bit, I guess. He'll be all right, though, if he can find his son. He has his older son's navy sword which is probably worth an 'undred guineas. That'll do him a while…

"Anyway, Captain McNeill didn't want to go to Gibraltar, but we crossed *Stork*, Lieutenant Mewes' advice boat, before reaching Malta and I went aboard with him for the ride to Gibraltar. You could imagine the commotion in Gibraltar between the blockade at Cadiz and the battle at Algeciras. We chose to leave there before some ship conscripted me… I think we were only minutes ahead of the shore boat coming to get one of us.

"My intention was to come straight here, of course, but there's no letting a British naval officer loose without good reason these days. We crossed Captain Rowley's squadron under way for the north of Spain. I was foolishly standing on deck with Lt. Mewes and they spotted me, and Captain Rowley called me aboard *Boadicea*. The only reason I'm here now is because he sent me back as Prize Commander with three Spanish ships we cut out at Corunna."

"So that's why you disappeared. Your mother and sister were after me, afraid you'd gone missing again."

"Do they know I'm back yet?"

"I sent word the minute I got your note from Plymouth."

"Thank you for that."

Neville continued with the details of his run from Toulon and the cutting out at Corunna, concluding with, "I only took a night to have my uniform cleaned and rest my bones in Plymouth before I came up here. The ride up from Plymouth was awful – ruts and dust."

"I can understand why Captain McNeill needed to be back on station," Mulholland said, returning to the previous topic. "Things became much 'warmer' there after you left. The *USS Enterprise*, a big two-masted schooner commanded by a Lieutenant Sterret, engaged a fourteen-gun Tripolitan corsair on first August and gave her a great thrashing at no cost to herself. We're watching the situation carefully. Having you there as a liaison was not a bad idea, but now we've something else for you to do."

"I look forward to it."

Sir William noticed the tone. "You may be successful in action, young man, but you must learn patience. You might warm to one of my ideas, although I'm not sure how you will take to this one… Jamaica."

Neville held his tongue for a full minute or more. *Do I dare?* He wondered. "Go on," he said.

"I received the papers you picked up in Toulon and had a chance to look them over. There is some silly stuff in there, I think – maybe even stuffed in by our counterpart in France as deception. There is one piece – the one in English which you probably read – the one from a Mr. Chester Stillwater to Citizen Sysson in France. I think Stillwater may be spying against us." *Ahh – M. is for Mister, not Monsieur.* "The letter mentions an attachment – a list of his rum prices. I find no attachment, however. It could have been anything…

"The whole situation of being watched and followed is telling in and of itself. The French might know of the activities of M. Badeau and Georges Cadoudal. That situation would be unfortunate, indeed. And this Chester Stillwater may bear some watching."

"And where is he, then?"

"As I said… Jamaica"

"Why would you choose me to watch him?"

"Because his business is trading in rum; which is to say, 'shipping', so 'watching' will require the navy. If I remember correctly, you have some knowledge of the place – not just Jamaica, but the Caribbean as a whole – you speak both French and Spanish, and you have certainly distinguished yourself in just about any situation you find yourself. He's American, by the way."

"Who is?"

"Mr. Stillwater, of course. Don't play thick, Neville. I don't believe Citizen Sysson in France is a rum customer, either. I recognize the name as one in the government – an aide to Napoleon. Are you interested?"

After another long pause, he answered, "Certainly, Sir, If you wish it. How do I go?"

"Since you've managed to have yourself pitched off the *Elephant*, you'll be assigned to *HMS Vanguard* and go aboard as one of her lieutenants. Your seniority date – and therefore position aboard - will fall where it may, I suppose."

"I imagine so. How am I supposed to watch this Mr. Stillwater if I am a mere lieutenant aboard some ship in the harbor? Where is he in Jamaica, by the way? And I have another problem..."

"I cannot tell you how to do it from here. You did well on your own last time. He's in Kingston, across the harbor from..."

"I know where it is," snapped Neville... "I am sorry, Sir William. I was quite out of line."

"You were, but I understand. And remember my adage, Neville: 'some solution will usually present itself'. What's the other problem?"

"Not what... who: Admiral Nelson."

"Admiral Nelson? What business of yours is he?"

"I promised him my reports of liaison with the Americans. I've sent him two, so he knows I was accepted on the *Boston*. Now what should I do?"

Sir William blew out slowly though his teeth; almost a whistle.

"I will handle it," he finally said. "I doubt his interest is much more than curiosity, and I understand he is not well."

"Thank you."

"Do you need some time? The *Vanguard* sailed for Cadiz on the nineteenth, I think, and will be there for some time. You could take a few weeks to go home. We'll find some little ship going that way to take you."

"I was quite surprised to hear you were home, Major Hall," said Neville to his brother-in-law. Neville had just walked into the Angel Hotel foyer with Mr. Blake for late afternoon tea. "Elizabeth makes me believe she never sees you at home here in Bury St. Edmunds."

"In truth she doesn't much," confided the major. "This last posting to India will continue for some time. I am just lucky the hostilities have died down for now; I petitioned for a short furlough. And you? How do you come to be home now? I am led to believe the navy is throwing everything it has at the French these days. Does it have anything to do with the arm? I understand you've had a bang-up."

"No, not at all. Some Frenchmen smacked me with their batons, but now I've had some rest, it's going away. I should be all well before I go back, thank you.

It is true the Navy's quite active, but sometimes one is just lucky enough to catch a break. Sorry your parents couldn't make it, Gage. And what of little Gage," he asked, inquiring after his nephew. He's what, four now?"

"Five, he is. Ahh, here's Mr. Blake, now."

The three shook hands and they moved to the table where two women sat ensconced at a table by the windows.

"You already have your tea, Ellen, I see," said Mr. Blake to Neville's mother. "It's a good way to pass an afternoon like this one." The rain drummed lightly on the panes and dribbled downward in little rivers.

"Yes. This is a good spot for a proper English summer day."

Small talk related to the happiness of being home – or having the men home – gave way to ordering a bit of food and drink. Mr. Blake, a local corn merchant and Neville's step-father, then summoned the bravery to ask the question that turned the talk to the subject the women did not really want, but knew would come: "What of the war, gentlemen?"

Gage gave his knowledge and impressions of the situation in India and Neville spoke of the Mediterranean and the Americans there. He did not mention his escapade in Toulon. That would open a Pandora's Box he not only didn't want open, but also was required by his orders to keep shut.

"What next, then, Neville?" his mother asked.

"*HMS Vanguard* and the Caribbean, I'm afraid. Captain Sir Thomas Williams."

"The Caribbean again," said Ellen, "You'd better write this time. No disappearing for three years!"

"Yes mother. I promise to write."

"Why 'afraid'?" asked Gage. "Is she not a good ship? Or not a strong captain?"

"I've not heard a thing about Captain Williams," Neville answered. "As a ship I'm sure *Vanguard* is just fine. She's only about fourteen years old, I believe, which is far better than many, but she's a seventy-four. I'm afraid the big ships are not really my 'cup of tea', as they say. I'll be one of six lieutenants. I hate the politics of all that, and they carry sixteen midshipmen, for all love; boys running all over the place. Most sail like pigs, and the admiral will normally call them all up in a line beside the enemy to make a battle of it. I like my frigates. Strategy, maneuvering… using your speed to win the battle, not just pounding away at the enemy. The *Elephant* was not a terribly bad sailer, but I got crossways with the first lieutenant from the get-go. He had me put off to the Americans, as I've told you. Sir Mulholland has been good to help keep my career on track – have me sent back on the *Vanguard*. I have this time away now, though, because *Vanguard* sailed on nineteen August for Cadiz. They won't much miss me for a few weeks - probably don't even know I'm coming."

"Sir Mulholland?" asked Gage. "What's **he** to do with the navy?"

Neville winced inwardly, realizing he had divulged something he should not have. He picked up his teacup and took a sip to allow himself time to compose a reply. He decided that something close to the truth was his best route. "Ahh. I am sorry. He asked me not to say anything. He doesn't officially have anything to do with the navy. A friend of mine described him as 'a senior bureaucrat' though, and such people can pull a lot of strings if they have it in mind. He wrote me a letter, is all."

"I see," said Gage; he politely left it lie. The women didn't pick it up either, probably in hopes the whole discussion of war was done.

"The sun's coming out, look," said Elizabeth. "Let's go for a walk, Gage."

8: *Vanguard*

Neville was pleased he'd gone home when he had the chance, although there had been far too much time alone with his unhappy thoughts. He'd not had much time for such self-indulgence during his escape from France or the escapade in Spain. He argued with himself continually about Maria's death. His anger had mostly subsided, but he still found it almost impossible to believe Maria was gone. If only he had insisted on an earlier marriage, the awkwardness of her pregnancy would not have been the cause of her death. *My fault. My own fault.* The thoughts continued as Neville sailed toward Cadiz in *Hirondelle,* the little hired fourteen-gun cutter acting as packet-boat for the Cadiz fleet.

"There they are, Sir," said the master, pointing forward on the tenth day out of Plymouth. The coast of Spain to the north had been visible since daybreak after they had rounded the westernmost point of Europe at Cape Farol, but the coast at Cadiz was as yet too far off to be visible. The offshore squadron could be seen, though. A long line of topsails dotted the sea several miles ahead, and shipping bound for Gibraltar could be seen to the south.

"Aye. Not a bad passage, was it, Mr. Goodard?"

"Not bad. Even the Bay of Biscay behaved itself. It's a lot warmer here, though."

"There she is – *Vanguard*," announced Goodard a half hour later.

"Excellent. I'll make sure my sea chest is packed and strapped."

Just before dark *Hirondelle* backed her sails in the lee of *Vanguard* and put her jolly-boat over the side. After a short row between the two, the little boat discharged Neville to *Vanguard's* gangway ladder. A rigger's line was already on the way down for his sea chest and a mail packet brought by *Hirondelle*.

I'll remember to keep my footing this time. Neville stepped over the brow and turned aft. Two or three hundred eyes were on him, he knew. He saluted the colors and then touched his hat to the lieutenant – probably the officer of the watch - who had been observing his arrival.

The man touched his hat in response, "Welcome aboard," he said, then extending his hand, "We've been wondering if you would show up before Gibraltar."

"You knew I was coming, then? I wondered if you would."

"We didn't know who, but we are short one lieutenant, so we had every hope someone would come. I'm George Thurin, fifth. Mebbe I'm sixth now."

"We'll see, won't we? I'm Neville Burton. What was your comment about Gibraltar?"

"It's where we'll be in another few weeks. We'll be provisioning for a cruise to Jamaica."

"Well, that makes sense."

"Makes sense? Why would you say such a thing? Why would you not expect us to stay on blockade here?

"Just something I heard. Nothing official." *Just something of Mulholland's doing.*

"Wilson, Ganges, there!" yelled Thurin, "Get this chest down to the wardroom."

HMS *Vanguard* swung at her best bower in Port Royal Bay, Jamaica, in January of the year 1802. Her 3rd Lieutenant Neville Burton found the situation more emotional than he had expected. Here he'd loved Maria Fuller and lost her, and he had not yet accepted the loss into his heart. He knew where her house was – on a former sugar plantation now surrounded by the sprawling city of Kingston, but he did not know its occupants. Her father, Thomas, a man he had also come to love as a father, was also gone. He stood at the larboard rail on the poopdeck studying the details of Kingston – or what details he could see from this distance. He watched a flight of pelicans swoop low over the water, skimming inches above it for yards in rigid formation, looking for their breakfast. *Maybe writing a letter home will take my mind off these memories.* The birds rose and wheeled about for another pass.

> *HMS Vanguard*   *January 27, 1802*
> *Jamaica Station*
>
> *Dearest Mother and Elizabeth,*
>
>   *Our passage across from Gibraltar was smooth enough. The wind is almost always at one's back across the Atlantic in those latitudes, and the sun warm. It has been over a year since I have been here – juste exactly here, in Port Royal Bay. I know I haven't told you of it because I am not permitted to do so – it's where I was when I "went missing". I can tell you some personal things that have been too painful to mention, though. I think*

Elizabeth smoked it that I had a girl here. I was to be wed, but she was killed in an accident. Enough said there for now.

Vanguard is a reasonable happy ship. Any ship with this many men aboard is a difficult thing to manage, but my fellowe officers are a capable lot. Captain Williams is a fair man, and stern. I've only met him at dinner twice, so I don't know muche more. I joined her off Cadiz and we patrolled a while to keep the Spanish in, but then went off to victual and provision at Gibraltar before we sailed for here in December – but I guess I've writ you most of this before.

First Lieutenant Joseph Dagleishe has become a particular friend. That's a pleasing change from Elephant. Second Lt. Otto Stolz is a rather thick and didactic German, and can be quite rude at times, though I'm not sure he realizes it. I'm third, as I've writ before, and I've not changed my opinion of the other lieutenants.

Mother, I am amazed to report that I've got your letter about the New Year's party at the Corn Hall. It must have come straight across as soon as you wrote it. Pass my regards and thanks to Mr. Blake for treating you so well. I'm happy of it!

We should be here quite some time, so if you can send me word of Daniel and his Dad – and Gage, of course - I would appreciate it. I would love to hear how they're getting on.

All my love,

Neville

The winter months of 1802 brought very little excitement to *Vanguard*. A few patrols in the waters of the Greater Antilles kept the ship's company from sheer boredom. March saw her returned to anchor in Port Royal. The hiatus in sailing watches gave Neville time to sit and think – which was not entirely a good thing.

Why do I go see that Mulholland? he wondered. *Every time I go, he has another impossible thing for me to do. How am I supposed to research this Stillwater chap when I'm in harbor aboard a seventy-four? We lieutenants aren't just allowed to do as we wish. And here in Jamaica, of all places. I would give my arm to be able to go ashore and see Maria. But she's not there, I know, although it seems impossible. Enough. Enough on that. It can't happen and crying won't help.*

"Halloo. Burton, there. Come hear this," said Dagleishe, who had just dropped himself down the main companion stair. "Come off your letters. And grab Lieutenant Thurin over there. He'll be glad to hear it, too."

"First, the captain has granted us some privilege, as long as we police ourselves, he says. We should be spending quite some time here, on and off, so rather than have us pester him individually, he will leave it to us to schedule our own shore leave. That includes our warrant officers. And while we're ashore, we are to assess the situation for allowing the men leave as well."

Jolly good. Now I know how I get ashore. "At least it's not like the old days…" said Neville in a low voice – almost a mumble.

"How's that, Lt. Burton?" asked Dagleishe. *He's got sharp ears, don't he?*

"I, ahh… was referring to the old Port Royal, Sir. I've read about it." *I'm going to have to be more careful.*

"Oh, right. Haven't we all? That brings me to the next item: Our war with the French and Spanish seems to be going quiet. They are about, though, as are pirates, so we will be making cruises up the Windward Passage to the north to keep an eye on them -

and the slave rebellion that's been going on in Saint-Domingue since '97. It's a French problem, not ours, but we're to keep a watch. We don't mind that it bedevils the French, but we don't need it spreading to the British islands, do we? That's all I've got."

"**I** have just received the news in today's packet, gentlemen. We are no longer at war with the French," announced Captain Williams at an unexpected gathering in the wardroom in mid-April. "A 'Treaty of Amiens' was signed last month – on the 25th of March, to be precise. Lt. Dagleishe, I'll leave the rest of it to you."

"There's not a lot more to it," said Dagleishe. "To us here in the Carribees, it means we'll have to be careful not to capture the wrong vessels. Pirates are still fair game, of course, but it probably means we'll be assigned to even more dull duty – such as convoys."

"If there are no questions, it's back to your duties," Dagleishe concluded.

What does this mean to me? wondered Neville. *If we are not at war, then there is no such thing as spying for the other country, is there? I'd best lay off my enquiry and write Sir William.* Not that Neville had managed to investigate Mr. Stillwater very deeply. Most of his efforts were lonely and thankless work consisting of asking questions around the waterfront. He couldn't talk to anyone about it and required him to step away from various occasions when his peers would get together for a pint or a dinner ashore. He had learned that some sort of costume would be needed to do much more; his enquiries, as an officer in uniform, were often met with unusual facial expressions, blank stares, or outright scoffs. Too much more poking about would certainly come to the attention of Mr. Stillwater himself. He had also learned enough to raise his suspicions that there might indeed be something to Sir William's curiosity. It seemed to Neville that Stillwater – or some minion – was always about when a prize came in. They would buy any unopened rum – presumable for resale – that had not been appropriated by the prize captain. Chatty salesmen were to be expected, but 'excess rum' would always be a rarity. Moreover, during the transaction, their questions seemed far more than appropriate. *Were they just particularly gossipy fellows, or was there more? Is hanging around the docks just part of their sales approach, or did asking a lot of questions mean they expected to learn something?*

Neville sat the very next day with Lt. Dagleishe in the Morgan Arms in Kingston overlooking the harbor. Each had a half pot of ale in front of them, and the crumbs of their meat pies. February's afternoon sun glinted off the water into their eyes.

"I say we move table, Joseph," said Neville. "This spot will be very hot in a few minutes."

"I'll just finish my cup here and move on, Neville, I have a couple errands to run. You need a tailor? Hey, look there, the packet arrives. I'll have a letter from home, for sure."

Neville looked out to where the sails of a small ship were rounding the point at Fort Charles. "It's amazing. They come like clockwork these days. I remember when…"

"When what?" asked Dagleishe. "Why wouldn't they…? Never mind. I'm off to the tailor."

Fine, then. I'll be off to 'investigate' the mysterious Mr. Stillwater, thought Neville – *however one does such a thing. I suppose my first task is to find out where he lives and works…* "Barkeep, can I ask you about someone 'round here?"

HMS Vanguard   *September 23, 1802*
Jamaica Station

Dearest Mother and Elizabeth,

We have had a dreadful summer here in the Carribees. It has been beastly hot and the rain incessant. The two together have inflamed the diseases. We had a scare just two weeks past when Lieutenant Stolz died of something we thought to be the ague, but if it was, by God's grace it did not spread through the ship. I am second now, and I think I will remain so, since the Captain has promoted Mr. Entwigg from Midshipman to Acting Lieutenant. That means he probably won't be looking for a replacement on this cruise. I always feel a sadness for this method of rising to the top, despite that it is in my owne better interest, and is the way of things.

We've not had muche in the way of action – juste several cruises Northe into the Windward Passage and to the Southe of Spanish Cuba. There were two great Stormes that blew several days each, but the locals did not regard them as Huricans. We were thankfully in Porte for each. One man was injured when the Winde tore loose a Boat from the very deck, but we lost no one. Three small Vessels in Harbor were sunk by it.

I shall continue to take the utmost care, and pray you do the same,

Neville

The Caribbean Islands

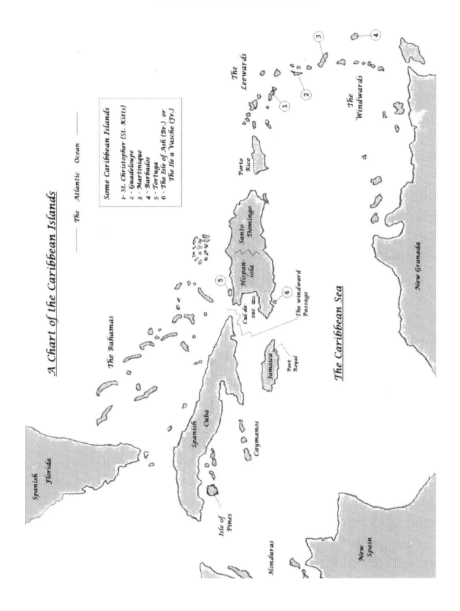

9: *Marion*

"**A** party for the new year of 1803? This is most unusual, isn't it, Joseph?" Neville asked.

"It is, indeed. I don't think I've ever been treated to a soirée ashore; New Year's or not."

Neville put on his haughtiest air and said, "Well, I have: the Governor's ball in Newfoundland when I served as a midshipman in *Castor*."

"Must I bow and scrape to you then, my liege?"

"I could do with proper respect on occasion, if you feel so inclined."

" 'Pfft', is my professional response to you, sir."

"To be honest," Neville said, "the event was what they call a 'command performance' – a military affair in which I had no choice. It was quite enjoyable, though."

"I hope this one is, too. The captain tells us we are not required to go, but I think if this Mr. Stillwater wishes to buy me a dinner that is better than what we have aboard and offer me a free taste of his rum, why should I turn him down? I'll warrant the pusser will not. Ho, ho."

"And I would wager it will, indeed, be better fare than what we have aboard. We cannot even be sure we have much better than ship's stores in the wardroom because of the poor victualing situation here in Jamaica," Neville groused. *I can't tell Joseph that because it's Mr. Stillwater's rum company, I would be derelict in my duty not to go until such time as I can determine Sir William's intentions, even if Stillwater is no longer a spy.*

"**M**ost officers from the ships in the harbor must be in here, Joseph," Neville commented after some time milling about the ballroom at the Stillwater mansion.

"And most of the merchant masters, Americans, and councilmen of Jamaica, too, I'd wager," said Dagleishe.

At Joseph's comment, Neville looked about the room, wondering if he knew anyone. It took only a moment before he realized the absurdity of his thought. There would be nobody from this council he could possibly know. Those men were all dead and gone.

"And Kingston's prominent businessmen," Dagleishe added, "Did you try that French wine from the drinks table in the corner? It's wonderful. I would have thought it would be all rum here."

"They enjoy their rum here, there's no question of it. Who is that lovely creature over there?" Neville asked Dagleishe, indicating a petite girl in a light blue dress on the far side of the room. A small group of officers surrounded her, and she obviously enjoyed the conversation and attention.

"I wouldn't forget that beauty. She's our host's daughter, Marion Stillwater. You should have met her, too, standing in the reception line to the left of her father."

"She must have stepped away when I came through," Neville said, now realizing that his heart was racing. He hadn't seen her face yet. *The hair is the right length, but the color is off… her figure is quite similar. It is Jamaica, after all. Such things couldn't be, could they?*

In all the questions I've asked about Chester Stillwater, nobody has said anything about her. Why would such a pretty woman not be one of the first things mentioned? Does she not live here? I went in to the Stillwater office once, and she was not there. But then, I can understand her not being involved with the business.

"I must say hello, Joseph."

"It won't be easy. Have you noticed she's surrounded? In addition, I'd wager most of them are your senior. I might add that more than one is a captain. They'll not be brushed aside by 'Excuse me, Sir'."

"I'll begin with the wine you suggested," Neville said. *I see she has a glass in her hand that is almost empty.* He began his adventure with a trip across the floor to the drinks table. *This makes me feel untrue to the memory of Maria, but the similarities are undeniable. I simply must meet her. If naught else, I must see her more closely. Furthermore,* he rationalized, *it is my duty to find ways to investigate her father. I must have an honorable ruse. I certainly can't be the oaf who stumbles into her.*

At the wine table, he selected two glasses, and then turned toward Marion. Her dress, empire-waisted as currently the style in England, showed her well-formed young figure extremely well. Hair of a color between brown and blond hung to just above her shoulders. The young lady was very straight of posture, bringing her up to about five feet and two inches in the thin blue pumps which occasionally peeked out from beneath her floor-length dress. Glasses in hand, he walked directly toward her.

Neville's dilemma of finding a way into the circle was solved when one lieutenant brushed another, sending a small stream of rum onto a third. Being on their best behavior in the situation, they all three stepped aside in a cacophony of 'Excuse me's', 'So sorry, old chap', and such, leaving a gaping hole in the lady's defenses. Neville stepped boldly in, raising the glass he had brought for her.

Quietly, he asked in Spanish "¿Ha estado esperándome usted? (Have you been waiting for me?)

"I am sorry, Sir, I do not speak... Spanish, I would guess from the Latin roots – not Italian?"

He looked her directly in the eyes. Pale green eyes, like the peridot. "Oui. (Yes.) Vous avez une bonne oreille. (You have a good ear.) Et François? (And French?) J'ai demandé si vous m'avez attendu. (I asked if you have been waiting for me). I'm told your name is Marion."

She looked back at him with the same confidence Maria had worn so well. The smell of plumeria from the flower in her hair – just as Maria had worn – threatened to turn him feeble. She accepted the glass after a short pause, and quietly responded, "C'est possible, Monsieur. (It's possible, sir.) Puis-je avoir l'honneur de savoir le nom d'un officier anglais trilingue avec de tels yeux bleus? (May I have the honor of knowing the name of a trilingual English officer with such blue eyes?)"

"Neville," he said, returning to English. "I'm sorry, miss. Second Lieutenant Burton of the *Vanguard*, here in the harbor." *Of course she knows I'm from a ship in the harbor. I make a fool of myself.* "May we speak?"

"Neville, is it?" she queried through a soft smile. "I hope we can talk more later – on the veranda after dinner, perhaps – but I really must go."

She turned away then, taking the arm of a large man in a civilian suit who led her away toward the head table. The quick action left the group of officers who had been surrounding her somewhat at a loss. Six officers were staring at Neville. He stated the obvious to no one in particular: "Good evening, Sirs. It must be time for dinner."

The dinner 'casually invited' guests were only loosely organized. Ship captains and masters, local politicians, noteworthy businessmen and friends were consolidated near the host's head table furthest from the doors. The remainder generally found their own places with their fellow shipmates, meaning Neville sat with the officers from *Vanguard*. Lively conversation with the officers of two other ships seated at the same large table helped pass the time quickly.

Marion lit up the room beside a silver-haired man that Neville knew was Mr. Stillwater because he had greeted him in the reception line. He distinctly remembered his awkward feeling - ashamed or duplicitous or something - for accepting of the hospitality of a man who might be his enemy. But this is war. Or it was. What now? What feeling might I be allowed to have for his daughter? He couldn't force himself to ignore her, and before the desert arrived, he was quite sure he'd caught her eye at least twice. *Such similarities to Maria. How could it be? Is it good that this woman brings back my memories of her? Is it bad that she stirs feelings I thought were dead? And who is the big man on the other side of her?*

The dinner passed and the room returned to general milling and mixing until rum and cigars were suggested for the men. The few women present opted for sherry. "Shall we step outside for a bit of fresh air, Joseph?" Neville suggested.

"Yes, let's. I don't think it's a hot night, but it's gotten quite warm with all these people in one room."

Outside on the veranda they were pleased to find the beginning of a very pleasant evening. "It's not hot at all. Look, there goes the sun just now. Whoa! It flashed a brilliant green. Did you see it?"

"No. I must've looked elsewhere for a second. I don't believe there is such a thing anyway."

"Well, I just saw... Oh, hello."

Marion appeared as if from a mist. Neville might have been warned by the smell of plumeria, but the flower's fragrance hung in the air everywhere. A huge tree stood not forty feet away.

"Hello, again," she said to him. She was, indeed, a petit girl. Her small face, slightly tanned due to her tropical life, encompassed a short nose and thin lips. She smiled with the enjoyment of the party, her eyes twinkling in the last of the sunlight. "You also appreciate Jamaica in the evening, I see," she said. "And we have yet another handsome officer. I must say, gentlemen, in my opinion, this is the smartest-looking collection of officers the English fleets have ever put ashore. I simply must learn your ranks someday."

Neville could see Joseph was blushing and he felt the warmth of the same. "We aren't used to such compliments at all, Miss Stillwater," said Dagleishe, "particularly from beautiful women, but we thank you for them."

"Miss Stillwater, may I present my particular friend, and *Vanguard's* First Lieutenant, Joseph Dagleishe."

"There, you've been introduced. As the hostess, I may now say what I wish; and I wish," she said with a perfect smile and a wink in his direction, "for another glass of the wonderful red wine Neville brought me before."

"First names, is it? Certainly, miss. I know which it is; I'll be right back."

With Marion's comments to Dagleishe approaching what Neville took to be interest, he had felt himself approaching panic. The feelings – *my silly, inappropriate feelings* - evaporated when Joseph took the hint and went for the wine. He looked at her. They both watched for a few minutes as the glow of sunset faded to gray from the previous oranges and patches of azure blue. She turned to him and their eyes met for a moment, but no words were spoken.

"I feel as if we have met," she finally said. "Have you been here before?"

"Yes," he said after a pause, "but it's been a long time. I certainly wasn't second of *Vanguard*." *No, I was captain of the frigate Experiment.* His head began to swim with his continuing notice of similarities to Maria – height and size, eye shape and hair style – although not color – certain mannerisms and strong self-assurance; and the plumeria.

"How about you? Did you grow up here?"

"Yes, right here."

"Yet you speak French. Quite well, I must say."

"My mother's influence. She had me taught 'proper European ways', including French and Latin, but not Spanish, as you have discovered.

"So where is your mother? No siblings?"

"Mother died three years ago, and my older brother Freddie was killed by French privateers just last year. It has been a hard time." A tear dripped from her left eye. Neville fought the urge to grab her and hold her in his arms. It would have been most inappropriate.

"I'm sorry... Has your father been in this business long? Pardon me for being curious, but you certainly appear to live well; this is an amazing estate."

"You really hadn't heard of the Stillwater Rum Trading Company before now? That's us. Our business is rum. It's probably aboard your ship."

"Very impressive. I know this is very forward, but may I see you again?"

Marion might have blushed, but it couldn't be seen in the gathering gloom. "I would hope so, in time, but father doesn't approve of navy men calling on me; certainly none beneath the rank of captain."

Dagleishe arrived with the wine before Neville could form another question, and just following his passing it to Marion, another fellow arrived.

"There you are, Marion," the stranger said. "Your father requests your presence." He spoke with a flat accent containing a hint of American southern drawl, akin to what Neville had heard in Norfolk in the American colonies. Fashionably dressed in civilian attire, the man appeared to be thirty-five or so, a robust fathom of height and square-jawed as a marine sergeant. Together with the question he just asked, the smooth good-looker's confident approach indicated some familiarity with Marion. He had obviously noticed Marion standing with only one officer, not six or seven. He somehow had managed to brush Dagleishe smoothly aside.

"Second Lieutenant Neville Burton of *HMS Vanguard*, please meet Mr. Michael Stearns of the Stillwater Rum Trading Company," said Marion. *That explains the familiarity, I hope.* "I'm afraid I must go. Some other time, perhaps?"

"I hope for it, Miss Stillwater."

10: Prizes

"**W**elcome to convoy duty, gentlemen," Dagleishe announced to his gathered officers in the wardroom after dinner in late January, 1803. "We have orders – orders to do the something different than we have been doing for the past year." Light applause greeted the announcement.

"You have undoubtedly seen the shipping congregating in the Bay and heard the rumors. Between now and May we will have two more transits of the Windward Passage: One to the north -- as far as Florida to guard a convoy to Halifax – and one back south after we wait for another coming south. We should be back before the hurricanes begin."

Victualing for a voyage that might last longer than a few months began, as well as taking on water and wood, and giving extra attention to sails and spars and cordage.

"Our two weeks are up, Neville, and we're finally about to weigh anchor," Dagleishe said. He turned and yelled down to Boatswain John Waters, "Heave the anchor short." The familiar tramping of eighty or so men at the capstan began.

Neville, watching other ships in the fleet through his glass, reported, "The others are heaving short as well, Sir."

Captain Williams climbed the stair to the quarterdeck. After a short look around, he gave the order: "Raise anchor."

"Mr. Waters, raise anchor," repeated Dagleishe.

"I begin to wonder, Joseph, what our purpose is. Compared to previous passages I have made from Jamaica to North America, this one has been particularly unremarkable. We have had no clashes with pirates, no significant storms, no particular fear of privateers from the United States, and no expectation of encountering any enemy French."

"Anchor's aweigh!" Waters called from the bow.

"We have to be somewhere, don't we, Neville? If there is one thing I have learned in life, it is that I can never be 'nowhere'. If this really is peace, I would not be surprised if we are sent from Halifax to England, never to see Jamaica again, and maybe they pay us off and we find work as farmers or, God forbid, bankers."

Vanguard sailed with her convoy into the blue waters to the north of Jamaica. Neville shivered inside. There was a time when he expected to spend the rest of his life in Jamaica. Most feelings had drained out of him when Maria died; he had felt them drain - but now at least some were back. *This girl Marion...*

He had eaten breakfast in the wardroom, but taken his coffee to the leeward rail to see the last of the Jamaican coast sink into the sea. He found it comforting to see the flock of pelicans sweep past and the little white birds perched upon turtles. Joseph Dagleishe came on deck looking for a quiet place to finish his coffee. He spotted Neville leaning on the rail.

"Good morning, Neville. I am most glad to see you this new day."

"Early April is a beautiful time of year in Jamaica, Joseph, but I can feel the cold creeping in as we move north."

"Aye." They both sipped their hot liquids and watched Jamaica sink into the sea.

"Tomorrow's make-and-mend," said Neville. "Be sure your larbowlines are sewing themselves some warm jackets. Remind them of the climate ahead of us."

"*Bellerophon* is signaling us to keep station again."

"You see? Everyone has to have something to do."

A gale of wind blew off North Carolina. Manropes were rove to insure the ship's company remained aboard. Off the rocks by Gloucester, Massachusetts, it snowed. The ratlines froze solid; one man died when he lost his grip on a yardarm covered with sheet ice. Given the circumstances, the ship would not turn back to search for him. It wasn't often that being aboard a seventy-four, rather than his beloved frigate, gave Neville cheer, but when the spray from the pounding bow flew all the way back to drench the three quartermasters hanging on to the helm, he enjoyed having something to duck behind, whether it be the boats, the huge mainmast, or just the distance to the poopdeck.

In Halifax, a new captain came aboard. The first thing he said, after he read himself in, was "Lieutenant Dagleishe, pass word that war with France is again likely." He went below.

"Captain Walker has given me a bit more information, gentlemen," said Dagleishe at supper in the wardroom. "The King has apparently decided France's 'imperialist policies' in Switzerland, Italy and the West Indies are not acceptable to us. Our King has not declared war yet, but it could come soon. The West Indies, mates, will be in the center of this if it does, indeed, come to war. Expect a little more gun drill on the way home."

"More drill is fine by me," said Lt. Thurin. "My men could use a bit of action to keep their minds off the lousy food." He glared at Dagleishe as if it were his fault.

"Regarding our departure date," continued Dagleishe, "we will be on our way as soon as they put together a few merchants to go south." The time came a week later.

The weather warmed as they sailed south. They flew only topsails from Halifax to Massachusetts. They added the main course and sheeted it home for the first time off the Island of Nantucket. Full courses were not abroad until they could see the shores of New Jersey.

"Captain's a bit cautious isn't he, Lt. Miller?" Neville said to the fourth lieutenant. Miller's bashfulness continued to surprise Neville. He was younger than most, which might have explained it. He seemed more intelligent than most, as well. Those things might account for his passing for lieutenant so early in his career, but since *Vanguard* had seen so little action in the time Neville had been aboard, he had no idea of the man's mettle. "What would you do here?" Neville asked Miller.

"Do, Sir?"

"With the sails."

Miller thought for a minute. "Same thing, I suppose. We could sail faster, but we have to keep station with the convoy. They depend on us."

He looked at Neville for a minute through unhappy eyes, and then said, "Anything else, Sir?"

"No, Lt. Miller. Nothing. Good night." But Neville knew. He had spoken very little with Miller, but right then he knew. If ever he needed a man to take with him to another ship, it would be Miller. Miller was dead here, just like Neville. The young man needed speed and action, tactics and bravado to wake him up, unlike

Thurin, for example. His words were good, but it meant he was awake here. A seventy-four fit him well, as it did most of the others. The only thing Neville did not know – and maybe he never would - was whether Miller could survive life on a frigate.

HMS *Vanguard* returned to Jamaica Station in early May, dropping her anchor in the warm water of Kingston's harbor under a blue sky and hot sun.

"Well, that's it, then," said First Lieutenant Joseph Dagleishe to Neville, "Another voyage completed."

"I had hoped we might encounter the French in the Windward Passage, after Captain's news of possible war," commented Neville, "but the return passage was as unremarkable as the passage outbound."

"They're too busy on Hispaniola right now to worry about a few English ships going by."

"Too busy? Why do you say that?"

"Despite the fact that the entire island of Hispaniola has been under French control since '95, I'm told the slave rebellion is getting even worse in the western half of it. The French may be lucky to get out alive."

"Look. Here comes an advice boat already. I hope this doesn't mean we're going straight back out."

Midshipman Grimes waited in the main chains to take the advice boat's painter when it came alongside, but the boat did nothing more than hand a packet to Grimes and shove off. Neville and Joseph stood waiting for the packet to be brought their way. Since Captain Walker had not come up to investigate, it would be Dagleishe's duty to deliver it.

"I must say, I see almost no difference between Captain Williams and Captain Walker, as long you stand between us," said Neville.

"There isn't, really. Captain Walker's a bit fussier on the paperwork, and a bit more stand-offish."

Grimes handed Dagleishe the packet. "Thanks for the lesson on island politics, Joseph," said Neville, "Let me know if I've received mail."

Having nothing much better to do on a ship in port, Neville remained at the rail observing what little he could see of life ashore. Joseph returned in a half hour with a lighter packet.

"Personal post," he said. "Three for you. There's something to be said for being in port."

Neville took his letters below.

Neville continued to sit on his bunk after reading his letters, and another thought formed in his mind. He had a cache of silver here in Kingston – or at least he did when he was last here almost three years ago. With his personal money running low, it might be a good time to go collect it.

Shipping no longer landed in Port Royal. That city had been destroyed by an earthquake a hundred years earlier, and this new city of Kingston had arisen on the other side of the bay. The trip from Kingston's waterfront to the Fuller house – now the Verley house, behind which his cash was hidden – would be much shorter than it would have been from Port Royal. Neville cleared his absence with Lt. Dagleishe and went ashore. The walk to Verley House took him only 45 minutes. On his previous visit he had knocked at the door and been confronted with an old man who clearly preferred Neville to leave. He avoided the house and went straight into the brambles by the big tree behind. The brush growing in the forgotten cemetery had become thicker and larger since his previous visit, making it harder to find the two things he sought. First, he found the grave of Thomas Fuller. While it was not one of the two things he sought, it gave him a reference to find the others. Through the tears Thomas's grave brought to his eyes, four feet to the left, he found a flat stone on the ground marked 'Maria Fuller'. There he knelt and kissed the stone, even though he knew she did not lie beneath it. He allowed himself only a few minutes before continuing his search. He easily found the tiny stone building using those landmarks, and he slid the roof aside. His silver cobbed coins were there where he had left them – more than he had remembered - but there on the spot he decided to take only what he needed for current expenses. It had proven to be a good hiding place – a good place to store money for emergencies. He had all he needed at Hoare's Bank on Fleet Street back home in London, England.

The fleet did not sail directly, but orders were not long in coming to do so. *Vanguard* spent the last of May victualing. Another letter arrived in mid-June. He recognized the handwriting, but was reticent to open it. He finally decided there nothing to be gained from procrastinating…

Bury St. Edmunds,   *25th May, 1803*
Suffolk, England

Neville,

  By now, you must know that the clouds of war again spread over us. With this news, I know I must respond to your last with an affirmation of your previous project. I'm sure you expected it, but I nonetheless wish you the best.

Your Godfather,   W'm M.

The clouds of war, indeed. Dark clouds. Clouds that make the loss of Maria feel even worse.

The noise of a great commotion on deck became loud enough to be heard in the wardroom. Neville thought to investigate, until he realized the reason for it. His was not the only mail confirming the news of war. The secret was out.

Vanguard spent the remainder of June working her way north out of Jamaica with Commodore Henry Bayntun's flagship *HMS Cumberland* and several others who were seeing another convoy off. 30th June, 1803 promised to be like other Thursdays – make and mend in the heat and passing showers.

Neville stood with Joseph at the lee quarterdeck rail with glass in hand. "That's the last of them, Joseph. The convoy has gone beyond our horizon west'rd above Spanish Cuba. We've seen 'em safe off. What now?"

"Our orders are to blockade the island of Saint-Domingue."

"Joseph, pardon my... curiosity... but how is it you propose to accomplish such a thing with a single squadron?"

"It's just an island, Neville. Why would you ask such a thing?"

"Britain is an island, Joseph. Would you propose to blockade it with a half dozen ships?"

"We're not alone. The Barbados station has charge of the eastern end."

"Hmmm. There are a dozen little ports in the Cul-de-sac, and pirates have been known to favor the waters on the north between Hispaniola and Tortuga. We could face significant resistance."

"I really don't know where you get your information, Neville. This end of the island has been involved with a slave rebellion for the last dozen years. Don't you remember my lesson on island politics? The French have their attention on the rebellion. I can't imagine they could put ships out against us. On the north, however, I suppose some French navy ships might ignore the local hostilities and sail over the top of the island, thinking to come down on Jamaica."

"I know we're back at war, but I think I have some stockings needing a bit of darning, and I have only another hour before the larbowlines go on watch, so if you'll excuse me, I think I'll take my needle and go at it."

Neville paused before walking off. "Oh, and by the way, if I were Sailing Master I'd shorten sail a bit before we reach that headland or something might just carry away. Just conversation, mind you."

"Lieutenant Burton, if I didn't know you better, I'd think you were trying to tell the captain how to sail his ship. Don't you think we've been through this passage enough to know our way?"

"I would never suggest to Captain. That's why I'm happy to be friends with the First Lieutenant. Remember, though, that whenever we've come north on convoy, we've been on the far side of the Windward Passage. For all the times we've sailed here on patrol, we've never rounded this point close in. So much for our experience. The nor-east wind comes down above the island and bounces off the hills to the west, just there." He pointed at the headland ahead and to starboard. "Personally, as I have told you, I've been here before – although I can't tell you when or why -- and found the effect to be quite impressive… Oh, look, there goes *Cumberland's* main t'gallant sail, and maybe the t'gallant mast with it. But I'll just mind my business and go darn my stockings."

"Oh, no you won't…

"Lt. Thurin, halloo! Have Bo'sun call all hands." Dagleishe yelled to the Officer of the Watch. He walked off briskly to speak with the captain.

Neville's two midshipmen had no sooner reported sails reset for the windward beat to Tortuga Island north of Hispaniola an hour later when the mainmast lookout called down, "Sail, ho!"

"Where away, man?" Dagleishe hollered back.

"For'ard - four points larboard, Sir, and a signal from *Cumberland*: Enemy."

"Hoist acknowledge, Thurin," said Dagleishe.

He yelled up again, "Can you make out her course?"

"*Cumberland*'s falling off to loo'rd, Sir. Enemy course West to Nor-west."

Captain Walker, who had been pacing the windward rail, walked over to Dagleishe by the binnacle, and began speaking in a voice loud enough for Neville to hear: "*Cumberland* must think she has a chance to catch her. We are closer and at a better angle to the wind. Reshape our course to cut her off, Lieutenant."

"Sailing Master Boyle, call all hands. Fall off five points to loo'rd."

"Aye, Sir."

Neville sauntered forward to his post by the mainmast bitts to observe the performance of his midshipmen and their charges. He saw no need to rush yet; he had only to walk fifteen feet, and the bo'sun's mates had just begun at their pipes.

Only half a glass of sand had run through the neck of the glass before they knew they had a good chance to catch the French ship ahead of them. She bore two points free of the starboard bow now, and *Cumberland* remained on the starboard beam as far as a league away. *Vanguard* had the better chance.

"She'll run for Inagua, perhaps, Neville?" Miller asked. His eyes were wide open and he seemed as alert as Neville had ever seen him. "Why do we not crack on?"

Dagleishe passed an order to Master Boyle, and a moment later Thurin yelled, "Bo'sun! Loo'rd stuns'ls!"

"We do, then, don't we, Miller?" answered Neville. "She may simply be hoping her safety lies in the open sea. You'd best see to your foremast."

Sails reset, dinner just over, and rum served out, Dagleishe yelled, "Clear for Action!" He finished fumbling in his pocket for a watch and raised his head to observe. The ship came fully alive with the sounds of men running to their stations, tramping marine boots, whistling bo'sun's mates, and the slapping of hundreds of calloused bare feet.

"Guns out, Sir?" asked Thurin.

"You presume to give me orders, Lieutenant Thurin?" While Neville had a fondness for each, they had run afoul of each other some weeks back. Neville remembered his personal experience vividly, pleased that this discontent seemed minor. He wouldn't have to worry about retribution by Dagleishe against Thurin unless Thurin committed a truly serious error.

"No, Sir,"

"Our chase can't come up higher on the wind and hopes to outrun an old seventy-four close-hauled," Neville instructed Miller once the hubbub ceased, "She can't fall off, either. You know why, Lt. Miller?"

"Aye, Sir. *Cumberland* is far enough to his wind'rd that even a slow ship would have her. And we can fall off as easily as she might, so she's forced to keep her course and hope for the elements to assist her."

"Very good, Lt. Miller. We can't tell whether she might have the speed to outrun us, but we do seem to be catching her up. Go aloft, would ye, with your pair of good eyes, and see what she is?"

Miller called down not three minutes later, "A frigate, Lieutenant Burton. A large one."

"Keep your eyes on her."

"Thank you for that, Lt. Burton," said Captain Walker directly to him. "I was about to send someone up."

"You are most welcome, Sir. I couldn't contain my curiosity; thought of giving it a climb myself."

The captain returned to his pacing. In a half glass, he ordered Dagleishe to have the foredeck gunner test the range of his chase gun. The 'bang' of the gun could be heard on the quarterdeck despite the following breeze, and the smoke from it, due to the wind direction, blew swiftly away to leeward, posing no visibility problem.

"Half cable short and to loo'rd as well," yelled Miller from above.

"Excellent, Lt. Miller," yelled Dagleishe. "Come down.

"Lt. Thurin, run out starboard, if you please."

Miller landed on the deck by the backstay with a thump. "Her name's '*Créole*'," he said, and trotted forward to his station at the starboard guns on the lower deck forward.

"Thank you, Lt. Miller," Dagleishe yelled at his back.

From the position Neville had taken on the gangway, he could observe *Vanguard* slowly overtaking *Créole*. The latter had little chance of escape. A foredeck twelve-pounder fired. The shot obviously stuck *Créole*. Large pieces of wood could be seen to go flying. A second shot from the forward upper deck made a great hole in her mizzen course. She did not return fire. Her sheets flew to the wind and her French colours began to drop.

As best they could manage while busy with their work of loosing sheets and backing a few sails to stop beside *Créole, Vanguard's* company threw up a cheer. *Cumberland* sailed by with no evident intention of stopping.

"Lt. Burton, step over here, if you please," said Dagleishe after they had the smaller ship grappled alongside.

Neville joined the two on the poopdeck.

"Captain says you are to be prize captain. He knows you speak French. That should simplify things. It should only be a two- or three-day sail depending on weather. Take another lieutenant, the Master-at-Arm's mate, bo'sun's mate…"

"I know the drill, Sir. How many men?"

"You've done this before?"

"Several times, Sir. Thank you for your confidence."

Captain Walker and First Lieutenant Dagleishe glanced at each other, and Neville thought he saw a slight shrug on Dagleishe's part.

"Forty should do. Send the same back."

"Aye, officers and captain. I'll take Lt. Miller, if I may."

"Miller? He's our youngest. Are you sure?"

"Yes sir, I'm sure, and it should cause you the least inconvenience."

Supper had just been served out aboard *Vanguard* when lieutenants Burton and Miller followed eight marines aboard *Créole*. Neville sent four marines to the quarterdeck and four to the foredeck.

"Observe carefully, Lt. Miller," Neville said. His stomach growled. "I hope you will have cause to repeat it many times."

After he returned the salute of the captain of the forty-four-gun ship, Citizen Le Ballard asked in English, "Will you take my sword, Sir?"

"Not I," said Neville, "but you may offer it to Captain Walker once you are aboard. I would like this transfer to go as quickly as possible," he continued. "We will exchange forty able seamen – you see ours coming there already in the boats – a few officers and so on. You are familiar with this, yes?"

Le Ballard drew himself up straight and replied, "I have never been taken before."

"No prizes, either?"

"Only one," Le Ballard answered with less bluster.

"Do you have wounded? If you do, do you have a doctor?"

"Of course we have a doctor. Our two wounded are already in sick bay."

"Very well, then, please take your commissioned and warrant officers into the boat we came across in. I will ask your mates to send out forty men to be exchanged. No man will be hurt if he cooperates, but I expect they will be held in Jamaica until our governments wish to exchange prisoners." He touched his hat to the captain and held out his hand in a 'please step to the sally port' gesture.

He then walked, with Miller behind him, up the steps to the quarterdeck. "There's the bell, there," he said to Miller, "Please ring it a dozen times – just make a racket."

Miller did. Neville stood at the forward rail between his marines and motioned with his hands for the frigate's crew to gather in the waist. "Boatswain's Mate, please step forward," he called out in French. A short stump of a fellow wearing a frayed white shirt, orange trousers and a rope for a belt stepped forward.

"Have all weapons piled here below me immediately, and then have your men step back and wait for further instructions."

Only an hour later, Neville looked up from the frigate to the larger vessel's quarterdeck and yelled, "Permission to release grapples, Sir?"

Captain Walker looked down over the side. To Dagleishe he said, "Just an hour, and he thinks to be off?"

"Yessir. There's a frigate captain for you. Always in a rush; something to prove."

Walker nodded, and Dagleishe yelled, "Release grapples.

"Good luck, Lt. Burton. See you in Jamaica."

"Acting First Lieutenant Miller," Neville said over the noise of unfurling sails, "I believe this will be your first opportunity to see what sailing a fast frigate is like, yes?"

"Aye. You speak French?"

"It would seem so, wouldn't it? One must have something to read on those long days on the ocean. Have you paid enough attention to what Lt. Dagleishe does above deck to mimic it?"

"I think so, but what of our sailing master?"

"We two together are the sailing master, and we should get a bit of help from their mate. He certainly wishes his ship no harm, and he knows we'll know if he tries to take us where we don't want to go. Furthermore, if he hasn't been in the Greater Antilles before – and I suspect he hasn't – then I know these waters far better than he does. I should ask him, I suppose."

The French Frigate *Créole* slid slowly into Port Royal Bay three days later in the calm before a strong blow hit the island. Most of the ship's crew who were not handling sails or preparing the anchor were at the railings observing their surroundings.

"Shouldn't we…?" began Miller, looking about the decks.

"Where would French sailors go in an English port, Lt. Miller?" interrupted Neville. "Let them have their look. The home guard will be out to take them away soon enough. Here they come now, see? They'll want to tell us exactly where to anchor."

Five days later *Créole* swung easily at anchor in a remote corner of the harbor. Her remaining company were enjoying the peace of having only forty-some men aboard. Lieutenants Burton and Miller watched the squadron arrive and drop anchor one after the other.

"Personally, Lt. Burton, I am glad we got in before the blow. They were probably in the middle of the Windward Passage when it hit them pretty hard two days ago. A few of them appear to be missing a stick here and there."

"They've got another small ship with them, as well," said Neville. "We aren't the only prize."

"*Vanguard* took that ship there the same day as us, I think," said Miller. She's a small schooner – French navy; I watched her sail right in to our squadron."

"Look there, at the harbor mouth. There's two more. If they're also prizes, the squadron's been busy, indeed. Have the captain's gig swayed out, if you please, Acting First Lieutenant. I suppose it's time to go home."

"Aye, aye, Sir," said Miller. "If I might be forward, I wish to say that the experience has been the best I've had in my years in the navy, and I'll always remember you for it. It's just a shame we didn't come across another Frenchman to fight."

"A nice sentiment, yes, but with a company of Frenchmen aboard, we would not have given much resistance to recapture."

"Always a lesson, hey?"

Seventh July found Neville back aboard *Vanguard*. Seaman Banks approached him in the waist. He touched his forehead with a bent finger. "Beg pardon, Sir. Captain's compliments, and will you please lay aft."

On Neville's approach to the captain's cabin, the marine sentry came to attention and then rapped on the door frame. "Lt. Burton, Sir." Neville came to attention, hat under arm, and knuckled his forehead to Captain Walker and Lieutenant Dagleishe. He said nothing.

Neville had always been impressed with the spaciousness and luxury of a captain's cabin on any ship larger than a frigate. *Vanguard's* was no exception. Walker's personal desk had a matching table that would seat six – *all in cherry wood*, Neville mused – and all were polished to a gleaming shine.

"As you know," began Walker, "we have captured several ships. The frigate *Creole* you brought in and the corvette *Mignonne* must be sent to prize court. There are also the privateers *Superieure* and *Poisson Vollant*. The latter two will, in time, be taken into our service here, I expect.

"We have no excess of captains here in Jamaica. The first lieutenants of our ships of the line and frigates have chosen to stay where they are rather than move to unrated ships. We have therefore chosen two lieutenants from the fleet to command them. I will not go into the details of the selection process, but *Vanguard* took possession of her, so you are offered the option to be Master and Commander of the fourteen-gun schooner *Superieure*. Would you accept the posting?

"May I ask a question, Sir?"

"Go ahead."

"Is she to stay here on the Jamaica Station or sent elsewhere?"

"Admiral Duckworth will keep every ship he can get hold of with the war on again."

"Then, I say 'Aye, Aye, Sir', with pleasure."

"Gather your kit, then. Commodore Loring has ordered us to sail again in a week. Your compliment is seventy including the marine complement of fifteen. The marines ashore will arrange a troupe for you, but you will probably be hard-pressed to scrape the rest from the fleet, what with *Poisson Vollant* doing the same. You'll not get them all, so plan on petitioning Admiral Duckworth for landsmen and boys from the island. You'd best hop to it."

Lieutenant Dagleishe, with Captain Walker's permission, allowed Neville use of the captain's gig for his first ride over to his new ship. "For practice and exercise of the gig's coxswain and crew," he said. "I'll come along, if you don't mind. I would like to have a look at such a small ship."

"That explains why you didn't want the posting. You think it's a toy, don't you, Joseph?"

"I said no such thing. Keep in mind that I hold a position of great respect at the moment, and my name keeps rising up the Navy List."

"Yes, well… take us 'round her before we go aboard, if you please, Cox'n."

Superieure boasted fore-and-aft rigged fore- and main-sails on two masts with a square topsail and topgallant on the foremast. She was flush-decked - no raised quarterdeck or forecastle. A little jolly boat hung on davits astern.

"Those raked masts give her a very swift look, don't they?"

"Aye, and she's the latest American design – built just two years ago. She should go to weather quite well."

The two lieutenants climbed the few steps of a small ladder to board. There were no pipes or drums, no sideboys and only two saluting redcoats. *This seems a familiar situation*, thought Neville. Save a contingent of three guards, the vessel had nobody aboard. Even her standing officers were missing. Even if a French privateer carried the equivalent of gunner, carpenter, and boatswain, they would not serve in the British navy. Joseph and Neville walked up the deck and back between ten squat, ugly eighteen-pound carronades to the foredeck where two long brass twelve-pounders and a swivel gun were mounted.

"Well, Neville, you are well-armed," said Dagleishe. "Smashers and chasers."

At the stern, they found two more of the long twelves, one on each side of the chicken-coops and a pig pen. Neville was surprised to find the pens occupied. The guards had at least thought to provide water for the miserable creatures inside the pens. The ship's barge was upturned and secured amidships.

"I've not seen one of those in some time," said Dagleishe, pointing to a huge tiller.

Neville grimaced. "It's efficient," he said.

"And simple," added Joseph. "I'll send you over one each boatswain's, carpenter's, and gunner's mates, if Cap'n permits," said

Dagleishe. "I'll see if I can roust caulker and cooper's mates from the other ships, if I can, and a cook, of course. If we can get you five men from each of the big ships, then you'll need maybe…" Dagleishe calculated in his head a minute; "five boys and fifteen landsmen. I would think it unlikely Duckworth would disallow you a few men. Maybe there are even a few foreigners from her last crew who would serve."

Belowdecks, Neville led the way back to his cabin, ducking his head under each successive deck beam. *I'd about forgotten this.* "Here it is, Joseph. My place of splendor." The captain's cabin on *Superieure* was larger than his cabin aboard *Vanguard*, at least, although without the headroom; two men could sit opposite each other at a small desk for a private conversation. Two small portholes aft allowed in some light from astern. The rest would have to come in through the hatch above, deck prisms or oil lamps and candles.

"Better you than me, then," said Joseph. "I think I'd become claustrophobic. At least she's new."

"Aye, and will sail past you upwind…

"Joseph," Neville then said, "I could do with a bit of instruction. I must admit to being unsure of my role."

"The role of Captain?"

"No, not that. I know what it is to serve as a lieutenant on a seventy-four – and on a frigate." *I also know what it is to captain a frigate in a solitary role of defense, but I can't tell him that.* "I've never performed the command role in an unrated vessel associated with ships of the line in a squadron. What is my ship's duty? I doubt the Admiral wants me to chase after enemy frigates or attack shore batteries with fifteen marines. I have seen the un-rateds chase about willy-nilly during battles, but I never paid a great deal of attention to what they were doing, other than fishing men out of the water."

"In this instance, Neville, I cannot assist you much. I've seen the same. You may be called upon to act as packet, signal ship, scout, rescue boat and general annoyer of the enemy. Your complement of seventy is justified by the latter. If I were you, I would expect to be involved in actions against other small ships."

"That's fine by me. Thank you for your advice."

"Best of luck to you, then, Neville," said Joseph, giving him a warm handshake. "I'll find my way topside. Anything else you need? I can send it over with a few men and your chest…"

"Nothing else I can think of at the moment, thanks. Cheers." Neville made a quick inspection of the cabin's contents, found a quill and paper, sat at the tiny desk, and began to write lists.

11: *A Company Collected*

Men began to come aboard. They were delivered by boats from the other ships of Commodore Loring's squadron. Small groups came from *Vanguard* and *Theseus,* and in ones and twos, they came from smaller ships. Eight marines and two boys came from shore. In all of these, some were excited at the prospect of life on a small ship. Some were sullen and argumentative. When Neville noticed a small group of the latter, a terrible thought occurred to him: some ships would take the opportunity to unload their troublemakers on him and on the *Poisson Vollant.* A ship full of cheerful men might be quite different from a ship with a troubled element. *What was I thinking when I took this posting? I should have thought of this. The situation is not at all like when I took command of the Experiment.*

Despite the normal practice of a captain 'reading himself in' as soon as he stepped aboard, Neville waited.

"It's been three days, Sir," commented his new Second Sailing Master — an unrated ship the size of *Superieure* wasn't authorized to carry a fully-warranted Sailing Master. Martin Catchpole might have stood close to Neville's height but for his stooping posture. He was slender as a rail, with a rough complexion left over from smallpox or a bad case of acne as a youth. He never seemed to pay much attention to his hair from what Neville could see, and his upper teeth stuck out at an unusual angle. Neville had barely managed to stifle a laugh when he first saw the man, because with his oversized round ears, the appearance of a rodent was overpowering. Nevertheless, Catchpole claimed to be proficient with his navigation and ship-handling. "Mustn't you read yourself in?"

The question surprised Neville. Not because the question itself was odd, but because of the forwardness with which the mousy Mr. Catchpole had asked it. "First of all, Mr. Catchpole, would you have made such a suggestion to your last captain?"

"To Captain Bligh of *Theseus*? Oh, no, Sir. I would never."

"Bligh. **The** Captain Bligh, of the *Bounty*?"

"No, Sir. This is John Bligh, but still, I…"

"Well then, don't do it here, either. If it relates to sailing this ship, you may speak as you need, but outside of that, you may only ask if I want your suggestions. We should get on just fine if you but follow a few of my simple rules."

"Aye, aye, Sir."

"As to your question, I would expect nothing outlandish to occur in the next two days. I would like to address as many of our company as I can, but I can't address men who are not yet here. Look, here comes yet another barge-load, as you can see. Tomorrow, maybe. Do you know if anyone has come aboard yet who is to act as boatswain?"

"Dunno, Sir. I would've thought he'd report to you direct-like."

"Oh, this boat's from *Vanguard*. Maybe it's my 'birthday package'." He held a small glass to his eye.

"Sir?"

"Yes, I believe it is, Mr. Catchpole. Prepare to receive our boatswain and… gunner, I think."

Gerald Johnson, former Boatswain's mate of the *Vanguard*, pulled himself up the boarding ladder with ease. Gaining the deck, he looked about curiously, as though he were wondering if someone had hidden the rest of the ship from his view. He looked skyward. There were only those three yardarms; pitiful little things on the foremast. More men came up the ladder behind him and shoved him aside – rather gently, it seemed to Neville, who was observing the whole event closely – as if this new arrival were a man of some stature.

Bulging forearms – possibly as large as Catchpole's thighs were the first things one noticed about Johnson. Neville thought he had some slight remembrance of him from *Vanguard*, or someone he'd seen elsewhere before, but finally decided he didn't, but this must be his man, regardless; he sent a boy to fetch him. Neville saw the boy speak with Johnson, whose head jerked toward the quarterdeck after listening to a few words. He would probably not have expected a request directly from the ship's captain – certainly not the moment he stepped aboard – since he wasn't an officer. He walked straight back to where Neville stood, removed his squatty hat, and touched a beefy knuckle to his forehead.

"Boatswain's Mate Johnson reporting for duty, Sir." He stood with a straight posture to six foot and two inches. On closer inspection, Neville did remember him from *HMS Vanguard*, but there he had always been a minor player. His head carried a boyish face of clear complexion and bright, clear gray eyes. He certainly had a quick-witted look about him. Neville guessed him to be of Swedish descent and having lived maybe twenty years. He kept his blonde hair, which was apparently going prematurely gray, combed back neatly and held with a string of small stuff into a ponytail in back. Neville knew he might be wrong on first impression, but he expected he would have to thank Dagleishe for this one.

"Good morning, Mr. Johnson," said Neville. He repeated Johnson's gesture. "I am Commander Burton. Perhaps you remember me from *Vanguard*?" He then extended his hand.

Johnson looked quite cautious as he reached out to take it. He had probably never shaken the hand of a ship's captain before.

"I do, Sir, yes. Do you remember me?"

"Only vaguely, I'm afraid. Did Lt. Dagleishe send you?"

Johnson hesitated for a moment, and then he answered, "Aye, Sir, zackly."

"Are you ready for this? It's a bigger job than being mate on a seventy-four, even though we have fewer men."

"Certainly, Sir," replied Johnson. Neville thought he didn't seem sure of it.

"Was there a gunner in the boat with you?"

"Aye, Sir, Mr. Skullen. He's the best we had aboard *Vanguard*, if you ask me, but he got crossways with Chips, the Carpenter, if you remember him. He's a grouchy one, anyway, so it's no..." He stopped there, obviously realizing his audience "Sorry, Sir. Don't mean to be passing rumor."

"Not to worry, Mr. Johnson. Welcome to *Superieure.*" He touched his hat, and the interview was done.

Two barges full of landsmen arrived from town, and four more boys. Eight more marines came in another boat. Their commander, Sergeant Denby, reported stiffly upon arrival and hurried his detachment off to sort their quarters, all clinking and stomping.

"**M**r. Johnson," Neville said at the conclusion of breakfast two days later, "Have the men lay aft."

As the ship's company shuffled back toward him, he climbed up on the taffrail and stepped forward onto the lid of the hog pen, then climbing to where he could stand with a hand on the main boom. He withdrew his posting letter from his jacket pocket. As with his taking command of the frigate *Experiment*, which also happened here in this harbor, he made short work of reading himself in:

"I am Commander Neville Burton. By these orders I am to repair aboard his Majesty's ship *Superieure* now lying at Port Royal, Jamaica and to take command as Captain and to discharge my duties as directed by Commodore Loring and also by the Admiralty as I may receive such orders from them. I am now your captain."

These men had heard such before and gave no indication of any joy of a new undertaking. They stared back at him silently. He recognized a few faces from *Vanguard*.

Neville then said almost the same words he had spoken to the *Experimentals*, although he doubted the effect would be as successful:

"There's more I wish to say. Under my command, discipline is of utmost concern. We are – we will be - a small ship in a vast sea, often with little or no help close at hand." He paused, and thought he detected stiffening amongst the men. "We are English," he continued, "and we will do our duty because it is our duty – not because we fear the starter or the lash – but because if we don't, we will all die together. Proper discipline comes from trust and respect for your mates, not from me. Petty officers and sergeants are not to use their starters unless it is truly deserved, and we will not have the cat out of the bag for a minor offence. It is not me you should fear, but the French and the pirates. You will obey your orders without backtalk or this ship may soon belong to the enemy and they may cheerfully feed you to the sharks – or worse."

Someone in the back threw his hat up and yelled, "Hoorah! Let's see you mean that!" The comment set off a general round of tentative cheering and scattered smiles.

That's good enough for now, thought Neville. "We sail a week tomorrow on the mid-morning tide," he added, "so we need to sort things quickly.

"Officers step up here, if you please." Neville jumped down off the hog pen and walked forward, closer to the mainmast. The jocularity ended quickly.

Johnson, Catchpole, and Denby of the Marines glanced about themselves, but proceeded directly to walk the few feet closer to their new captain. Not being used to any such notoriety, Midshipmen Framingham and Foyle both looked about anxiously, but did not move. Mr. Skullen, the Gunner, stood firm.

"I trust you have met these men already, but if not – here they are. Their orders are to be obeyed.

"Mr. Johnson is our Bo'sun," announced Neville.

Johnson took a step forward, raised his hat, then placed it back on his head and stepped back.

"Sorted him on *Vanguard,* they did," said a voice in the crowd. With the gathering being informal, without officers overlooking their divisions, no speaker could be determined. It was the sort of heckling that would get a man's grog stopped, if not normally worse.

Neville knew the comment would cause a raging rumor about the ship, spreading no good. The company fell quiet; he knew they would expect a response from him. Some captains would go into a fit of rage at such an outburst, stop all grog and tobacco, and mount an inquest into the identity of the 'mutinous cur'. He decided to hold his retort until he finished introductions. "Mr. Catchpole, Second Sailing Master."

"And him – on *Theseus,*" said another heckler.

Neville walked slowly back to the taffrail on a dead-quiet ship. He climbed back to his place on the hog pen and stared forward at his men for a long moment before speaking.

"And the third man there is Marine Sergeant Denby," he began. "Will anyone else have a remark?"

The men remained quiet, save the occasional clearing of a throat a small cough, while Neville waited in the stillness.

"I thought not," he said after taking an intentionally long few minutes to organize his thoughts.

"You are lucky men," he announced. The remark was greeted by a general growling. "In most ships I'll wager the two of you foolish enough to make those comments would be found and punished harshly. Your captain would probably also punish the lot of you for not throwing those same men down before him. I also suspect most of you have been sent here from your former ships because you made mistakes. Some of you may continue to make mistakes, thinking I will tolerate insolent, sloppy, or lazy behavior, but if you do, you will suffer for it. You are lucky men because there will be no punishment today at all. I will not search for the men who just made their first mistakes aboard my ship. You are lucky men because you have been given another chance. I am aware that Mr. Johnson and Mr. Catchpole made small mistakes where they were before, but I am not concerned by it. They will have their second chance and they will serve well here and prosper. All of you have the same opportunity.

"I will introduce three more of my officers, and there will be no remarks. Have I made myself clear?"

A general chorus of "Aye, Captain," rolled across the ship's deck.

Again, Neville hopped down off the hog pen and walked forward. "Gunner and Midshipmen step forward, if you please," he said.

When they had done so and he gave their names, the company stood silent. "Do not disobey the orders of these men, either, and see to your duties with good cheer, and we shall have a happy barky." When he added, "Report by divisions," there confused inactivity ensued.

Neville turned to the men he had just announced, and ordered them to "Line the men up by rating. For now we'll have the marines around the stern rails behind me; landsmen, boys, and anyone else who has no idea what I'm talking about over there" – he pointed center ship to the larboard rail.

"Waisters to the center 'round the boats; able seamen move to the mainmast. Those who would be topmen come here to my right. The rest of you, who should be rated ordinary seamen, move toward the bow."

"One of you to each group," he said to his officers. "We need all the names to make our muster lists. Most of the ships sent no lists."

The men all began shuffling in the directions he indicated.

"Waisters," Neville yelled out, "do any of you hold the King's warrant?"

An average-looking man with muscular arms waved his neck kerchief and yelled, "Aye, Sir. Carpenter's Mate Church, here."

"Welcome aboard, "Mr. Chips," quipped Neville, "And, who's our cook?"

A man stepped forward and made his announcement: "I am, Sir. Pickering."

"He's not a cook!" someone forward yelled. "If he is, lash him up. The food stinks!"

"And he's got two good legs; cain't be no cook!" yelled another.

The first remark struck Neville as another of the sort he had just cautioned the men about, but the second might have been good-natured. Before he could respond, another man stepped forward from the ranks of the able seamen. His motion was so abrupt that Neville thought he might have been pushed.

"Captain, Sir," the man began, holding his hat in his hands and twisting it cruelly, "Me 'an the men here wots' been aboard three day wants to know if you're going to do something wi' this food. And the water... The water stinks, and we ain't even left port yet."

"Hear him," another man yelled.

A hand reached out and gave the speaker a rough push on the shoulder. After a pause, he continued: "An' when does we get our pay and shore leave?"

When he'd finished his questions, Catchpole leaned over to Neville and whispered in his ear, "That man may have a wild moment here and there, but he's a dullard, mind you. I doubt those are his own thoughts."

Neville turned slightly to hear him, and then replied, "Despite our earlier conversation, Mr. Catchpole, I thank you for your input. Fetch me a goblet of the water, if you please."

He yelled forward, "What's your name, man?"

"Thomas. Thomas Sudpen." He did not add the customary 'Sir'.

The ship's company grew quiet again. Unless they had been at the mutinies at Spithead or the Nore back in 1797, they had probably never witnessed such open challenge to a ship's captain.

Neville had been there. He recognized what stood in front of him — a demand to negotiate -- but he had no immediate answer. If some of these men had also been there, then this might be an even more dangerous situation than it appeared on the surface.

"Mr. Sudpen," began Neville, "I have not been here any longer than most of you. I have no idea when the water came aboard, nor the victuals. For that matter, most of it is probably French, and we should be pleased at what our cook, Mr. Pickering, there, has managed to do with it."

"Thankee, Sir," Farnsworth interrupted.

"I will look into your complaints, but I will not investigate pay and shore leave now. I just told you that we are to sail in a week."

"Here's the water, Sir," said a small voice behind him. Neville turned enough to take the battered pewter goblet from a black-haired brown boy of about eleven. He lifted it to his nose and smelled. The glass held green pond scum and smelled of months in a cask; not the worst he'd ever drunk, but there was no excuse here in the harbor. They hadn't been on blockade duty for the last six months — and they certainly didn't need to leave port with foul water.

"It must be French," he announced. He raised it above his head and poured it on the deck. "Start the water — all of it overboard," he ordered … loudly.

A hearty cheer rose throughout the company. Within ten minutes, the clunk of a pump could be heard below, and the stream of green water squirting over the side emitted a stench that enveloped the ship in an unpleasant fog.

"Let's get these names down on paper. Jamaica Station should have reports from the fleet. We can check against those."

"That did not go as well as one might hope," said Neville to his officers when they gathered by the ship's tiller half an hour later to sort names for the muster lists. "I do not count myself a suspicious man, but that smelled closely of mutiny – mutiny for no particular reason I'm aware of," he added.

"I agree," said Catchpole. "I can't put a finger on any man, but there are some on board now of a type I have seen on many a ship – those who will be happy with nothing you do for 'em.'"

"I agree, too," said Midshipman Framingham. He was probably the only other officer other than Gunner Skullen old enough to have served aboard more than one or two ships.

Skullen remained silent, but Johnson said, "There were a few aboard *Vanguard*, too, Commander, but Bo'sun Waters had us watch them close. Master-at-Arms had eyes on them, too, so they never did much. Most of the men were Man-o-War's men. You saw the bad apples at the gratings often enough."

"Keep a close watch. I fear we have a great collection of apples from the bottom of the fleet's barrels. We'll pray we have enough good men to outweigh the bad, but we need to know who might be leaders. Sudpen might be, but Mr. Catchpole doubts it."

"**W**ater hoy's a cable off, Sir," Catchpole announced into Neville's cabin three days later.

Water hoy! Neville wondered to himself. *When I was here before we had to roll the barrels down and bring them out in boats.* "I'll be right up," he yelled back.

Neville arrived on deck just as the hoy thumped gently alongside *Superieure*. "Here's a good ship-handling captain," said Neville.

"Aye. He scarcely flattened the fenders," responded Catchpole. "No extra paint detail today."

"Send my compliments to Mr. Johnson, if you please; ask him to lay aft with his report on the victuals as soon as he sorts the water pumping. I'm becoming anxious about our schedule to leave in four days."

Johnson appeared in Neville's cabin just ten minutes later with a fist full of papers.

"You don't look comfortable, Mr. Johnson. Is something wrong?"

"I think we're doing fine, Sir, but it's complicated. I'm sorry, Sir but I've never had to work the vittles." The man was obviously flustered. "The Pusser handled all that," he continued." It's all comin' from Station in a big jumble, Sir, an' they're askin' me to sign all these papers." He held up his papers and shook them. "I'm sorry Sir, but maybe it's too much for me."

"Bring your papers, Mr. Johnson, let's go look. Have you chosen three mates yet?"

"Only one, Sir." He followed Neville up the companion stair.

"There's your first problem, Mr. Johnson. You can't do this alone. Who do you have to choose from?"

"I'm down to four, Sir, but I haven't…"

"Send them all to Mr. Catchpole in the next ten minutes. He'll give you two, and I'll send them to help you. I'm going to speak with him now, and then we'll all meet in the galley. Cookie will give you his advice on where he wants everything so he can get at it. We'll go with that."

A man unfamiliar to Neville lurched suddenly up the bilge ladder, dripping wet from the knees down. He stopped when he saw his captain, stared at Neville for a moment, and opened his mouth as if to speak. He closed it again, knuckled his forehead, and then rushed past and vanished up the main companion stair.

"Who was that man, Mr. Johnson?"

"Don't remember his name. One of the new carpenter's mates, I think; maybe the one standing for cooper? He's probably just checked bilge..."

Catchpole came hopping down the companion, two stairs at a time. "Ah, there you are – both of you. If you would follow me, please. Mr. Phillips..."

"Phillips, that's it Sir. Zackly." interrupted Johnson. "The man who just went up."

"Yes, of course, Mr. Johnson.

"Mr. Phillips reported what of the bilge, then, Mr. Catchpole?"

"Three feet, Sir. Our draft is nine, and two feet would be high normal, as you know. The hold had but one foot and a half yesterday, if you remember. Have we sprung a leak?"

"When it rains, it pours, does it not, gentlemen? See to what I asked before, if you please. Mr. Catchpole. You are to interview Mr. Johnson's four candidates for his mates. Choose two in the next half glass and send them to the galley. Have Mr. Phillips send me Chips forthwith."

"Oh, here's 'Chips' now. He's heard, then...

"Mr. Church, get some light down there and tell me as fast as you can if the water is rising. I would be truly mortified for us to founder in harbor on a calm day. Send a report to my cabin in ten minutes with your answer, if you please."

Neville departed with Johnson's papers, thinking he would spend a few minutes organizing them to keep his mind off the bilge water problem. Ten minutes pass quickly when one is preoccupied.

Mr. Church soon stood in front of Neville's little desk with Johnson. Both wore serious faces.

"Well, out with it, please, gentlemen. Have we the worm so bad we can barely float? I can't imagine that on such a new ship…did we hit some rock somewhere?"

The two looked at each other before Johnson spoke. "No, Sir, worse. It didn't take long to find the problem. There is some skullduggery afoot. The water's not rising at all, and there's not much taste of salt to it. Several of the new water tuns have been turned on their sides and the bungs knocked out. They're floating about now, as well."

It had been some time since Neville's temper has risen so quickly. He could feel the flush rise up his neck into his face. He sat fixed, however, with no immediate solution coming to mind. "Who would do this?" he queried.

"Almost anyone could sneak down there at night, Sir," Johnson continued, but that work would cause some noise. Somebody must have heard it. We can ask about."

"Why, though? Do they think to delay our departure – make the ship look bad? Gain some shore leave? Or just to play the devil with us? Most importantly, I need to know how much good water remains. We are only scheduled to be out three weeks. I must know if we can leave with a short supply. See to it immediately, Mr. Church. Pump the bilge down, Mr. Johnson – and pass word for Sergeant Denby. We'll post a sentry at the bilge ladder."

"Stores are aboard, Sir," reported Boatswain's Mate Gerald Johnson three days later. "Here's the last of the papers. We sent a request to Station for more water, but they would only respond that it had been sent over Tuesday last. I don't think they read the message you..."

Neville held up his hand for Johnson to stop. "What have you found from the men aboard, Mr. Johnson... about the bilge... incident?"

"Not a man is talking, Sir. I think they are afraid of somebody – or some group."

"Hmm... back to the water then; I think there is enough aboard for three weeks."

Another knock came at the door; the younger midshipman was admitted directly.

"P-p-pardon me C-C-Captain, but *Theseus* signals p-p-prepare to sail."

"Now, Mr. Foyle?"

At being questioned, Foyle's stutter worsened. "S-s-sorry, S-s-ir, b-b-but what it be t-t-tomorrow."

"Thank you, Mr. Foyle. You may go.

"Mr. Johnson, have the men lay aft. I wish to speak to the men about our situation – let the scurrilous dogs among them know their efforts will not stop a King's ship, and that they have only their own actions – or inactions – to thank for any suffering ahead."

"Aye, Sir. Another word?" requested Johnson.

"Go ahead."

"Thank you for the help choosing my mates. Mr. Catchpole did a fine job. I am pleased with his recommendations."

"At least something's gone right, then. Carry on, Mr. Johnson."

With a reasonable understanding of her duty, *Superieure* sailed before the van of Commodore Loring's squadron, pointing her nose toward the blue water beyond Fort Charles.

"Wind nor-east, Commander," offered Catchpole, "about force three; and I don't think that over there will blow our way atall." He pointed southeast to where a distant squall was dropping rain over the water. Above them, the sky remained bright blue with patchy white clouds. Another flight of pelicans in military formation crossed their bow.

"Aye," said Neville. "It's perfect for leaving the harbor and beginning our beat along Jamaica's south-eastern shore. The squadron will tack north for the Windward Passage once we've got sea room from the island."

"Verily, Sir… Sir?"

"Go ahead."

"Do you think we'll have trouble with the men?"

"I think we already have trouble. Do you have any word on the spilling of the water?"

"No, Sir. Nothing yet."

"I didn't care to make that speech to the men yesterday, Mr. Catchpole. You know it never works to ask Jack Tar to tell tales against his own. And, it's not my way to run a ship – threatening the lash to maintain control."

"I've seen naught else, Sir. What other way is there?"

"My way, Mr. Catchpole. My way. We tell the men the mission. We act fair with them and expect them to do their duty. Only serious offences receive serious punishment – not every little complaint. This is a tough life, and you know it. I have always seen fairness make a happy barky. It may be a hard sell here, but we must try it... Harden courses, if you please, Mr. Catchpole."

Soon after Neville's order was repeated forward, however, an outburst of yelling began between two men.

"Who's playing at silly buggers, there, Mr. Johnson?" Neville hollered forward. "Bring those two here."

More trouble, and not one day out, ruminated Neville. His stomach tightened as the men approached.

The two, one walleyed ordinary seaman of the mainmast and his petty officer, a Mr. Downey, were marched back to where Neville stood by the helm near Johnson.

"What's all the fuss?" queried Neville.

"This man back-talked Mr. Downey here, for all of 'em to hear."

"Well you said, Sir..." the man began, but Johnson cut him off short.

"Hold on. Nobody's talking to you yet."

"I said?" asked Neville. "What did I say to do with you back-talking your superior?"

"Beg your pardon, Sir, but you said they ain't supposed to use their starters on us for naught. Smacked me right mean, he did, and I was climbing." Neville noted the surprisingly forward manner by which an ordinary seaman would address him. He gave the man his best 'mind your manners' scowl, and then turned to Downey.

"True, Mr. Downey?"

"He weren't moving at the proper speed, Sir."

"So you did hit him prematurely?"

Downey, a good half foot shorter, with long greasy hair and a drooping black mustache, raised his chin to look directly into Neville's eyes. "I did, Sir, and he'll get another next time, too."

"Find me a witness, Mr. Johnson. You ask him what he saw and get back to me.

"Mr. Downey, wait by the chickens a minute."

Johnson was back in two, and he said, "Mr. Downey hit him, Sir. Hard, Seaman George says, and as he could see, 'twas only because he let one of his mates have the next rung up on the ratlines."

"We're not waiting for punishment day, Mr. Johnson. Trice Mr. Downey on the main shrouds, and I'll speak to the men."

With the hubbub of setting sails complete, the Boatswain called the ship's company back to where Neville could address them from a perch on the mainmast bitts.

"I told you all," he began in a voice loud enough to be heard above the wind and waves, "that we would have firm but fair discipline aboard this ship. Mr. Downey there is to be respected, and I will have no one telling lies about him after he's cut down, but he – and all the rest of you petty officers – will respect the men. If they are going about routine duties in a reasonable manner, keep your starters still. I said it, and I meant it, as you can see. You may warn them first with a touch and a word, but if you hit first and question later, you will be with Mr. Downey there – or worse. Return to your duties."

The company shuffled back to work with a great deal of hushed mumbling, and Mr. Johnson came back to ask, "How long's he stay there, Sir?"

With a nasty grin, Neville said, "Cut him down when he wets his pants."

"Aye, Commander; zackly. Sailing orders, then?"

"Same as before, Mr. Johnson, as I've instructed Mr. Catchpole. We go up 'round Tortuga and look for the enemy. If I were you I'd be praying we find some little ones we can chase after ourselves for a little spending money." *I'll just let that thought go 'round the men after the last thing.*

"How did you come to be here, Mr. Johnson? Did you volunteer?"

"I did, Sir, zackly." Johnson said nothing more.

Neville felt the rise and fall of the waves as the little ship slid away from the protection of land. The feeling was nothing like being aboard a seventy-four. Here you could really feel the sea. A slightly stronger puff of air passed, and *Superieure* instantly leaned away and began to accelerate. The larger ships scarcely changed their attitudes at all if it wasn't blowing a gale of wind. *So many feelings at once. It was a day like this and right about here when I made my decision to stay forever in Jamaica with Maria.* The gurgle of water from *Superieure's* wake increased.

"When you came aboard, Mr. Johnson, I thought you said Lt. Dagleishe sent you. Were you encouraged to volunteer? Don't you consider a seventy-four to be the best of ships?"

Johnson seemed to become a slight bit defensive – or offended? Neville had no reading on Johnson's feelings about the punishment, either.

"I told 'em I'd had duty on a revenue cutter before, Sir, and I thought it every bit as good."

Neville had been studying the sails. He turned to the Sailing Master: "Mr. Catchpole, will you bring the main in a bit and see to the forestays'l? I'd wager we can go a bit faster on this wind."

"But don't we have to keep…"

"I doubt it," Neville interrupted. "Until they tell me otherwise I don't think we're expected to 'keep station'. I expect they'd rather we went scouting out ahead. Don't worry. I know these waters very well."

Neville returned to his conversation with his boatswain: "Mr. Johnson, will you step over here a minute, please?"

Once downwind of the helmsman, and unfortunately also the hog pen, Neville leaned close to Johnson's ear and asked quietly, "Did you indeed see duty on a revenue cutter?"

A very frightened look crossed Johnson's face and his color flared red. He paused before responding, "You doubt my word, Sir?"

"Should I?"

Johnson paused again and appeared to have made some decision. "I'm a troublemaker, Sir. They wanted me off the ship." His posture did not relax, though he seemed to hang his head slightly.

"How is it you make trouble, Mr. Johnson? I don't remember anything about you on *Vanguard*."

His tone changed to something more like a desperate need to explain himself – not belligerence. "T'weren't me, Sir, honest."

The helmsman looked over his shoulder at them.

"Carry on, quartermaster," snapped Neville. The man's head jerked forward where it belonged.

Johnson continued in a lowered voice, "I got off on the wrong foot wi' Bo'sun Waters the minute I stepped aboard, Sir. I din't know who he was an' I made some remark about the ship being untidy. He's 'ad it in for me ever since, and he don't like Swedes anyway – thinks we're all stupid... Looks like it'll be the same here, don't it, wi' you catching me at a lie on the first day out?" He clammed up.

"Come walk forward with me," said Neville.

"Lovely, Mr. Catchpole. She's pulling much better now, don't you think?" Neville said on the way past the helm.

Neville and Johnson walked forward to an empty spot between the larboard rail and the boats. "Take a look under the boat, Mr. Johnson. See if we have any shirkers – or ears." He leaned on the rail watching the verdant hills of Jamaica slide slowly by to larboard.

"Nobody, Sir. Why you smilin' so big, if I might ask? Is it at my expense?" he asked, a touch of anger returning to his voice.

"Your situation, Mr. Johnson, is very much like mine. I know exactly how you feel. I came across on *Vanguard* because they threw me off *Elephant*. But on *Vanguard* things went very well for me, as you might guess now."

"You? Why would they…"

"I got off on the wrong foot with the First Lieutenant. Does the story sound familiar? Don't spread it around. It would be just like passing around that they wanted to toss my Bo'sun off *Vanguard* – although I think the rumor has been around already. Wouldn't be good, would it? I like what I see in you already, Mr. Johnson, and I understand the lie. I'm telling you you're in a new situation and you have the world before you. Do right by me and you can tell Mr. Waters to 'sod off' one day." *So Dagleishe did us both a favor by sending him over, then.*

Johnson grinned ear to ear.

"Two more things, Mr. Johnson…"

"Aye, Sir?"

"No more lies to your captain."

Johnson touched his forehead, "Ne'er happen, Sir."

"And treat the men with respect, but I don't mean to go easy on them. I've just told Mr. Catchpole the same. We need them doing their jobs **and** we need 'em on our side."

At five bells of the afternoon watch *Superieure* tacked northwest, then running parallel to the lead ship of the squadron, the thirty-two-gun frigate *Tartar*. When eight bells of the afternoon watch tolled, only the shadows of the sails and occasional patchy clouds offered protection against the hot sun. Neville waited patiently, sweat running beneath his blue uniform, to watch the ship's first supper under way proceed smoothly before he went below for his own meal.

"From the smell of it," Midshipman Framingham commented on his way by, "Cookie is trying to improve his reputation."

"We can pray for it, Mr. Framingham, both for our bellies and for the happiness of the ship."

"Aye, Sir," said Framingham. He'd certainly heard that 'Burton and Johnson had already had words', and was not going out on any limbs with his new captain.

"Don't hesitate to call me if there's any need." Neville emphasized his first two words, and then added, "I'm going below."

Below, in his cabin, he found his coxswain busy in the cupboards. He wasn't sure what to make of this fellow who was, as best Neville could guess, slightly his elder; he'd never been good a guessing age anyway. Mr. Hajee Ayoub was a five-foot tall fellow from India – or some Arab place – with a poor brown-skinned complexion, wavy black hair, and English that was difficult to understand, at best. Although not Christian, he seemed an efficient servant. Neville's supper arrived in short order and the man inquired about mending his uniform... *or I think that's what he meant, so I told him 'yes'.*

At Sea – Windward Passage   *July 20, 1803*

Dear Mother & Elizabeth,

    There has been muche happen since I have last writ. I have been so busy that I fear you think me lost again. You see the Name of the Ship that I am in (below). She was French until a few weeks ago, but Vanguard Captured her at the Northe of Hispaniola (with no loss of life) and I am made her Captain because she is small and 'unrated', as we say, so none of the Firste Lieutenants of the fleet wanted the Command. Suche gives me the rank of Master and Commander, whiche sounds lovely, and should be a posting of great dash and excitement, but I wonder that I am up to it. It's not that I haven't Commanded a ship before – during my absence, I acted two years as a Frigate Captain – but Superieure is so small that I have very Limited assistance to Command her. I have but two Midshipmen, and I think one very young and green, and the second a questionable older fellow. Then there is a Second Sailing Master and a young Boats'n who was a junior mate on Vanguard. And there's worse. The other ships of the fleet have sent me many malefactors in the rush to complete her complement. I don't mean that I fear Mutiny, but I may have to go against my Personal Principles of Command and serve out far more punishment than I approve of.

    This is a lot of grousing, I know, but I am feeling very isolated in this Tiny Boat, and Grumpy, perhaps, for what might prove to have been a poor decision to take the Posting. I shall bothe keep my sword handy and pray for Guidance.

I pray this finds you well and happy as when I last saw you,

Love, Your son/brother

Nev. Burton, Master & Commander, HMS Superieure

Neville completed his letter and went back topside to enjoy the setting of the sun and the cooling air.

"Midshipman Foyle, how goes it?"

"All f-f-fine, Sir."

He said no more. Neville didn't complain about the ensuing quiet, which gave him a moment's peace to get his bearings. Jamaica was still visible to larboard, with a ridge of white cloud upon it like a lady's sun bonnet. The north-northeast breeze had stiffened a bit, though Neville expected it would die with the setting sun. They were moving well – five or six knots of the log he judged, with a small sea running against the starboard bow – and he could see the sails of the fleet behind: as much as a league, already. *This little barky really does run swiftly.* He turned to face his Midshipman of the Watch.

"Mr. Foyle," he said, "Let's get something straight between us right off."

Foyle, a gangly lad of about thirteen years with bushy blond hair, gave him a horrified look, but didn't say a thing for over a minute while Neville did his best to glare at the boy without snickering.

"Your silence, Mr. Foyle. There's the problem. You haven't said anything."

"W-w-what sh-sh-should I s-s-say, Sir?"

"I am the only commissioned officer aboard, as I am sure you have noticed. Beyond your commander, we have you two Midshipmen, Second Sailing Master Catchpole, and Bo'sun Johnson who is in truth but a mate. Marine Sergeant Denby and Assistant surgeon - Trimbley or something, I haven't even met him yet — and all the waisters aboard, are not involved with sailing this ship. What I am getting to, Mr. Foyle, is that there are really only five of us who need to communicate clearly to the others our sailing information — course and speed; that sort of thing. When I come up and ask how things are, if there is no emergency, I expect you to tell me those things, and you must always tell them to the relief of your watch, and particularly at night. Your responsibility here is far beyond what is was on your last ship, even though your rating has not changed. Am I clear?"

"Aye, S-sir. Qu-quite."

Neville had also passed word for Denby and Johnson, and when they arrived, he said, "We'll need gun drill, gentlemen. Start with just running them out one side and then t'other today. Then bring them in and house them, and then do it all over again. We can't afford to meet the enemy as we are, having no idea how our guns work. Tomorrow we'll fire every other one and the next day a broadside. Remember to steer the landsmen clear. Many have probably never heard a cannon fired, and we certainly don't want them standing behind the guns when we fire them."

The two departed to organize the exercise.

"Who's on duty next, Mr. Foyle?"

"Mr. Catchpole, I think, Sir."

"Make good use of the chalkboard, then. No change to our course, and unless we get some wind there'll be no sails to tend. Good night."

"G-good night, Sir. Thank you."

12: *The Plot Thickens*

Thursday morning dawned gray. This time of year, observance of the weather was of paramount importance. July is the time of hurricanes. Neville could see the gray even before his head reached the deck. Low clouds covered the sky straight across. The hairs on the back of his head prickled at the thought of a storm, adding to his anxiety concerning his ship's company. He had considered posting a second sentry by his door, despite having a hard time accepting that his men would actually mutiny on him. He also wondered what sort of signal a second sentry might send them. He had decided on simply hanging his sword and a loaded pistol near the door and keeping a dirk with him at night. "What do you think of the weather, Mr. Framingham?" he queried, when close enough to speak to the Officer on Duty in a normal voice.

"Not to worry, Captain. Wind's been steady. A shower passed an hour ago, but it didn't seem different from any other morning. It's just another summer's day in the Spanish Lake, I'd say."

"Let's hope so… the fleet?"

"There, dead astern. *Theseus* keeps signaling some of them to stay on station, but there's been nothing for us."

"Thank you, Mr. Framingham." Neville took another swig of his rich Jamaican coffee, but his stomach churned again. He had experienced difficulty eating these last few days; appetite gone with the ship's happiness. He noticed Johnson and Foyle had been leaning at the leeward rail talking. They glanced his way every so often, but made no movement while he spoke with Framingham. When they saw him finish, they walked toward him with the apparent intention of wishing him a good morning. When they arrived, however, their faces displayed no joy of a new day.

"Excuse us, Captain," began Johnson. "Mr. Foyle has something of great gravity to report, but I think it must be as ... confidential ... as we can."

"My cabin, then. Lead on."

Neville's neck hairs prickled again. He felt eyes upon him. Looking about the ship as he descended the companion stair, he saw nothing unusual. With so many men aboard, at least one would always be watching him.

"Leave us a moment, please, Hajee," he said as they entered his little cabin.

"May I close this, Sir?" asked Johnson, referring to the hatch above his head.

"Serious, then?"

"Very, Sir.

"Tell him, Mr. Foyle."

"It were last n-night," began Midshipmen Foyle. "There's one of the b-b-boys who is mis-mis-missing this morning, Sir." Foyle's chin quivered. The lad was, indeed, only about thirteen; hardened by the service, but still young. "I think it's my fault."

"What do you mean by 'missing', Mr. Foyle? How can one be 'missing' from a ship at sea? And, why would you say it's your fault?" Neville could feel himself becoming impatient with Foyle's answers. "Can you assist, Mr. Johnson?"

"Mr. Foyle says he talked to the boy – Ralph Farnsworth – last evening..."

"He w-was a friend," resumed Foyle. "We t-t-talk of an evening sometimes. He's from C-C-County Nottingham, same as m-m-me."

"Then what's your point, Mr. Foyle?"

"He s-s-said something about the spilled w-w-w-water, Sir. He wasn't trying to tell me anything. He just slipped, I think, and then he re-re-realized it. He said he couldn't say nothin' or he'd be knocked on the head... anybody w-w-would be and nobody could t-t-t... say anything. There's a group of the able seamen, he said, who are the leaders. He wouldn't say more, and he l-l-left right after. I dunno if somebody listened. We weren't trying to k-k-keep it a secret that we talked – to begin with."

Foyle's chin quivered again. Neville's stomach tightened and his neck hairs prickled more strongly. A trickle of sweat worked its way down his backbone.

"I'll pass word for him to come see me after breakfast," Neville said after pondering what he had just heard for a minute.

"That's all I can find out, Sir," continued Foyle. "That's w-w-why I went to Mr. Johnson f-for help. Ralph's m-m-missing, like I said. I don't see him about this m-morning. He should be c-c-carrying the holystones up. I asked after him, and they all say, 'Not seen 'im, Sir,' or 'Dunno where he is', or some such codswallop. I think someone heard us and they've knocked him on the head, just like he feared... thrown overboard, maybe, hours ago."

Neville jumped to his feet. "Mr. Johnson, we can call a drill whenever we feel like it. Call the ship to clear for action and beat to quarters... now! Then run out to starboard. Be sure to put a timer on it."

Johnson and Foyle literally ran from the cabin. Johnson began hollering the moment he cleared the door, and then blowing his pipe. Three men arrived to remove Neville's cabin screens before he had taken a second swallow of his coffee. Four more came in for his personal gear as he strapped on his sword belt. He then took his coffee tumbler and strolled as nonchalantly as he could muster up onto the deck to the captain's proper station by the helm. "Good morning, Mr. Catchpole. You were quick, thank you."

"Aye, Sir, and good morning to you."

"Haul our wind three points, if you would, please."

"Haul our… now, in the middle of clearing?"

"Precisely now, Mr. Catchpole."

"Aye, Sir," he said, and hollered the order forward to Mr. Johnson.

The pandemonium increased only slightly. The watch on duty did not have much more to do than they were already doing – sailing the ship. Closer to the wind, the ship heeled slightly more, creating an increased feeling of urgency to every movement aboard.

"Five and a half knots, Sir," reported Framingham. The ship steadied on the new heading, angling slightly away from the fleet.

"Ready, Sir," reported Johnson. "Seven minutes, forty-five seconds." He said it bravely, with his head up, but he knew it would bring Commander Burton's wrath.

"Seven…?" Neville yelled in his face. "We could be dead men! Fire gun three!"

Johnson bellowed the order forward, and they waited. They waited thirty to forty seconds before the gun spouted fire and leaped back against its restraints.

Neville looked at Johnson. His face had drained of color. His mouth opened, but he said nothing.

"Aye, Sir. I understand," mumbled Johnson. "We'll have more gun drill."

"Have the men report by divisions. And, tell me in what division I should find Mr. Farnsworth."

"Right away, Sir. Mr. Farnsworth should be at the mainmast with the other powder monkeys."

Neville turned to Marine Sergeant Denby, who stood nearby, "Sergeant Denby, please follow to my cabin."

Once inside, Neville gave Denby a quick summary of the problem before them, saying, "I don't believe your marines are involved at all. You and my officers are the people aboard I most trust. I will call on you to do your duty, even if it must be against our own men. We'll begin with the search for a missing boy, if he is indeed missing."

Neville climbed the companion stair with Denby close behind. He walked directly to two rows of boys and landsmen at the mainmast. "Who reports these men?" he queried the group's petty officer.

"I do, Sir," replied one very nervous Mr. Trindle. "All present are sober, Sir. One man... boy... missing."

"Name?"

"Ralph Farnsworth, Sir."

"You, there; boy on the end. When did you last see your mate?"

The boy's chin quivered. His eyes welled with tears, and he began to shake. "I can't... I can't..."

"Answer your captain's question, Mr. Sears," Trindle ordered with a very hard edge to his voice.

"But I… If I…" He stopped there, with tears running down his shaking cheeks.

Trimble spoke again. "Where's Farnsworth, Mr. Sears. If you know, tell the Captain," he demanded.

"They threw him over the side in the morning watch," he blubbered. He was crying now, and began sobbing.

"Mr. Sears, can you manage to go to the helm and tell Mr. Catchpole to reverse the morning's course?"

"Aye, aye… Sir," Sears snuffled between sobs, and began his trudge of twenty feet to the tiller.

"Why did you not report this earlier, Mr. Trindle?"

"I didn't know. He just said it now. I heard it just as you did. How could I report something I didn't know?"

"Sir?" yelled Catchpole from the helm.

"Aye, Mr. Catchpole. Reverse course immediately."

Neville moved to within a foot of Trindle's face and said, "You knew, Mr. Trindle. It is your duty to know where your men are. You knew, and you said nothing."

He turned to Denby. "Sergeant, put this man in irons for dereliction of duty – or for assisting with a murder – or for mutiny – I'll decide later."

Sears returned. His sobbing had stopped, but he was looking about furtively as a recently caged animal might.

"Mr. Sears, you claim Mr… your mate, Ralph…they threw him overboard in the morning watch? As close as you can, what time would you say?"

"Three bells, Sir. Right on three. First the bells, then the splash."

"What did you do about it?"

Sears began to cry again. "Nothing, Sir. I didn't do a thing. I just stayed there under the boats and kept quiet as I could manage so I wouldn't be next over."

"We'll talk more later, Mr. Sears. Try to gather yourself."

The ship stood up straighter as she nosed through the eye of the wind. The main boom sliced through the air above their heads, and the sails were let out as the swooping turn to leeward began. The mild pounding of hull against waves ceased as the ship's attitude changed from beating to windward to running with the wind. A swishing sound of water along the sides and the gentle repetition of waves surging beneath the ship from astern replaced the pounding.

"We'll make some calculations," Neville announced to no one in particular. "We might find him alive. The water's warm here. A man could last for hours."

"Not him, Sir," said Sears.

"Why not, Mr. Sears?"

"Ralph couldn't swim… and they knocked him on the head first anyway. It were a horrible sound I'll never forget; sort of hard, but hollow."

"I'm sorry, Mr. Sears, I really am," said Neville. He walked back to the quarterdeck.

"Mr. Johnson," he said, "please complete the inspection of divisions. Tell them all we are very disappointed with their performance at clearing and they should expect considerable more drilling. Have them stand down after that. Pass word for Chips to report aft as soon as they put my cabin back together, if you please."

Tired. If nothing else, Neville felt tired. Yes, the anxiety wore on him. His stomach churned. He clenched his teeth. But being tired dragged on his soul. He'd felt the energy of the world not too many months ago. Three years ago, he was on top of the world. Nothing could go wrong! Now, everything had changed for the worse. Even his own men were against him. No, not all of them, but some. Most? Despite feeling almost exhausted, he vowed to find the answer to that last question.

"Mr. Church, please come in. Have a seat. Pardon me if I do not spend much time on formality."

Another knock came at the door before Church sat. The sentry announced Mr. Foyle.

"Mr. Foyle, this is not the time."

"I'm sorry, Sir. Signal. *Theseus* wants to know what we're about."

"Ahhh… yes, she would. Please respond 'sail practice' and advise Mr. Catchpole to return to our previous upwind course."

"Aye, Sir," said Foyle. He departed.

"I do not know you well yet, Mr. Church," Neville continued, "but we must gain each other's trust. I will not let out what you tell me until I have questioned – interviewed – many of the ship's company, so nobody will know who told me any one thing… unless, of course, you tell them what you've said. I am not looking to punish the entire ship for keeping secrets, although you can be sure I don't like it. Can you tell me who is keeping the ship in fear for their very lives?"

"First, let me offer you my thanks, Captain. I have no interest in discovering I have become a pirate or a deserter just because I didn't object to it all. We in the waist are kept out of it, mostly, so I can't tell you much. I can say that I know of two able seamen who…"

Neville held three other interviews – with the cook, Gunner Skullen, and the caulker. Mr. Phillips, the carpenter's mate acting as cooper, would be next. He heard a cry above: "Signal. Our number!"

With considerable trepidation, Neville went on deck to inquire about the signal from the flagship. On the one hand, he knew much more about *Superieure's* condition. On the other hand, knowing what he had just learned, he had greater concern about her ability to do her duty in the face of the enemy. When he stepped up, the weather had a bit improved from earlier. He had to remind himself that it had been several hours since the discovery of the missing boy. Most of the overcast of the morning had dissolved into a distant haze, but the wind persisted, raising a slightly larger sea.

"There, Sir," said Catchpole, pointing eastward to where *Theseus* could be seen. "She signals 'enemy… chase'."

"So she does, Mr. Catchpole. Where's our prey?"

"Hard to see, Sir. Very hard. Due North. A very small thing, I dare say, which is probably why they send us… I'm sorry, Sir. I mean no offense."

"None taken, I understand. What you say is logical. I see nothing there, though. Is there s glass handy?"

Framingham had anticipated the request and offered the long glass he'd fetched from the mainmast becket.

After a few minutes of steadying and squinting, Neville said, "Yes, I agree there's something there. I believe she's moving norwest toward Spanish Cuba. Signal *Theseus* 'acknowledge', and we'll chase the bugger. Drop us two points off the wind, Mr. Catchpole. Let us see how fast this horse will run."

Despite the tenseness of the day, Catchpole smiled large and responded with a hearty, "Aye, aye, Sir."

"After you sort the sails, Mr. Catchpole, bring yourself below and we'll look to our course across the charts."

In his cabin, Neville had the charts for the Windward Passage and for the east end of Cuba unrolled on his little desk. "I am concerned about our nearness to the Cuban coast," he said, when Catchpole appeared. "Can you prick our position?"

"Here's our last," he said, taking a minute to transfer latitude and longitude from the binnacle slate to the chart. "Course is thus." He drew a very light line north. "If our chase is small... let us say a schooner or small brig – not a lugger, or she will shortly be gone from us – then she must be low to the water and we could not see her from far. She must, therefore, be within three leagues."

"And, if we put her three leagues north... here," Neville interrupted, touching the chart, "and she runs for the north of Cuba, then she may be able to weather Punta de Maisi. From here, we would surely need to put in another tack, and she will be lost. We are ordered to chase, however, so we shall do. Between you and me, Mr. Catchpole, losing her may be a saving grace. You saw our gun drill. We are far worse than sloppy."

"Aye, Sir," said Catchpole. Rather than appearing concerned, he looked very relieved.

"However it goes, we shall be quite some time at it. Send one of the foremast petty officers down for a chat, if you would, please."

Neville contained his anger well as the picture of fear-mongering on his ship slowly presented itself through one interview after another. As the only commissioned officer aboard *Superieure*, he was alone, however, and quite conscious of it. This drastic situation called for drastic action. He no longer had any doubt there would be at least one hanging at the end of this road, and he didn't want to get it wrong. After another five interviews, however, he needed some relief. Without concern that mischief of a more serious nature would occur during the chase, he went topside to check on progress.

"We're well into the afternoon watch, Mr. Framingham," he commented, "Do we seem to be closing the distance?"

"Definitely, Sir. She's another Bahama sloop, similar to us, though not so well sailed, I think. She's to larboard of us now... there, see?" he answered, pointing. "Mr. Catchpole says we must stay on this heading, however, if we are to have any chance atall of weathering the point. The chase is surely going there, and he may know it well enough to sail close in. The wind has been veering these last few hours."

"It will, of course, as we reach the northern end of the Passage and gain the easterly effect of the trades, and it will not help either of us weather the point. Our fleet has tacked over to the east, I see. They leave us to pounce on our little water bug alone."

"Aye, Sir. Didn't even wave good-bye, did they?"

This Framingham has a sense of humor, at least. I wonder what his problem is. All the others seem to have something. Maybe just that he's older - thirty-two if I remember right - and hasn't passed for lieutenant. I suppose he just simply prefers the comfortable path. I'll have to hope his actions in battle are different.

"There are but three hours until the sun sets, I estimate. We should make some calculation... ahh, here comes Mr. Catchpole now."

"I have been ciphering, Captain," said Catchpole when he'd come close enough to speak without having to yell over the breeze, "Would you take a look? I've laid it all out on a mess table below,"

"I was just coming to that now," said Neville. "Lead on."

The two descended the main companion stair, which in *Superieure* led directly to the mess salon. "It's there on the table to starboard, you see?" Catchpole directed, waving his hand in the direction described. "What the bloody…?"

"What is it, Mr. Catchpole?"

"Look! It's been torn apart. Our small chart of this region is in shreds under the table. We have mutinous curs aboard, indeed!"

"That does it," said Neville. "Pass word for all officers to report here immediately. Have Sergeant Denby post two guards by the helm before he comes."

"Before they get here, Mr. Catchpole, what is the gist of your calculations?"

"Unless the wind veers four points or more, we'll not catch him, Sir. We're closing, but not fast enough to round the point in daylight. He can point as well as we can into the wind, but he's higher on it than we are to start with, and thus probably has a few extra cables offing to spare. If he knows the water, he could chance close in, but there's no light on the headland. We'll not be able to go so close in the dark."

"We can go close in if we can see," said Neville. "I've been there."

"Been there? Did you not just come across on *Vanguard?*"

"This time, yes. Let's not question. So, we shall follow until it is certain we cannot, understood?"

The officers had appeared by then, Denby arriving last. Commander Burton made his announcement: "I am sure the rumors are around and around again by now. Everyone knows I have spoken to a dozen people about our problems, so I sincerely hope no one person is singled out for more mayhem. Young Mr. Farnsworth was knocked on the head and then thrown overboard in the night, so we must determine his murderer. We have a mutiny in progress… the water barrels, probably the sluggishness displayed during our preparations for action, and now this," he said, waving his hand at the torn charts. "Someone aboard simply hates the navy, it would seem, and wishes us all ill. I suggest you all arm yourselves before our next step, but I will have the marines behind us. I have two names. Mr. Johnson, we will create a bit of distraction by clearing for action and beating to quarters as soon as I am finished here. Sergeant Denby, bring four marines and two sets of manacles. You and I shall make the arrests. All ready?" He looked quickly at the grim faces around him, and saw no shirkers.

Johnson went up the stair first, crying out to clear for action and blowing his pipe. Denby left to find his preferred assistants. Neville walked aft to his cabin for sword and pistol before the clearing crew packed it all below. When Denby rejoined him on deck, he led the way forward.

There! he thought. *That great hulking mass of a landsman holding a bucket. He's just as described.* "Mr. Wallis! Put down the bucket," Neville yelled. He continued walking toward the culprit, a man at least eight inches taller than Neville, and certainly heavier; his shape suggestive of the center drum of a capstan – wider at bottom than top. He sported dark, unkempt hair – greasy, long, and untied – and a scarred face. One eye was partially closed from a multitude of fights in his past, and his nose flat for the same reason. The permanent sour look on his face turned to a snarl at being called out, and his first instinct was to heave the bucket at Neville's head. Neville ducked, which proved to be unnecessary. Denby had chosen well. One of the marines instantly swung the butt of his musket in front of the bucket as if he were at bat in a Sunday game of cricket. The other two marine muskets came up almost as quickly, but they were not batting. The clicks of the two being cocked rattled across a now-silent deck.

"Hold!" Neville yelled. "Don't fire unless he attacks. We'll let this one sit in irons until we hang him.

"Mr. Church," he hollered, "Hammer the manacles onto our murderer."

"Sergeant Denby, send him to the hold and bring your next two men with me." He resumed his walk to the foredeck.

"Mr. Stiles, Able Seaman, show yourself!" Neville yelled, "Come out and surrender!"

At this call, unlike with Wallis, several men began to cheer. "Huzzah… He's got 'em both… Stretch their necks…," and then someone yelled, "He's up here!"

"Tall and lanky, Sergeant," said Neville to Denby. "Long dirty blond hair… usually wears a red jumper."

"Oh, I know the one," said Denby. "He's a nasty piece of work, that one. I don't see him up here, though. Don't see anyone."

A man hanging in the starboard forward ratlines pointed down at a jumble of white cloth – a recently-doused pair of jibs.

"Oh-ho!" exclaimed Denby. "We can enjoy this! Start thumping this pile with your muskets, men. Maybe some vermin will crawl out. Ha, ha!"

"**H**ow convenient," said Neville to Johnson the next morning. "Something's going right. Today is Saturday. We'll have punishment. I don't normally look forward to punishment day atall, atall, but today is very different. We'll start at six bells. Right now, I need to meet with Mr. Catchpole and sort out our course to rejoin the fleet."

"Thank you for breakfast, Sir."

"You're quite welcome, Mr. Johnson. With our chase gone off 'round Punta de Maisi in the night without us, we're not in such a hurry any more."

"Sorry about that, Sir."

"No matter. It may have saved us. If we engaged an enemy of similar size with mutineers among us and our gun-work as slow as it is, we might not be the ones losing our ship. And, if we bested them, how do you suppose I could have split off a prize crew?"

"Hmm… I shouldn't like to think about that."

"Plan on quite a bit of gun drill over the next couple weeks. Take a pot of coffee with you, and pass word for Mr. Sears."

"Mr. Sears," Neville said when the boy arrived, "how are you feeling today?"

"I'm fine Sir."

Someone must have told him he is only supposed to speak when I ask him a question. "I don't want to ask you this in front of the men, Mr. Sears. I have words from several others, but I want to hear it from you. Did we arrest the right blackguards?"

"Aye, you did, Sir."

"How do you know? When they knocked Farnsworth on the head, which one did it?"

"It were Wallis, Sir."

"Did you see him do it?"

"No, Sir. I was under the boats, like I told you."

"Then how can you claim witness?"

"Feet, Sir. I could see his feet plain enough. On his left foot, he wears a silver ring on his big, fat toe. And his feet is fatter than anyone else's anyway. Stiles weren't there. The whole company knows he does the telling and Wallis does the doing."

"All right, Mr. Sears. I won't ask you anything at punishment time. Off you go."

"Twelve strokes each," pronounced Neville in sentencing two similar cases. "Let this be notice to those of you who would talk back against a superior who makes a lawful command. I told you when we began that I'd spare the lash, and I have gone easy, as you know. Even as I make this promise, you must know that gross insubordination cannot be accepted here. We have the French to fight, not each other. Boatswain, do your duty."

The two man-o-war's men took their punishment with no more than a few grunts while the marines stood in a line athwartships behind Neville. Their mates sluiced the blood off with seawater at the completion and carried them below to sick bay. Before the flogging was complete, five of the landsmen and one of the boys, having never seen such punishment before, fainted dead away to the deck.

Three minor cases followed. The guilty parties received light punishment. One of the foremast jacks had saved up enough of his rum ration to become thoroughly intoxicated the evening before, whether because of or in spite of the day's events. Neville stopped his rum for a week. Another was accused of stealing a mate's knife. Neville stopped his tobacco for three days, knowing his real punishment would be served out by his mates.

Then the gunner of gun three – the only gun fired – had his grog and tobacco both stopped for a week for dereliction of duty. Neville would have preferred a harsher sentence, but because improved gunnery would be stressed, he wanted the man's attention and relative health.

Neville had reviewed the Articles of War – those same Articles of War that he had read to his company time after time to be sure they had no misunderstanding – and decided he did not understand his own role. A captain's words were law, yes, but did he have the power to hang these men here and now? He did not doubt that waiting for a court martial would not be required if he was sailing alone... but as part of a fleet, with numerous captains available within days, was he required to hold these men and convene a court martial as soon as one could be gathered? Finally, he decided it was critical to demonstrate his lack of tolerance for mutinous behavior. He could not wait to rejoin the fleet. Something more might happen between now and then.

"Finally, we come to the matters of murder and mutiny," he announced to the assembled ship's company. "Sergeant Denby, bring the prisoners up."

Wallis and Stiles were led to the mainmast, and their chains temporarily locked to the bitts.

"A murder was committed," Neville stated. "You are all aware of it. We have witnesses. Mr. Farnsworth was struck dead by Mr. Wallis – who may have had assistants – and his body thrown overboard in an act of pure evil. Since he died before going over, his murderer is Mr. Wallis, not some shark. You must all watch yourselves, though. If Mr. Wallis had help, his accomplices are still out there among you, and the danger to each and every one of you is still very much alive. Does anyone have anything to say in his behalf on the matter of this murder?" He looked about into the silence. "Will he die alone, then, or does anyone confess to being an accomplice, or to knowing another who might be?"

The sudden shrill call of a flock of gulls flying overhead raised a murmur of amusement amongst the men, but otherwise, the sounds were no more than wind in the rigging, water along the hull, and the rhythmic creaking of masts and yards.

"I thought not."

Neville turned to Wallis, who glared back angrily, but said nothing. "Mr. Wallis, in accord with paragraph twenty-seven of the Articles of War, you shall immediately be hanged by the neck until dead from the forward yardarm.

"Sergeant Denby, do your duty."

A dramatic fifteen minutes passed while Wallis was dragged forward to the foremast, where a yardarm waited with a rope and noose. After slipping the noose around his neck, he was hauled ten feet off the deck. Neville waited for his twitching to cease, and then ordered him to be dropped to the deck and pronounced dead before moving on to his last case.

"Lastly, we have the matter of mutiny," Neville announced. "I am not one who normally enjoys speech-making, but on this I cannot remain silent." *I can't wait for a court-martial. I must lay down the law now, before any more get the idea to finish whatever it is Stiles hoped to gain.* He then read the Articles of War paragraphs eighteen and nineteen, which describe mutinous behavior and the duty to inform superiors of any suspicion of mutinous behavior.

"This man Stiles has been made known to me by several of your mates as being the fomenter of mutiny among you. According to the articles I just read you, many of you are also guilty of mutiny by your involvement – for your failure to report Stiles' activities to your superiors. I believe I could hang several of you. Maybe I should. However, I also understand Stiles had Wallis keep you in his line by threat of violence like that visited upon Mr. Farnsworth.

"It is my desire, of all things, to let you know that inciting others to mutiny cannot be tolerated. Neither can hiding any men who would harm your ship. After this, I will continue to listen very closely for any such activity, and I expect anyone who hears of such activity will inform his superior without delay. I will deal with any further mutinous activity quickly, and I ***will not keep trash*** like Mr. Stiles aboard."

A few moments of grunting and murmuring passed through the ship's company – not the rousing cheer Neville had hoped would arise.

"Mr. Stiles, in accord with paragraphs eighteen and nineteen of the Articles of War, I find you guilty of mutiny and sentence you to be hanged by the neck from the forward yardarm until dead.

"Sergeant Denby, do your duty."

13: Revenge

Superieure was a calmer ship for the next two days as she crossed the north end of the Windward Passage bound for rendezvous with the fleet at Isla Tortuga.

"The men seem less strained, I think, Commander," said Framingham at mid-cruise.

"I agree. They seem to be going about their duties more... I can't put a word on it... smoothly, maybe."

"I caught one of them whistling last evening. Seaman Phillips, I think."

"You didn't stop him, did you?"

"Oh, no, Sir. I wouldn't. He's an excellent whistler, for one, and I do enjoy a good tune."

"That's good to hear, but we still need to get busy at gun drill. Mr. Johnson will be calling it up soon. Our time to clear yesterday was four minutes flat. Much better than the seven minutes and something before the... the murder."

"Land, ho!" cried the lookout at the mainmast tree.

"Where away, Mr. Fishe?" yelled Neville. He began walking back to the quarterdeck where he had just seen Catchpole go.

"Two points on starboard bow."

"That's good, isn't it, Mr. Catchpole? Right where it should be?"

"As long as it's Saint Nick's Mole, aye," responded Catchpole.

Johnson's piping began, and immediately following, the hubbub of clearing and beating to quarters.

"Still a half day out of our rendezvous, if the…"

The rumble of guns running out on both sides was enough to stop the conversation. The deck quivered beneath their feet as tons of metal moved on little wooden wheels. Neville had one eye on the activity while he spoke to Catchpole.

"…if the trades don't pick up and come blowing straight at us 'round that…"

After those words, they had to wait for a rolling alternate-gun broadside to be fired from each side of the ship.

"…that point," concluded Catchpole.

"Much better, Mr. Johnson!" Neville yelled forward. "We might be able to fight, after all."

"We should join the fleet in early morning, then, Mr. Catchpole, "depending on where we find them."

Superieure's anchor splashed into the turquoise waters of a small southern bay near the eastern end of Isla Tortuga at five bells of the morning watch on the humid and overcast eighth day of August. The green mountains of Haiti were visible to the south, with a stretch of boisterous blue water between.

"There's n-n-not a ship here other than our f-f-fleet," Foyle observed. "I thought we were supposed to meet p-p-p-pirates and Frenchmen."

"Patience, Mr. Foyle. Enjoy the peace and quiet while you can."

"Signal, Sir. Repair to f-f-flag... at noon. All captains."

"So I see. I'll hope for a fine dinner. Please have my 'gig' ready." He chuckled again at the thought of his 'gig', which on *Superieure* was simply the little jolly boat hanging on davits astern.

"Sorry we can't do better, Sir," said Johnson.

"What do you mean, Mr. Johnson? This little boat will do fine."

"Them, Sir. Look there." He pointed to the *Vanguard's* gig, just passing by them on her way to report. Captain Walker's dozen oarsmen, in a gig twice the length of *Superieure's*, were turned out in matching blue jackets and palm frond hats. Each hat had a long yellow streamer embroidered with the ship's name.

"Oh, yes. I'd forgotten. The rest will be the same way, I imagine. I'm afraid our six must go in what they have. I must be on time, however. The simple commander of an unrated vessel will have to wait to board last, but wait I must. I dare not be absent from the gaggle floating about the flagship." The last thing he wanted was to be remembered. He did remember his previous experience very near this location, however: being summoned to Commodore Wright's flagship *Mary* several years before.

"Aye, Sir. She's ready."

Neville was thankful for the calm bay, for he knew that if this meeting had been called on the open water he would be jostled horribly by even a small sea, and would most likely arrive soaking wet. His turn to board finally came after the all the fleet's captains had been piped aboard, one after the other. He swung himself onto the ladder and began the climb, which was not unfamiliar; this ship was the same size as *Vanguard*. Although he knew his status as Commander of little *Superieure* would necessitate his being piped up the side, a small part of his brain wondered if he would get the same treatment he received from Wright: no pipes, drums or salutes. No, in this modern Navy he was properly piped aboard, met by a lieutenant, and ushered to Captain Bayntun's cabin.

Neville found the room full of spirited conversation despite the near-oppressive warmth of the place. He felt out of place here – a lieutenant among captains. He would mind his manners and speak only when addressed. He had time to view the scene. This ship was slightly less ornate than *Vanguard*, but the Captain's cabin on a seventy-four was always impressive. He could see the western end of Isla Tortuga through the expansive stern gallery. Because of this event, every pane of glass had been cleaned of salt spray, leaving the view almost 'picturesque' through the sparking clean glass. Inside, the four cannon that resided within the cabin were covered with some smooth blue cloth. The traditional black and white checked floor cloth had obviously been scrubbed clean in the morning, and the captain's furniture and wooden joinery of the room were freshly polished. Bayntun's tea service was in use, as were his crystal rum and wine glasses.

"Wine, rum, or tea, Sir?" asked a Midshipman acting as waiter for the meeting. "Captain has a fine claret. The rum is Jamaican – Stillwater's top shelf, of course."

"Stillwater, is it? I must give it a try. Thank you."

The officers in the room divided themselves by rank. The senior captains – Bayntun of *Cumberland*, Walker of *Vanguard*, and Bligh of *Theseus* were engaged in some conversation that sounded political, as best Neville could hear. *Cumberland's* three most senior lieutenants were in attendance, likely for the opportunity to meet the fleet's captains, but stood in a conversation of their own. Two younger captains stood apart near the aft guns. Neville's curiosity drove him to shuffle himself slowly around the perimeter of the room, after receiving his glass of rum, to determine the cause of their animation. Not only did their conversation promise to be more interesting, but also, one of the two was a Negro. Neville had heard of such a man – the Navy's only black-skinned captain, Captain Perkins of *Tartar* – but had never met him. His reputation was considerable. He stood within earshot for only a minute before they noticed him.

"Hello, there, Commander," said Perkins. "Are you from *Superieure?*"

"Aye, Sir. Neville Burton. Most pleased to meet you, Captain Perkins. I've heard tales…"

"Most are rubbish, I should think," he interrupted in good English with a slight Jamaican accent. "How do you find your schooner? I've had many a…"

A little bell rang, summoning the officers to dinner. "Perhaps a chance to speak to either of you later?" queried Neville as they all moved toward the table.

The seating was pre-arranged, as Neville expected. Captains Perkins and Ross were between pairs of senior captains toward the head, presumably as an attempt to be sure they were included in the senior officers' conversation. Neville sat between Captain Bligh and *Cumberland's* First Lieutenant. His opposite was their Second Lieutenant. Neville felt comfortable that this end of the table would not be required to propose much conversation.

"Good afternoon," he said quietly to those around him – more to the lieutenants than to Captain Bligh.

"Good afternoon," responded Bligh. The other lieutenants said the same, after hearing from Bligh.

Commodore Bayntun soon stifled Neville's hope for some conversation to soften the edges of formality by offering his description of what he knew about the status of hostilities between England and France, and then possible incursions of the French against British Islands, and then the greater plan for Britain's defense of the Caribbean. This monologue lasted though the starter

– a rough pile of tiny batter-fried minnows – and well into the first course of fresh fish. Neville recognized it as the dorado, or 'dolphin-fish'. He remembered taking note of the abundance of these in the waters north of Cuba.

Neville and the lieutenants around him were silent, yet pleased to enjoy the meal. Captain Bligh asked some question about Bayntun's concept for the defense of Jamaica. Bayntun answered. Captain Walker asked a question.

The fish finished, plates were removed and replaced with a course of fresh ham.

"I say!" said Captain Walker suddenly. He leaned forward and peered down the table. "There you are, Commander Burton. What caused all your chasing about in the Passage, pray tell? Sail practice, really?"

"No, Sir; a 'Man Overboard' search, actually," said Neville. He offered no more, any explanation having not been called for.

"Called off so quickly? Why so?" pressed Walker.

Neville, paused, and then decided he had best tell all. "We learned one of our boys had been murdered before being thrown over in the night, and so gave up…"

Table conversation ceased. A few utensils clinked as they were set on plates, and he heard the clunk of two or three glasses being set on the table. Neville felt the stare of eight red-cheeked men – and more around the edges – quiet, as if holding their breath.

"… the search," he concluded, looking round the table and setting his fork down.

"Murder?"

"It was part of an attempted mutiny, Sir."

The silence now went deeper, if such were possible. The mizzen mast creaked as a slow swell rolled lightly beneath the ship.

Somebody on deck dropped something so heavily that half the room started.

He looked at Commodore Bayntun and said, "It's in my report, Sir, but I don't know the reason for it. I make every attempt to run a fair ship."

"A fair ship? – what rubbish," interjected Captain Ross.

"What steps have you taken to safeguard your ship, Commander?" asked Bayntun.

"I made numerous inquiries among the men... interviews... We found the murderer and the leader of the dissident group."

"You've brought them here to be court-martialed, I presume?"

The silence in the room continued.

"No, Sir. I hanged them... a Mr. Wallis and a Mr. Stiles."

"Oh," said Bligh, "Wallis; a nasty piece of work, indeed. I'm afraid I sent him over to you. I should have hanged him myself a time or two."

"You didn't think there would be enough captains here for a proper court martial?" pressed Bayntun.

"I felt I couldn't wait, Sir. I needed to make a show of force immediately. I don't know if I will still have trouble. *Superieure* has a great collection of malefactors aboard."

Captain Perkins broke the silence by beginning slow clapping. Captain Bligh at Neville's elbow began the same, and then Captain Ross. In a moment, the entire assembly was in general applause. Neville's skin prickled. He felt a trickle of sweat run down his backbone.

"Congratulations, Commander; and you, Captain Walker," said Bayntun when the applause died, "It seems you chose the right man. I had my concerns."

"I'd say you'll do well," said Captain Perkins to Neville.

Neville's fleeting moment of glory passed, followed by a luscious aroma of some local herbs in butter, and the last course – fresh chicken – arrived. It was heartily devoured during a very changed, enthusiastic, general discussion of the need for swift retribution against mutineers. Neville was embarrassed to discover he was the temporary hero of the day – for taking an action he had hoped he could always avoid.

Commodore Bayntun wagged a finger in request of the cheese tray, and changed the subject. "Since we have found no French here – the frigates have investigated Cap Francois – we shall return to Jamaica," he said. "Commander Burton, you will accompany the frigates *Tartar* and *La Desiree* on reconnaissance of the cul-du-sac on the way back to Station. If the enemy is discovered, *Superieure* will carry the message out to the fleet and we shall sail in. We will otherwise not stop. By the way, Commander Burton, what happened to your chase?"

It's my day to squirm on the hot seat, is it? mused Neville. "She was a small brig, of similar sailing qualities to us," he began. "We followed well for some time, Sir, but she was higher on the wind and therefore able to weather Punta De Maisi in the daylight. We could not. With the extra tack required for us to weather the point, it would have been dark, and our chase far downwind. Also, Sir, the mutiny was afoot, giving me concern I might not trust a prize crew if we did catch her, so I declared her lost to us, and we came about to follow the squadron."

"Hrruumph," Captain Bayntun finally grunted. "A new American schooner not catch a brig? Hrruumpf. I would say you still have more sail training in your future."

Captain Perkins, always bold, broke the uncomfortable silence a second time. "A toast," he offered, "to the confusion of mutineers."

"**I**'m looking f-forward to a few days of stretching m-m-my legs ashore," announced Midshipman Foyle when *Superieure* jerked her anchor cable tight against an unusually stiff easterly breeze in Port Royal Harbor.

"So am I, Mr. Foyle, though I already suspect we might not get such a treat," responded Neville.

"Why s-so, Commander?" Foyle turned his head to follow Neville's gaze toward the point on shore from whence the Station's boats normally launched.

"We don't usually get such a prompt greeting if we don't have a prize in tow, do we? What do you suppose this fellow wants? Meet him at the chains, if you would, please."

A few large fish had congregated below the main chains in the ship's shadow. Foyle waited patiently there, watching the fish evade Pickering. The cook already had his fishing line in the water, hoping for something special to offer the officer's mess. The fish weren't biting. The shore boat came and went quickly, only passing up the advice packet for Commander Burton and interrupting Pickering's efforts. Foyle took the packet straight to Neville, who went directly below deck to open it.

Neville reappeared on deck in five minutes with a serious look on his face. "Have our officers lay aft, please," he said to Foyle.

When they had gathered, Neville made his announcement. "I am sorry to advise you that we are to go right back out, on direct orders from Admiral Duckworth. There is some pirate annoyance reported in St. Thomas Parish on the east end of the island's North Shore – attacks on small towns and remote plantations. Not a great force, the message says, so it's just us going to see if we can squash it – or just chase them away. Reading between the lines, I think we are expected to deal with it very quickly and be back in a week. How's our water, Mr. Johnson?"

Johnson made a face and sucked on a tooth a moment while he thought on it. "I'd better check," he said. "Just a week, you say?"

"Aye," said Neville. Johnson hurried down the main companion stair.

Neville lowered his voice and asked the group before him how he thought the men would take it.

"I think that without Wallis and Stiles aboard, the ship seems to function well, Commander. Wouldn't you agree?" asked Catchpole.

"I would," answered Neville. "Almost too well, I hate to say... not a soul offered up for punishment in the last four days."

"That's bad?"

"Absolutely not – but not normal, either. If someone is playing games with us, we just might find out soon if we go right back out. They wanted to talk about shore leave and other things, but if we're not in harbor..."

Johnson returned. "Water will just do a week on full ration, Sir; a few days longer if we need to cut it."

"There it is, then," stated Neville. "Let's break the news and get the anchor up. We'll go hunt pirates. Mr. Johnson, heave the anchor short, and then send the men aft, if you please."

By the time the ship's people were gathered by the mainmast to hear Neville's words, they already knew there would be no time ashore. The only reason to heave the anchor short is to prepare to sail. Neville stood at his customary perch on the hog pen and made a short speech describing their mission. He concluded with, "Are we ready, Mr. Johnson?"

"Straight up and down, Sir," Johnson responded.

"Haul away." Johnson and his mates began twittering their pipes.

Neville watched the men go to their work before asking Foyle, "What do you see here?"

"See, Sir? For our c-c-course out of the harbor? We'll have to p-p-pinch tight to miss *Bellerophon*, b-b-bu…"

"No; within the ship – the men. Is this what you'd expect?"

Foyle thought a minute, looking forward at each knot of men working to set the sails. "Something seems odd, n-n-now that you m-m-mention it, Sir… but I can't n-n-n-name it."

"Usually, when we leave port, I'd say they are quiet. Most take a few days to drop their thoughts of land and set their minds to being at sea. But look out there. Many seem cheerful; anxious to go, even. I've told them we're after pirates. It could be dangerous work. The group by the foremast, just there, they seem quite excited, indeed."

"Maybe it's b-b-because we never really set f-f-foot here. Their minds are still at s-sea, as you say."

"Maybe; I don't know. I suppose as long as they're not sullen, we should be pleased with it.

"Mr. Catchpole, bring the small charts for this end of Jamaica to my cabin, if you please. You come along, too, Mr. Foyle. We're almost clear of the port now." *Superieure's* movement as she left the smooth water of the harbor and regained the open sea returned to the surging motion they had all endured for the previous several weeks. A rain squall threatened from a distance, but the cloud formation gave no indication of anything worse to come, despite it being hurricane season

"You may remove your jackets for a few minutes, gentlemen," Neville said to them below. "There's no reason for us to suffer in this miserable heat while we study the charts. So, Mr. Foyle, you heard the mission. How would you go about this?"

"I m-m-m-must defer to Mr. C-C-Catchpole, I should think."

"Propose your plan to him then. It's time we move your training from mere navigation to planning where we go."

"Aye, Sir. You say w-w-we are directed to p-p-p-patrol the North Shore, but I sh-sh-should think we should stop in here," he said, indicating the small bay at Port Morant. "I know it's on the South Shore, bu-bu-but just. As I hear it, p-p-pirates tend to be undisciplined about where they go. They m-m-might get it in their heads to g-g-go 'round the p-p-point. It's along our way, at any rate."

"I agree," said Catchpole.

"After we are around the p-p-point here to the north we should p-p-p... stick our nose into each one of these." He tapped his finger on several little bays, as well as the port at Antonio. "I dunno how f-f-far we should go if we d-d-d-don't find anything." He looked up at Neville.

"Let's make it here," said Neville, indicating the large point of land on the north shore. "The bay is labeled...Port Maria." Neville's surprise at seeing the name caused him to pause momentarily. *I can't believe the name of the place is Port Maria,* Neville thought. *Here I am back in the world of my lost love and I am faced with ending a search in a place bearing her name.* He continued, "The Admiral's orders don't tell us to chase all 'round the island."

"By leaving in the afternoon into this fresh breeze," Catchpole continued, "we'll have to stand off all night and go into Morant in the morning, Commander. It's only about ten leagues."

They found nothing of note at Port Morant, either, except for the opportunity to take on two barrels of fresh water. The shore boat coxswain asked if there had been any offense to the town, and were told there had been neither visitors nor trouble. The question itself so concerned the townsfolk, however, such that they promised to set a shore watch. Another day found them in Port Antonio.

"Nothing here, either, Commander," Framingham said.

"I wouldn't expect a lone pirate ship would have the nerve to come in here," said Neville. "The town is large enough to defend itself, and most of these merchant ships you see here know how to use their guns, even if they don't carry many. Pass word for Mr. Johnson to drop anchor. We'll rest a bit here, and tomorrow will be another easy sail to Buff Bay."

Given a free evening, Neville decided he should take time to write a letter about a subject that had been worrying him.

HMS Superieure   *14 August, 1803*
St. Thomas Parish, Jamaica (The North Shore)

Sir Mulholland,

I apologize in advance for this empty report. I have not had an opportunity to advance the investigation you set me to this past Monthe and more. Please allow me to make my excuses: Vanguard was at sea for several weeks. We saw muche in the way of action and captured several ships. I was set upon the Frigate Creole as Prize Captain, and then offered the chance to Command this small vessel – an unrated American Schooner. To my great disappointment, she has been completed with the dregs of humanity from the larger Ships in the fleet, so we have had a Murder and almost a Mutiny. We seem to be in order now, but I have got no closer to Stillwater in all this than a glass of their rum aboard the Cumberland.

I shall endeavor to resume my investigation when we are returned to ~~Port R~~ (pardon) Kingstowne, which should be when I post this in about a week.

My Best Regards,

I remain, your humble servant, etc., etc.

Cmdr. **Ne. Burton**

"It's Buff Bay 'round this point ahead," announced Framingham to the deck the next afternoon. He took the little glass down from his eye, but before carrying it back to its becket on the binnacle, took another glance forward with his naked eye. "What's this?" He raised the glass again. "A ship's coming out."

"Sail, ho," hollered the lookout above.

"On the bow? What is she?" Framingham yelled up.

"Aye, on the bow. Can't see but half of her yet. Maybe a lugger."

Another moment passed. Neville and his officers moved to the larboard rails for a better look. They were much closer than they would have been to first notice a ship at sea. This one became suddenly visible as it emerged from the land not two leagues away.

"Merchant, maybe," the lookout hollered, "No flag of country."

Neville, having gotten out a larger glass, announced to those on the deck, "No flag of country, no; but she carries a flag… red field. My experience tells me she's a pirate. We'll see black bones or swords or the like upon the red when we catch her.

"Mr. Johnson, call all hands to clear for action and beat to quarters, then fire the signal gun.

"Mr. Catchpole, up two points and set sails to chase."

The usual noise ensued as partitions were removed below decks and gear not needed for battle hurried below. Dozens of feet slapped the decks in response to the ship's single drum banging and Johnson's whistlers all blowing hard as they were encouraged by the shouts of the petty officers. The squawking of the ship's chickens and bleating of goats added to the urgent atmosphere. *Superieure* began leaning to the pressure of the afternoon breeze which began rising onshore after the usual noon lull.

"She's not wasting time waiting for us, Commander," said Framingham.

"I would..." The forward signal gun fired.

"...not think she would. She's adding sail, not taking any down. She heels easily, I see. These barcolongos are like that. We might have a chance; she'll cross our bows. Pass word to Mr. Skullen, if you please. Tell him to take a shot with the bow chaser the first chance he gets.

"Up another two points, Mr. Catchpole. Our chase is turning further north. She'll risk a close brush with us in order to gain an upwind course rather than a downwind run, I suspect."

The sails were hauled tighter as *Superieure* strove to sail closer to the wind before the lugger crossed her course.

The roar of a cannon forward gave everyone to know that Skullen had made his try.

"Right in f-f-front of her, Commander!" yelled Foyle.

"Fire the first two larboard guns and the chaser again!" yelled Neville.

The pirate would never be closer, unless they could cause her some damage. She now sailed at a good seven knots, throwing white spray from the small waves striking her bow. She fired back – probably more out of amusement than any expectation of harming

Superieure. They watched a small ball skip across the water to windward of them and disappear into a wave.

Superieure's two larboard guns fired.

"I thought I saw her wiggle a bit commander, but nothing's carried away."

"No, and I don't see any holes in the sails, either," said Neville. "If we're lucky, we holed her hull and she'll slow as she takes on water."

Skullen's chaser fired again.

"Still n-n-nothing," said Foyle.

"She's passed us now, Mr. Catchpole. Let's haul our wind. Follow in her wake, if you can. We can see her colours clear enough now. Black swords crossed on the red field. No doubt now she's a pirate, and proud of it. Her name is *Revenge*, as best I can read it."

"Clap on, you!" shouted Johnson to one of the landsmen, "Haul away!"

A loud bang rang out somewhere aft of the mainmast. It wasn't a gun or some equipment flying loose.

"What was…?" yelled Neville. He didn't need to finish his question. The main boom began a wild swing off to leeward. It began jumping up and down as its sail began flapping with the noise of a hurricane.

"Mainsheet's parted, Sir," yelled Framingham.

"I can see, Mr. Framingham. Don't stand there, man! Get a line on the boom.

"Mr. Catchpole, loose the forecourse!"

Superieure lost speed rapidly as the helmsmen struggled to prevent a sudden change of direction from causing even more damage. Four men were immediately dispatched to control the main boom. Neville saw one go down hard against the larboard rail when the boom hammered him.

The noise of the flailing mainsail ceased ten minutes later when the remaining three men finally heaved a heavy line over the boom and secured it.

"Orders, Commander?" asked Johnson. "We can reave a new mainsheet in five minutes." He appeared very nervous, shifting his weight from one foot to the other. Such rigging was his responsibility.

"You may do so, Mr. Johnson, but there is no hurry. *Revenge* has gone to the horizon in the manner of a lugger. We'll not have a prize today. Pipe the men off quarters and put the ship back to rights. How's our injured man? I hate to lose anyone."

"He'll be all right, Sir. Broken collarbone and a broken arm," said Johnson.

"Mr. Catchpole, sail her smoothly as Mr. Johnson directs to effect his repairs, and when he waves you clear, turn back for Buff Bay," ordered Neville.

"You there, have you nothing to do? And what's to smile about? What's your name?"

"Sorry, Sir. I'm Whitmore, Sir. Just marveling at the Lord's mysterious ways, Sir. I'll be getting on. Sorry, Sir." He put a knuckle to his forehead and hurried down the companion.

Superieure's return to the coast and entrance to Buff Bay went easily. She sailed in before darkness fell.

"I don't see any d-d-damage ashore here, either, Commander," added Foyle. "There are t-t-t-two buildings and some fishing sheds at the far end of the s-s-strand, but they look to be in p-p-p- good condition."

"I expect there's not much to interest a pirate here, either, unless there's some plantation we can't see up in the hills," responded Neville. "The next bay is called Annotto. The chart shows a bit of a town there. We'll drop the anchor here, though. It's only another two leagues to Annotto, and I don't wish to enter an unfamiliar bay in the dark."

"What is it, Mr. Johnson?" asked Neville in the morning. He tapped his biscuit on the table a few times in hopes of scaring out a few weevils, and then dipped it into his coffee cup. His plate of collops contained only a few scraps of uneaten egg.

"They cut it, Sir," answered Johnson with his most serious face.

After taking a bite of the softened biscuit, Neville decided the coffee had cooled enough to drink, and raised it to his lips. "Who cut what, Mr. Johnson?"

"The main sheet – yesterday, Sir. Cut halfway through."

The coffee was still too hot, and Johnson's announcement caused Neville to gasp, giving him a mouthful of the steaming brown liquid. It came out faster than it went in – in a great coughing gush that sprayed Johnson and every paper on Neville's desk.

"Shite!" he yelled. "Ow! Damn! Cut? Cut by whom?"

"Sorry, Sir. Here's a cloth. We don't know; it could be anyone. We can ask about, but almost all of 'em carries a knife, and half the company can be back near the mainsheet at one time or another." He spread his big hands in a helpless manner.

"You'd better be asking, then, Mr. Johnson. Our troubles have not gone away yet. The cut in the sheet can't possibly be left over from Stiles and Wallis. I'd have Denby set a sentry by the mainmast, but we can't guard everything. What's next?"

Neville finished dabbing the spots of coffee off his stockings. "And send a boat in to ask – if they can find anyone ashore – if anyone from the lugger came to visit."

"**D**rop anchor again, Mr. Johnson," Neville ordered upon arrival in Annotto Bay. "The evening is calm, and this place seems fairly sheltered against this breeze. We'll take a boat in tomorrow morning and ask if the people here have seen anything."

After Neville's favorite breakfast of collops and coffee, he called for his gig, two marines and six landsmen to row, and departed for shore. He needed to set his feet on land and move about to clear his head and calm himself. Two civilians waited for them on the strand. Probably because they could see from shore that *Superieure* was British Navy, only one of the men had a weapon, and that only a shovel. Neville allowed his boat crew to take a walk down the strand and back while he chatted with them for about half an hour, after which they returned to *Superieure*.

"What did you find out, Commander?" Catchpole asked when Neville had collected his officers by the helm.

"We might be on to something, after all," he reported. "They say a small ship with a large number of men on it sailed in two days ago. They sent a boat in, just as we've done. The ship wasn't British Navy, and certainly not a merchant they recognized, so the villagers hid their women. You can see it's a fairly shabby place, so the townsmen weren't questioned much when they told their visitors it's just a fishing camp, and that most of the townspeople left long ago. The leader and a couple others from the ship took a walk through the village, and then asked whether any tobacco or cane is being grown around here. The townsmen told them about the Smithwick plantation inland, but after the pirates – as they were presumed to be – learned the plantation is close in to Kingston, they argued amongst themselves and then went back aboard and sailed off to the east. Kingston is only about fifteen miles over those hills by land, and there's a fair road for chasing them back here if they tried anything."

"So, they sailed from here to Buff Bay, but noticed us before we saw them," speculated Neville. "All they did at Buff Bay was turn their ship about and sail out, as we saw. They have been sailing east, then. Now what? Have we chased them off? Will they go back into Port Antonio? Should we follow them to the east?"

"Aye, to the east," said Framingham.

"The breeze is steady, Commander," said Catchpole. "We could continue the original plan before going home. It is but three leagues and a mile more to Port Maria. We can be there easily by dinner and take our look. If it's all quiet, we can turn the bow for Kingston before nightfall."

"Quite right, Mr. Catchpole. We should do that much, at least."

"Has there been any word on the cut mainsheet, gentlemen?" Neville queried the group.

"No, Sir, nothing," they all mumbled in their way.

"Heave the anchor short, then, Mr. Johnson. No time to lie about."

"The chart has the name 'Cabarita Island' on that lump of rock in the middle of the bay there, Commander," said Catchpole during *Superieure's* approach to Port Maria.

"Do I see masts behind it, Mr. Catchpole? Is there a ship in there?" Neville asked.

"Mr. Foyle, pull yourself up there with Mr. Semmes and have him take a close look."

A few minutes later, Foyle yelled down from his perch, "Masts, Sir. Two. Not square-rigged."

"She could be a merchant of some sort, Mr. Framingham, but I'll wager she's our pirate lugger. Damn, she's brazen!

"Mr. Catchpole, does the chart carry enough detail to tell us if we can sail in 'round the island? Are there rocks, reefs, or shoal water shown?"

"Chart's not that good, Sir. Sorry."

"We must anchor, then, within range of the guns, if we can, and then take the boats across. Get the way off her, Mr. Catchpole. Slow us down so we can watch the bottom."

Neville directed his ship around the outside of the little island, toward the stern of the mystery ship. At least three telescopes were on watch as the stern slowly came into view from behind the island.

"Lugger for sure, C-C-Commander," yelled Foyle from the top, "with a long outrigger off the s-s-stern."

They were now within a mile, closing and slowing. The bottom could easily be seen here. It didn't appear to be rocky, but it was also impossible to tell the depth... twenty feet? Forty?

A small cannon fired.

"Was that shot from shore, Mr. Framingham?" Neville asked.

"Nossir. From the lugger. See the smoke of it going downwind?"

"She didn't fire at us, then. It was a signal for their men ashore."

It took Neville a moment to process what he had himself uttered. "They're ashore!" he yelled. "That explains the signal. Most of them must be ashore, causing what destruction they can. They won't have left enough men aboard to fight the ship.

"Mr. Foyle, how many men can you see aboard?" he yelled up. Most of the lugger was now visible.

Foyle stared for a minute. "Not m-m-many, Sir. Six, m-m-maybe."

"We must go at her now, then, Mr. Catchpole. Straight away! If the lugger has enough water between her and the rocks, then we must also. We cannot possibly draw much more than she does. Keep on. Sail straight at her. We'll go alongside and grapple on right there!"

"S-s-s-smoke on shore, Sir!" Foyle hollered.

"Mr. Catchpole, have Mr. Johnson beat to quarters. Which side do you choose for grappling?"

"Ahh... Starboard would be best, Sir." Catchpole began a strange gulping motion.

"Give me a glass, Mr. Framingham. Thank you."

"Where's the smoke, Mr. Foyle?"

"Beyond the strand; far to the left."

"Oh, yes. I see it now. That's not smoke from a kitchen fire. Look, it's a house just broken into flames," Neville announced to nobody in particular. "Someone's being dragged out. A woman, by God. We'd best hurry."

The men on board were running now, every whichaway, as they do when going to their posts. Johnson paused in his whistling.

"Mr. Johnson," Neville yelled, "Ready all boats to launch to larboard. Where's Sergeant Denby? After we grapple on, we must take all the marines and every other soul we can fit in the boats to shore and give those marauders a fight."

"Denby here, Sir."

"Did you hear?"

"Aye, Sir. Whitmore's gone down."

"Whitmore? Who's Whitmore?"

"Armorer, Sir. He's gone down to pass out weapons."

Oh, yes, I remember meeting Whitmore. He was the man smiling when the mainsheet parted…but I don't really know Whitmore, Neville thought. *We haven't needed the weapons before this – or trusted the men to have them.* This last thought gave him pause. *Calm your thoughts,* he said to himself. *We are united in a common cause. Wallis and Stiles are gone.*

"Mr. Framingham. Can you name the best men to go in the boats?"

"I think I can, Sir. I'll get on with it."

"Mr. Foyle, come down!" hollered Neville.

"Sergeant Denby, put your marksmen and a swivel gun at the bow. We shouldn't need to fire a cannon at them if there are only six aboard. Shoot anyone who sticks his head up. The minute we grapple, send your men to the boats. Sailors can board.

"Which b-b-boat do I take in, Commander," Foyle asked.

"You? None. I have the gig; Mr. Framingham has the barge, and Mr. Johnson the small launch. Mr. Catchpole stays with the ship, as you do. You are to command our guard – to defend the ships if we cannot stop them all from coming back out."

Foyle looked particularly dejected, but returned a resolved, "Aye, aye, Sir."

Superieure was merely two cables away from the lugger, whose name could now be read as *Revenge*.

At the bow, Sergeant Denby exhorted his men to keep low. They could see two men at the stern rail of *Revenge* preparing to fire a swivel gun at them. Thankfully, the louts made slow and clumsy progress, as if they had been drinking too much rum to be a proper guard. Finally, they were ready, but they waited for *Superieure* to be closer. At one cable away, *Revenge* fired. Whistling pellets and damage to *Superieure's* lines and human skin were felt before the flame was seen, the blast heard, or the smoke drifted shoreward. One of Denby's marines twirled and fell to the deck holding his arm. A chunk of the forward rail carried another marine sprawling onto the foredeck. Pellets from the swivel gun's cannister rattled through the rigging and punctured little holes in the jib and main course.

Superieure's forward momentum did not cease. The pirates had not fired a disabling gun. They had only discharged an infuriating annoyance. The marines began to fire. Although the show of force was understandable, their efforts were nonsensical at this distance. It had the effect, however, of delaying the pirates who were fumbling with the swivel gun. They ducked for a few minutes before realizing they were out of musket range, and then resumed the reloading of their gun.

Superieure closed to half a cable from the lugger. The marines were called to the boats. At quarter cable distant, *Superieure* fired her swivel gun. The two men were no longer there when the smoke cleared. Sailors began to amass at the forward starboard rail. A few sailors with muskets began to fire. Two more pirates appeared from below decks and ran to the gun. One lasted only a minute before he stepped back from the gun and dropped. The other, giving the appearance of being convinced there was no chance to reload and fire again, ducked below the rail.

The sound of wood against wood began. *Superieure's* gunwale ground against that of *Revenge*. Parts of the railings of both were flying to bits, and *Superieure's* men were beginning to jump on board *Revenge*.

"No quarter!" yelled one of *Superieure's* lead attackers, as he leaped from one ship to the other.

"Launch!" screamed Neville. He took the time to turn to Catchpole and say, "Splendid ship-handling, Mr. Catchpole; quite exciting, what?"

Catchpole stood rigid with his hands clamped onto the tiller, gulping.

Three small boats hit the water at almost the same time on the opposite side from *Revenge*, and men were scrambling – or just outright jumping – into them as fast as they could manage. Cutlasses and muskets were thrown down without regard to their usefulness.

"Commander!" yelled Foyle just before Neville jumped, "There are groups forming at the boats on the strand. One is launched and rowing hard this way, but the others are certainly in argument."

"Mr. Foyle, I promise two pints of straight rum to the gunner who blows yon boat out of the water before we get there, and another for the boat on the beach.

"Oars, men! Push off. Make way, all! Pull hard lads, we have a town to save!"

Three little boats and thirty-on men shoved their way clear of *Superieure* and began the row to shore. Once out from behind the two ships, two oncoming pirate boats were clear to see – yet too far to hit with a musket.

Given the inducement provided by Neville, he wasn't surprised when *Superieure's* stern chaser fired. The forward chaser couldn't fire with the lugger in its way, so the gunners had cranked the aft chasers around with crowbars to meet the need. Their first ball skipped across the water twenty feet forward of the pirate boat, bouncing once on the water, and then plowing into the surf just off the beach and rolling harmlessly onto the strand.

"There's a new one on me," said Neville. "Pull on, Lads!"

With fourteen men to pull, as opposed to the six on Neville's little gig, the barge led *Superieure's* boats toward shore. The barge carried the marines, and they were already standing forward and shooting their muskets when *Superieure's* second gun fired. For the most part, the shot missed everything except the very bow. The forward two feet of the pirate boat disappeared in a shower of splinters. The pointy end of it, designed to push the water aside and assure a smooth path through the waves, became a great scoop. The next great pull of the pirate's oars sent the bow of their craft diving for the sea bottom and exposing all the occupants to the marines' fire. Only two survived the musket fire and began swimming for shore. They were smote with oars as the barge passed through the detritus.

"Another boat is setting out, Commander," yelled Framingham from the launch.

"I have eyes, Mr. Framingham. Steer for it."

"Aye, Commander."

"Pull, lads, pull!" yelled Neville. There are only six of them in this boat ahead. "You two aft keep rowing. You four forward gather your arms. They will come near enough, I think, to be shot at. You two in the bow, take the muskets…"

"I c-can't…" stuttered the first oarsman.

"Who's the best shot, then? Pass the musket back."

"I never miss," boasted the aft larboard oarsman.

"Take it, then, and shoot the first man who stands. Move to the bow."

Neville drew his sword as the distance between the boats decreased to thirty feet, then twenty. The pirates were showing no sign of letting up. The boaster stood up in marine fashion, raised his musket, and fired. The pirate coxswain pitched over the transom of his little boat into the clear water of Port Maria's harbor. With the splash, the other musketeers fired into the pirate craft. No pirate stood to fire either musket or pistol before the two boats crashed into each other. From afar, the episode would probably have appeared laughable. The fearsome pirates smashed their little launch into another little six-man rowing gig, losing their leader and two other men before the crash even occurred, and then finding themselves skewered or hacked into little pieces even before their boat could sink.

The momentum of it shocked Neville, but only for a minute. "To the strand, men! Put your backs into it. We have women and children to save." A moment passed. "Thank you, Mr…."

"Davis," the marksman said.

"Thank you, Mr. Davis. You've earned a dinner in my cabin. I'll not forget this quickly."

"That last boat ain't coming out, I think, Sir," said a man forward, observing the activity of the pirates still ashore.

"They had an argument, that's sure. Those last must have decided they couldn't take their lugger back from the Navy."

"To shore," screamed Neville. He stood and waved his arms. "To shore!" he yelled again to the barge.

All three – the launch, gig, and barge – continued to row hard for land.

14: Shore Party

A small surf was breaking onto the strand – worse in the center of the beach than elsewhere. Neville had seen the pirate boats come out through it, and made a mental note that they'd had a rough go of it.

"We have to ride the surf in, men! Stay on the back of a wave. No cocked muskets, now. We'll hit the sand hard."

The coxswain of *Superieure's* barge, ahead of Neville's little gig, displayed his inexperience at surf landings. Rather than ride the back of a wave as he'd been instructed, he guided the heavy, twenty-foot boat to a position before a large wave. Its speed increased. When the wave broke behind it, the rudder lost its bite on the water, allowing the boat to slew to larboard. Then the boat dropped heavily when the wave dissipated into the sand. The starboard bow scrubbed hard on the bottom, stopping the boat's momentum which, in turn, threw its cargo of men forward and to their right.

A musket or pistol fired. The following wave capsized the barge, throwing everything into the shallow, albeit warm, water. The men began searching for weapons and struggling to shore. Two, gone limp in the crash, were dragged onto the sand.

"You see," cried Neville. "Go straight in on the back of the wave; not before it as the barge went. No turning, and get the boat out of the water as fast as we can." He could now hear the distant pop-popping of musket fire from shore.

Another of his men from the barge spun around and collapsed. The others began pushing the water-filled launch up on the sand. They turned it parallel to the shore and hid behind it. Someone had the idea to tip the water out of it and then inch it forward, at least until the wounded were shielded from further fire.

Neville's gig landed at the same time as the small launch about a cable to the east of the barge. Both had straightforward landings. Between the two, they discharged another sixteen men onto the strand. They all began running for the cover of the high-tide sand banks.

"Can you see where the pirates are, Mr. Davis?"

"I saw one musket-flash near the house just up from the barge, Sir. There are more than one, but I can't see 'em. Several muskets fired at almost the same time. There's no return fire from the barge, though. I can't imagine they have any dry powder. There goes a man from it, though, running for a rock." A musket fired, but the runner displayed no effect.

"I saw that one," said Davis. "I'll go get him." He ducked low and ran off into some bushes on the landward side of the strand.

"Come on, men," said Neville in a raised voiced, "Follow Mr. Davis." He and the other six crossed the twenty feet from the gig to the bushes without drawing any fire. They settled in a group near the burning house, close enough to feel the heat of the fire. They could hear the shrill screams of more than one woman from someplace farther inland.

"How many could there be?" Neville wondered aloud. "They might've had fifty and five on the lugger. They left six behind to guard it, so there were forty-nine went ashore. Ten came back out in their big boat, which Mr. Skullen put a cannonball through, bless his soul. Eight more we just put to rest on the way in. That's twenty and four less than they had aboard, I'd wager, so there are about thirty of the creatures here in this village. We began with the same, but we saw three down when the barge went all ahoo on landing."

"Good odds, if you ask me," spoke one of his topmen. "They've been drinking hard, I'm sure. Some will probably be in the gutter already, and the rest barely able to point a gun."

"Aye," agreed Neville. "We run for the shelter of the buildings along t'other side of the beach road, and then search out their marksmen."

The gig's men ran, one at a time, across the beach road to the buildings. The last man waved his arm for the launch's crew to follow.

"Four groups of four," ordered Neville. "One group down the beach side of these buildings, the next group down t'other side of them. You last eight go back 'round past the burning house and then divide up and start searching the back streets. Watch out you don't shoot each other."

"Now where has Davis gone? Has anyone seen...?"

A musket fired from the bushes by the strand fifty feet away. The instant result was a man who stepped out from behind a large palm stump another hundred feet off. He slowly pulled out his sword.

"That's Davis, there in the bushes," said Neville. "He's grown bushes for a hat, he has. He told me he never misses, but that man's alive and well." Neville rolled onto his belly and cocked his musket, with every intention of shooting the pirate down before he could charge Davis.

The pirate raised his sword across his body in a good position for a run, then dropped to his knees and fell flat forward onto his face on the gravel of the road, giving not another twitch.

Davis didn't miss after all, did he? thought Neville. His eye caught the motion of four other pirates abandoning their positions in the beach bushes and running into town. The door of a small house opposite them flew open and a man ran out from there, as well. All five disappeared into the sparse commercial district of the town. Several muskets behind him fired. Ten seconds later another three or four muskets were fired behind the strand's buildings.

"They're on a run!" someone yelled.

"Go after them!" screamed Neville. "Catch a couple, if you can, but don't go easy!" He ran down the strand to a point above the barge. There behind a large rock he found the one man who had run up. He handed him his musket and said, "Go chase with the rest of them. They're running."

"Come out from behind, men," he yelled to the barge. Most of the soaked marines charged out immediately, brandishing cutlasses.

"Sergeant Denby... one man was shot from shore. I doubt he'll make it. That one there is just full o' water from our tumble, though he may have a broken rib if the boat landed on him. Private O'Hanion's gone – shot through the head by our own musket what some twit had cocked. The rest of us just have no dry powder."

"Take your cutlass and get on with it, Sergeant," said Neville. "Your men are ahead of you and the pirates are on the run. I'm going to see if the townspeople are in need or if they can help us run these marauders to ground."

Neville checked his men on the sand before running up to join those in battle. O'Hanion was dead; no question. The man who'd been shot by a pirate had a hole through his leg, but he was breathing. Neville decided they had best just leave him for the moment. The man who'd been stove in by the boat complained about both his leg and his ribs, but remained coherent. Neville dragged him higher on the strand. "The tide shouldn't be this high before we get back," he said, "Just lie still."

The first things Neville noticed on crossing the road along the strand were four dead bodies. By his attire, one appeared to be a townsman. The second was the pirate Davis had shot, lying with his face smashed into the gravel. The next two also appeared to be pirates. They were dressed in the ridiculous clothing they often wore. They were dead, or at least bleeding badly.

Neville ran now, looking to join the action. Muskets were being fired straight ahead on this street. *It looks to be the main street of town,* he thought. He saw two more pirates lying at the first intersection of two sand streets. *These would account for the musket shots we heard when the pirates left their posts at the beach. Our men coming along behind the building got 'em.*

The door of a large building ahead of him creaked open, and someone stuck out a broomstick with a white flag on it. Neville dropped to one knee and pulled his pistol.

"Come out. British Navy!" he yelled.

The door opened farther, and a middle-aged man limped out onto a stone sidewalk in front of the door. "There were too many," he said. "Most of us were in the fields. They shot the first two of us they saw just to keep us in line. Not many here have muskets, and I don't think there's a pistol in town."

Neville stood and replaced the pistol in his belt. "Tell your story later, gov. Can you round up your friends and come help us drive them into the hills? Bring clubs or harvesting knives if you've naught else."

"I… yes, yes. They took women to the school, just there," he said, pointing to a low stone building behind some low trees.

"Some might hide there yet, if your men ran past following the buggers."

"Get your men into the school, then. Turn 'em out."

Neville resumed running. He passed a pirate in the gutter in front of some sort of warehouse. *This one looks more likely drunk than dead. He'll be dead when the townspeople get here, though.*

Running past the school, he thought he heard the muffled cry of a woman. He could already hear a growing chorus of yelling behind him, though, so he knew it would be only minutes before the townsmen stormed the place. *It might be better if I am not a witness to what happens,* he thought. *I won't even try to stop them from whatever they might do. Besides, I need to catch my men. I don't need them chasing pirates half way to Kingston.*

The road began to rise a few feet in every hundred as the last of the town's buildings receded behind him. It took a turn to the left behind an outcropping of rock. He joined four marines by the rocks.

"There's a group o' them curs just ahead, Commander," one of the marines offered. "We can't do much more than keep them from running back down the road here, what we've got no muskets. Four of ours went round the left and another six to the right. We should hear something soon."

The words were just out of his mouth when musket fire began very close ahead. "Three shots and four back, if my hearing's good," said the marine.

"Two more," said Neville. "They must all be reloading now." Six shots rang out almost simultaneously, followed by the clash of steel on steel.

"Come on, men," Neville yelled, "they've gone to swordplay." Once around the rock, they could see the skirmish ahead, a hundred yards or so. Four men were in the center of the road going at each other with cutlasses. An additional three pirates could be seen running on down the road. Another musket, fired by a man they couldn't see, dropped one of the fleeing pirates into the dirt.

At the sight of a navy officer and four marines, the sword-fighting pirates, knowing surrender simply meant hanging, took their final desperate slashes at *Superieure's* sailors. Then, they too began running down the road after their compatriots. Neville and his marine were only a few feet away by then. One of the marines removed a twelve-inch knife from his belt, steadied himself, and threw it at the retreating pirates.

To Neville's amazement, the knife stuck firmly in one pirate's right arm. The shock sent him sprawling into some brambles at the side of the road, screaming in pain.

"These will do nicely," said one of the marines who had picked up a pirate musket.

"Yes, they will," said another. "We have three now, and there's another in the road ahead, I think. Can we chase, Commander?"

"Four marines and five sailors, aye. An hour, no more. Then get back here, whether you've done for them or not. Keep a count on how many get away. Townsmen will want to know.

"You five, we're going back to town to see how we can help. Drag the bugger out of the brambles. I see the marine has just took his knife back and left the scum to bleed. Put a cloth 'round his arm and make him walk."

"Hello, Commander. I'm George Dorn of our town council," announced a man who appeared from one of the buildings on the edge of town. "Thank you! We would have been in a sorry state, indeed, in another two or three days, if you hadn't come along."

"Thank Admiral Duckworth at Jamaica Station, my good man. He sent us to find this lot. What is your damage, Mr. Dorn?

"Mr. O'Connell's house is burnt to the ground, as you can see. Our mayor is all but dead. They tortured him for the location of our treasure."

"Treasure? What is it?"

"That's just it, Sir – we haven't any. They cut off a finger, and then put a leather 'round his head and twisted till his eyes almost popped out, but of course he had nothing to tell. They took three women. The schoolmistress has had very rough go of it. I doubt she'll stay here. The other two were not treated properly at all, but you were soon enough to prevent a disaster. Our men found two pirates in the school, and they've been pounded to mush with hammers and rocks."

"Why have you no better defenses?"

"Another raid before this took almost everything. We have no gold or plate, but we had weapons they wanted. They were mostly English, though, and really meant us no harm personally. But these French curs, pfft." He spat on the ground.

The party of marines and sailors who had chased the pirates into the hills hove into view just then, walking down the street toward the beach. The each carried a musket. One man carried two. The man who'd been knifed stumbled along behind at the end of a rope. A local crowd soon gathered behind him.

"You caught some, then, did you, marines?" cried Neville when they were close.

"Aye, Sir. Three at the edge of town and another four who were silly enough to make an ambuscade. They wounded Michaels, here, but not badly." Michaels was walking. He had a bandage around his head.

"Where are they?" Neville asked.

The marine grinned. "We couldn't carry them down from the rocks, Sir. These muskets is heavy enough. Foxes could eat what's left, for all I care."

The crowd cheered.

"You have control, then, I think, Mr. Dorn. We'll leave you these seven muskets for your defense, and some powder. I calculate there are as many as nine pirates still up in the hills."

A gun fired in the harbor. "It's not a musket, Sir; something more. A swivel gun, perhaps," said Framingham

"Signal from *Superieure*, Commander! Something odd's happening!"

Neville ran to the large rock by the strand and climbed on it to see. "Signal, aye," he said. "Mutiny. Ship... secure. What's going on out there? *Revenge* is free of *Superieure* and raising sails. *Superieure* is adrift!"

"No, Sir," said Framingham. "There goes an anchor."

"Get a pole and put something up. Red and white for 'acknowledge'. A bloody shirt might do. There, the man Davis shot. His shirt will do. We can't do much else from here. Why don't they fire on *Revenge*?

"Mr. Dorn, we must go quickly. I'd put an armed guard on at night for a time if I were you. If you write us a list of critical supplies, I can see if Station will send them up. This man's coming with us," he said, referring to the prisoner on the rope. "We'll see what we can learn from him."

"No, he's not," blurted one of the townsmen. The man stepped forward and stuck a harvesting blade though the man's face. Another clubbed him to the ground with a heavy stick.

"It was his wife they took," said Mr. Dorn, holding his hand out to stop Neville's retaliation.

Neville took the rope from the marine who had been leading the pirate. He put it in Dorn's hand.

"Fair enough," said Neville. "His blood's on you.

"To the boats, men. Mr. Framingham, straighten up the barge and see if we can find anything of value in the water."

"Mr. Davis, where did you learn to shoot like that?" Neville asked his sailor on the row out.

"America, Sir, back in 1774. Queen's Rangers. I fell out of them; too old for all the walking, even then. Shooting that musket was just like old times, it was."

15: A Company Divided

Midshipman Foyle heard his commanders words: 'Mr. Foyle, I promise two pints of straight rum to the gunner who blows yon boat out of the water before we get there, and another for the boat on the beach.' He watched for a few seconds as his commander jumped down into his gig. "Oars!" Neville yelled. "Push off. Make way, all! Pull hard lads, we have a town to save!" Commander Burton's departure left Foyle in charge of the ship's defense. He had heard Commander Burton order it, and now he had three things to do at once.

"Did you hear him, Mr. Skullen?"

"I did, Mr. Foyle. You just stand out of my way… No offense. You and you, come wi' me. We've got a cannon to shift." Skullen trotted off to his game with great enthusiasm.

"You men," Foyle ordered, "get aboard the lugger and take control of those few men left standing. Clap them in irons, if you can find some manacles, or tie them tight to their mainmast."

His order slightly lagged the reality of boarding. Twenty or more men were already across. He followed. Seeing several men descending the main companion stair, he suddenly realized his biggest jobs might be to put some organization to searching the vessel for valuables and contraband and keeping his men out of the spirits locker.

"Mr. Church," he called to the carpenter, "I… I have… an un-un-un-unusual request. I have m-m-my short sword, but can you… will you p-p-please bring something for a w-w-weapon and accompany me below? There are no marines ab-ab-ab-aboard, and the situation seems, w-w-well… unstable. We need to r-r-restore order, and to check the captain's c-c-cabin for any useful p-p-papers, charts, orders, or what have y-you."

"Aye, Mr. Foyle. I'll bring a cutlass. Lead on."

Foyle followed the group descending the stair. He heard crashing and slamming forward, followed by cursing about the spirits locker being empty.

"Aft, Mr. Church, to the captain's c-c-c-cabin."

"Aye, Sir."

Below, Foyle drew his short sword and entered the open door of the cabin. Even the master's cabin on a narrow seventy-foot lugger is not large, but it had been luxurious one day in the past. It was no longer: any proper furniture had been removed, save a long trestle table in the center. One man of the boarding party – or Foyle presumed him to be – was digging in a locker to larboard.

The man looked up when Foyle entered. "You, there," Foyle said clearly, "stop your digging and get out." He was relieved to see the man obey orders. He recognized the sailor as part of the ordinary seamen from the starboard foremast crew, but he didn't remember the man's name – if ever he had known it.

The man stared at him for a few seconds, also seeing Mr. Church, and then picked up a musket and pushed past them out of the cabin.

A box in the aft corner held some papers. A quick search gave Foyle to know he would find no Letter of Marque. He took a quick look in a locker on the floor aft.

"Oh! Look at this, Mr. Church. It's the p-p-pirate's booty chest. Now the whole sh-ship knows it's here." There were table pieces of almost worthless pewter as well as a few silver plates, a bit of silver tea service, and all manner of coins form every country that had ships sailing these waters.

"I d-d-don't need to see m-m-more now," he said. "We'll have to p-p-post a guard on this cabin. Let's go up and find a few p-p-p-petty officers to organize things."

Foyle's chest had just risen above deck level when Gunner Skullen fired the chaser at the pirate boats. The surprise and shock wave of it, though not as large as he had endured in the past, thumped Foyle hard. He staggered back a step or two, but Church pushed him back up.

"You're all right," muttered Church. "I've had that happen a time or two." Skullen's gun crew was already aiming the stern chaser for another shot.

"Petty Officers," Foyle yelled, "come to me!" Looking about, he saw only one man walking his way from the bow. "Where are they all?" he wondered; formed as a question to Church.

"There." answered Church, nodding his head toward a knot of a half dozen men gathered around the lugger's tiller, where Mr. Whitmore was talking excitedly in a somber, low voice.

"What can he be...?"

Gunner Skullen's second blast stopped Foyle's sentence. The gun crew raised a cheer. All eyes followed the line of the pointed gun out into the harbor where there were now pirates swimming around their launch. They watched musketeers stand in *Superieure's* barge and fire into them, and then row through the bodies, striking two or three with oars. They didn't stop.

"What's Whitmore up to?" Foyle asked Church.

"Haloo, Mr. Whitmore!" yelled Foyle. "See t-t-to getting those m-m-men in irons. The ship is s-s-secure. Collect the weapons, if you p-p-please."

Whitmore jumped into the ratlines above the main chains are yelled back, "I don't think so, Mr. Foyle."

"This is our chance men, and we'll not get another! Shove that stuttering twit and all his little navy boys back on their ship!

Behind Whitmore, Foyle could see Framingham's overturned barge on the beach and his commander's gig landing. The shock of Whitmore's action and the realization that help would not be coming both hit him at the same time.

"This is our ship now," continued Whitmore. "Get back on your own deck, Mr. Foyle. All the rest of you what ain't with me, you get off, too, real quick-like.

"No you don't, Skullen!" cried Whitmore, noticing the gunner crowbarring the chaser around to point at the lugger.

"Go at 'im, Finn!" yelled Whitmore. Finn, one of the largest men in Skullen's gun crew, ducked low and charged at Skullen like a loose bull at a red flag. His shoulder hit Skullen in the stomach, tossing him neatly overboard. Finn then grabbed a musket from the nearest rack and began moving toward *Revenge.*

Foyle, by now back aboard *Superieure*, used the distraction to run forward. "That's it, Mr. Gains, the swivel gun," he yelled, "Let's give... What are you doing?"

"I'm taking this as my personal toy, Mr. Foyle. I wouldn't use it on me mates. There, it's off the rail, you see, and it ain't so heavy one man can't carry it."

"Carry it there, then," yelled Foyle, slamming his body against Gains and the gun, much as he had just seen Finn do to Skullen. The result was very similar, except this time the man going overboard took the gun with him. With the gun still on top of him for a few seconds, he was driven as deep as twenty-five feet before he got loose of it. His struggle to swim upward was visible to everyone watching through the clear water. The gun landed in a swirl of dust at the bottom of the harbor well before Gains burst through the water's surface, coughing and spluttering.

"One less gun for you, Mr. Whitmore!" yelled Foyle.

"Enough playing at silly buggers, lads!" screamed Whitmore, "Throw 'em back."

A row of mutineers formed on the lugger. They all raised muskets and pointed them toward *Superieure* or toward their shipmates who were obviously not part of their inner circle. "Not the rest of you louts, neither," he yelled at those who had not been immediately motivated by the call to arms. "You can just stay and be good little navy boys!" Finn and another man, both carrying their muskets, pushed their way through onto the lugger. They were not challenged.

"They've all got muskets and a blade in their belts," some landsman on *Superieure* yelled, "And we've got cutlasses."

"Which I give 'em each what I wanted, didn't I, you ninnyhammer," retorted Whitmore. "You think I'm a simpleton? You lot step back polite-like and we'll leave you all standing. You're not such a bad lot of shipmates, just too knuckleheaded to see your opportunities. And you can keep this one."

Three of his men picked up Mr. Sudpen, the dullard who'd made the ship's first complaint, and threw him bodily over the rail onto *Superieure*. "He's too dull to pound pegs."

Superieure's crew stood back against the larboard rail and watched, except for a man who threw Gunner Skullen a line. A man on *Revenge* did the same for Gains at the bow.

"You keep back along the rail. We're sending four men over to cut all your gun lashings on this side so's you don't get a clever idea to shoot at us when we leave." He ran his eyes down the row of landsmen, waisters, and specialists he left behind, and said, "I doubt you lot can't fix 'em fast enough to shoot, anyway – if you even know how. Ha, ha, ha!"

Foyle counted the deserters during the chopping of gun lashings. In the relative quiet, he could also hear the raised tempo of musket fire ashore. Fully seventeen of *Superieure's* complement were deserting.

The four axe-men finished, and they began climbing over the gunwales to leave. Sudpen again tried to join them. He stepped clumsily up on the rail to jump, but was knocked back to sprawl across the deck by a man who sneered, "You can stay here, Thomas. Sorry to leave you, but we can't afford to take idiots with us."

"Cut the grapples, mates, heave the anchor short, and raise the main course."

Whitmore couldn't resist another taunt. "There's a perfectly cromulent reason for this action we take here today," Whitmore began yelling to Foyle and Catchpole, now standing together by the mainmast, "If that redonculous captain of yours had even a bit of brain in 'is 'ed, 'e'd know what it is. You just tell 'im from me we thank 'im for the ride up 'ere to get us a nice fast boatie, and he needn't bother to chase."

"Raise anchor mates; sheet home," were Whitmore's last words.

Superieure, now free of *Revenge*, began to drift shoreward with the breeze. The only anchor down had been the lugger's.

Catchpole, in charge of anything related to sailing, managed through his gulping to yell, "Drop an anchor. I don't care which one, just drop one."

"Who can shoot a musket?" Foyle yelled. Four men stepped out or yelled, "Oi."

"All of you come get a gun, then, and we'll shoot anything you can hit over there." He ran down the companion for the armory.

By the time they had returned topside, *Revenge* was already sixty feet away. She had two sails up and was rapidly gaining speed. So far, there had not been a shot fired.

"Sh-sh-sh-shoot something, Mr. Catchpole," said Foyle, while he began aiming his musket at the departing Whitmore. "Sh-sh-shoot something big! Signal Commander B-B-Burton!"

Foyle fired his musket, followed by his three self-appointed marksmen. There was no visible effect on *Revenge*, but they could hear laughing and yelling. Five or six tiny puffs of smoke were seen at *Revenge's* stern. One musket ball whizzed past Foyle's cheek and another thumped into the main mast.

"But Mr. Foyle," said Catchpole, "You knocked the signal gun overboard."

"A big g-g-gun, then. Oh, here's Mr. Skullen. A larboard g-g-gun, Mr. Skullen. Any one you like, as quickly as ever you c-c-can… any direction."

"Reload your muskets, men. G-g-give it one more try."

Superieure jerked hard at her cable when the anchor set, stopping her voyage toward the beach. The musketeer next to Foyle fell hard against the rail. His musket discharged, sending splinters flying from the tiller just an inch from Catchpole's hand. Catchpole flopped forward onto the deck, motionless.

"What in Heaven's…?"

"You, there," he said to a man nearby, "see to Mr. Catchpole, if you please."

Foyle pulled the signals bag out of its cupboard in the binnacle and began rummaging for the flags he wanted. "This," he said to a man he recognized as an able seaman, "then this, this, and this. Get them to the masthead. Lively, now. Lively."

A larboard gun spoke, leaping back at its lashings and sending a great puff of dust into the sky from the small island. The gunner cursed his aim.

Revenge was moving fast now, leaning far over to the breeze in a full set of sails. The breeze also flattened a large square of red cloth rising to the peak of the mizzen sail.

"You'll b-b-be our lookout for n-now," he said to the man who had raised the flags. "G-G-Go on up to the t-top and call out if they signal b-back from shore."

16: *Shorthanded*

"**I** couldn't p-p-possibly give chase, Commander." Midshipman Foyle began before Neville's gig even handed its painter over to a man in *Superieure's* main chains. "We could, now you're back. There are enough men to…" Foyle hung above him in the shrouds like some jungle ape.

"Please, Mr. Foyle," Neville responded, "what I want to know right now is whether we still have a cook."

"A cook, Sir?"

"Aye, Mister Midshipman, a cook."

"Right here, Commander," said Pickering, grinning at being the first person requested by his commander.

Neville tipped his head back to look at a few puffy clouds drifting slowly westward across a bright blue sky and said, "Thanks be to the Lord."

He turned to Pickering, "What can you fix us all, Cookie? I'm starving, and I'm sure all these good lads are, too; and Mr. Foyle, although he is acting otherwise."

"Burgoo would be quickest," said Pickering.

Everyone in the boats who heard him, as well as everyone on deck, gave an immediate moan. Someone threw a wad of small stuff at him.

"If you can wait a bit longer, gentlemen," Neville yelled to the crowd about him, "I think it's time for the sow to volunteer. What do you say?"

Thence erupted the heartiest cheer Neville had yet heard aboard *Superieure*.

"**I** couldn't p-p-possibly give chase, Commander…" Midshipman Foyle began as before. Burton, Foyle, Johnson, and Framingham were sitting beneath a hastily-erected awning in the quarterdeck area enjoying a short glass of rum. Church and Skullen had been invited for the occasion.

"We couldn't g-g-go without our c-c-c – you, Sir. And our numbers…" Foyle rolled his eyes. "Only seventeen of us s-s-s-still on the deck – after we pulled the good Gunner Skullen out of the w-w-water, that is."

"I thank you for that," Skullen interjected.

"Most of our b-b-best sailors went with you," Foyle continued, "so we had landsmen and most of the w-w-w-w-waisters. We could never have fought the ship, even if we c-c-c-could have caught *Revenge*. Oh, and without M-M-M-Mr. Catchpole, either, to sail her p-p-p-properly."

"You needn't explain it all," Mr. Foyle, "It's perfectly understandable. I admire your pluck, however. No, we've done our job here. We'll return to Station. Now you mention it, where is our Mr. Catchpole? I haven't seen him since we returned."

"He, ahhh... he... Here he c-comes now. You shall hear his story from his own l-lips."

"Excellent. He looks a bit white, though. Before we get to Mr. Catchpole, Mr. Foyle, how is it Mr. Whitmore was the leader?"

"Here, Mr. Catchpole, have a seat and a sip of rum. We're celebrating this evening."

"Thank you, Sir."

"I don't know how he came to be the leader, but there is no question he is, right, Mr. Skullen?"

"No question at all, no. Go on, Mr. Foyle."

"Oh, yes, and he l-l-left a message for you. He used a n-number of very strange words, but the g-g-gist of it is that he had a good reason they d-d-d-deserted, and you would understand."

"Complete rubbish!" Neville blurted. "Why would I understand desertion?"

"Maybe it's a good thing, Commander," offered Framingham. "We've got rid of our bad apples, no doubt of it."

"So we thought when we hanged Wallis and Stiles," said Neville. He sat quiet a moment.

"We can hang Sudpen now, too," said Denby.

"That's a bigger problem for me," said Neville. "From what you say, there is no question of his guilt, but he is apparently so slow that he will go wherever he's pushed. Is it he who is guilty, or merely the man who pushes him? He's killed no one we know of. He may be just as valuable if we push him the way we want him to go..."

"He's in irons, at any rate," said Denby. "We have plenty of time to find out what he knows of Whitmore's plans."

"Sudpen just might tell us everything," Framingham suggested. "Mr. Foyle, here, says they threw him back aboard *Superieure* not once, but twice. He'll be feeling disappointed and mistreated, both."

Pickering himself walked up the stair to the deck just then, and shouted, "Fresh ham!"

"How many men remain, Mr. Johnson?" Neville asked during dinner.

"Only forty and two; might be three more if Denby's marine — the man hit by the lugger's first shot — and them as was injured ashore — all heal."

"So…mmm…twenty and four gone, if we include the two we hanged. I'm not saying you could have gone after them, Mr. Foyle, but now the shore party's back — even allowing for our injured and for several of us who must remain as waisters — cooks and carpenters, and the like — we still have more than enough to sail her," said Neville. "Possibly we could even fight one side, if we give a few waisters some gun training. It worries me to go back to Station and ask for more men, although I suppose we must. The thought of more bad apples scares me more now than before I learned the consequences of it."

"Oh, l-l-look. We have C-C-Catchpole back," said Foyle, snickering.

"Back from what, Mr. Foyle?

"Sick b-b-bay; injury in action, Sir. A m-musket ball stuck the t-t-tiller by his hand."

"And?"

"And he f-f-f-fainted dead away like a lady in a run-run-runaway coach. Ha, ha, ho!"

"Just what is your story, Mr. Catchpole?" Neville asked, suppressing his smile as best he could.

Catchpole glowered at Foyle, saying, "I'll return the favor someday, young man. He could've gone a year without hearing it."

"Well, Sir…" They cajoled Catchpole into explaining the incident, much to the amusement of the officers at dinner.

"We'll try not to surprise you again, Mr. Catchpole," Neville said at the end of the anecdote. "When it comes to interrogation, though, I believe we should go 'round all the men to learn what they knew, if anything. I, personally, would like to know how the secret was so well kept and a band of deserters selected."

"So would I," said Sergeant Denby. "You'll notice there were no marines with them."

Questioning began immediately after the next day's dinner. Sudpen was the first man called to the captain's cabin.

"Where's he going, Mr. Sudpen?" asked Catchpole.

"Wot? Where's 'oo going?

"Whitmore, Mr. Sudpen. Who else would we ask you about?"

"I dunno, who else?"

"Aaargh!" interrupted Neville. "All right, let's start over. Where is Mr. Whitmore going on the lugger?"

"Oh, him. He always said he would take his ship to the Bahamas. He made them islands sound so nice. Little bays to hide in, plenty of water, and rum from every ship that passes from the Caribbean to the Americas. What more could a man want?"

"The Bahamas, then. Anything more specific?"

"The Bahamas ain't in the Specific, no. The Bahamas are in the Atlantic, just north of here, they are. You need to get yourself a chart and look, or you'll never find him."

"What can you tell me about Mr. Wallis, Thomas?"

"Bad man. If you say anything, he will hurt you – good you hanged him. Better."

"And Mr. Stiles?" continued Neville.

"Stiles? You hanged him, too."

"Yes, we did. Did you like him?"

"Stiles was a stupid man, Whitmore says. I never saw Whitmore before you hanged Stiles. After Stiles was gone, it was all about what Whitmore wants. 'Come with Whitmore,' he says; 'you can have whatever you want; rum, women, anything!' But they didn't let me go. They threw me back! They hurt me!"

"I think we're done. Thank you, Mr. Sudpen."

"Who's next?" asked Neville.

"Mr. Henry and two of his mates of the forecourse – Maple and Turnbutter," answered Catchpole.

"Mr. Thrumpit asked me if I ever wanted to be a pirate," said Henry. " 'A life of freedom and luxury', he said."

"I told him: 'No way I wanted my neck stretched. He says, 'They never catch no pirates'. I say, 'You hears it all the time'. He says, 'When's last time you saw a row of men swinging on the gallows at Port Royal?' "

"They hangs 'em in the fort, I says."

" 'Women's talk', he says, and that was the end of it. He never talked to me about it again."

"Same for me," said Maple, "I didn't think more of it."

"Just about the same with me," said Turnbutter, "And together with Wallis, we understood nobody was supposed to say anything about it or we'd have him on us."

"I suspected, I suppose," said Maple, "but I wasn't asking."

"What about Whitmore?" asked Neville.

"We didn't know anything about him. We thought it would be over when you hanged Stiles."

This conversation went about the same for each group they questioned. They returned to Sudpen at the last.

"So, Mr. Sudpen," began Framingham, "We understand you were an important man in Whitmore's little band."

The words obviously appealed to Sudpen; they had made him feel important. It might have been the first time he ever felt important, and Whitmore had played him. "I was his top man," boasted Sudpen. "He told me himself. I still would be if that nasty bugger Williams hadn't knocked me back on here."

"Where's he going, Mr. Sudpen?"

"Williams? He's going straight to…"

"Not Williams, no. Williams will go with Whitmore. Where is Whitmore taking *Revenge*?"

"*Revenge*? Oh, the lugger-boat." He thought for a minute. "The Bahama Islands. In the Atlantic, remember? I told you. He talked about it enough."

"Mmmm, I see. What did you do for Whitmore? Why were you so important?"

Sudpen launched into a long and useless tale of fetching things for Stiles and Whitmore, reminding 'Stile's men' to keep their secrets, passing messages, and the occasional minor damage to the ship's equipment.

Midshipman Framingham, Catchpole, and Neville all soon tired of it, and the inquiry was finished.

"**Y**ou're Commander Burton?" asked Captain John Loring of *Bellerophon* a couple weeks later. He stared at Neville as if he had expected someone larger – or smaller – or something. He didn't stand or offer a seat. "I'll be Commodore of the fleet for the next cruise out. I've heard good things. How's that little ship?"

"Aye, Sir, I am. I'm honored to meet you, Sir. Thank you. She's quick, Sir."

"Excellent. You may need her speed on this next cruise. I understand you've had a few problems, however."

"Aye, Sir, I have, but we have them sorted."

"You think so?" Loring stared straight into Neville's eyes.

"Aye, Sir, I do."

"But you are short on your complement of... seventy, is it?

"Aye, Sir. We have forty-five aboard. We began one short at sixty-nine, had one murdered. Four were killed in line of duty I hanged two, and lost the remaining seventeen to mutiny. I've given a report."

"I've seen it." Loring was quiet for a minute. He must have been deciding what to say, or whether he would say anything at all.

"Look here, Commander," he finally said, "I understand how you came to have such a... problematic collection of men aboard, but it is not within the purview of your Commodore to solve your problem. I will pass word 'round the fleet, however, that you are again looking for men. You must ask them each yourself for assistance, of course. Some may take pity on you. Station can resupply marines, I should think, and a boy or two, and a few landsmen. You shouldn't have such a bad lot off them; you took their worst already, I assume. We're lucky to be rid of them, although I would have preferred a few hangings. You should have plenty of time; we're not scheduled out for a month or more. That's all, Commander – I just wanted to meet you."

"This is a beautiful day, indeed, isn't it, Mr. Framingham?" He and Neville stood in the quarterdeck area in the early morning with their coffee goblets, enjoying a view of Kingston in the cool of morning before the sun dried the dew.

"Aye, Sir. The only thing better I can think of would be looking out at England rather than Jamaica."

"Really, Mr. Framingham? You don't care for Jamaica?"

"It's not so bad really, but it's rather hot for my taste. I have come to feel somewhat at home here, but it's not like England."

"No. What would it be like at home on sixteen October? Short days and growing colder; leaves coming down all over. Time to hunt the fox and pheasant, it is."

"But here we are," said Framingham.

"And good morning to you, Mr. Johnson," they spoke in unison as he walked up to join them.

"This last little training cruise went well, didn't it?" queried Neville, "despite being five men short. This new lot will be suitable, it appears."

"Aye," said Johnson. "There's one might bear watching, but interviewing each one before we took them on was the right thing to do. I don't think Captain Bayntun enjoyed that we sent him two back."

"Let him keep them in line, I say," said Framingham. "Oh, here's Mr. Foyle and Mr. Catchpole. We'll just need a sixth for a good game of whist."

"Denby will be up in a minute, I'm sure," said Neville, "but I don't play at cards much."

"Commander," said Framingham. "There's something we've wanted to say to you."

"Really, gentlemen, I haven't time for another mutiny." Their faces remained serious. "Sorry, a poor jest. Go ahead."

"The last we were out – with Whitmore and them aboard – punishment was hard and often… almost as bad as we've seen on other ships. This last run was as different as we've seen in the Navy. We didn't know your way, Sir, but now we've seen it, we're most pleased, and we want to say we're proud to serve with you."

"Hear him!" said Denby, arriving with his pot of tea.

"Hear, hear!" the group chorused.

The fearless Commander Burton blushed. He said, "There's a boat coming… from *Vanguard*, I think."

"Fetch me… oh, thank you, Mr. Foyle." Foyle, anticipating his request, handed Neville the glass from the mainmast becket.

Neville squinted for a minute. "From *Vanguard*, indeed. It's First Lieutenant Dagleishe. He's up and about early."

"New orders, do you suppose?"

Vanguard's launch soon scraped against *Superieure's* hull. Dagleishe quickly hopped up the few feet from boat gunwale. "Here it is, Commander," he said to Neville.

"What, it can't wait for "Good morning?""

"It is a good morning, you'll see," he said. He straightened himself up, saluted the colours, and thrust an official Navy Office envelope into Neville's hand. "Here."

"What's this, orders?"

"Better, my friend. It's Christmas. Open it."

Neville popped the sealing wax off and withdrew an unfamiliar document. "Again, I must ask, what is this?"

"Your ship belongs to the Navy now, she does," He looked about, and then added, "even if she's a little thing. The Navy decided the prize money and claimed her for our own just yesterday. I was at Station, so I volunteered to carry your paper out."

"This is good news, for sure, but what you're telling me is that I've been doing all this – the mutiny, our sorties and all – on a borrowed ship? Have I been in the Navy, then?"

Joseph grinned. "I've told you my maxim, Neville. You must always be somewhere."

Wither From Here?

Appendix

The Square Sails of a Man-o-War

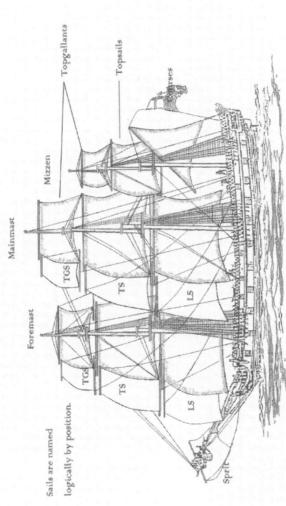

The square sails of a Man-o-War

Sails are named logically by position.

Foremast   Mainmast   Mizzen   Topgallants   Topsails

Sprit

The highest sail (topgallant) on the main mast is the Main Topgallant (Main t'gallant), etc.

This illustration shows studdingsails in use (stuns'ls) – but only on the 'weather' side of the ship, which is the side from which the wind is blowing – in this case into the page. The downwind side of the ship is the 'lee' side. There are no leeward (loo'rd) stuns'ls set in this illustration.

Here the studdingsails are labeled LS = lower stuns'l, TS = topsail stuns'l, and TGS = t'gallant stuns'l. They would be further described by the mast they are on... e.g. TGS on the mainmast = Main t'gallant stuns'l

The Fore-and-Aft Sails of a Man-o-War

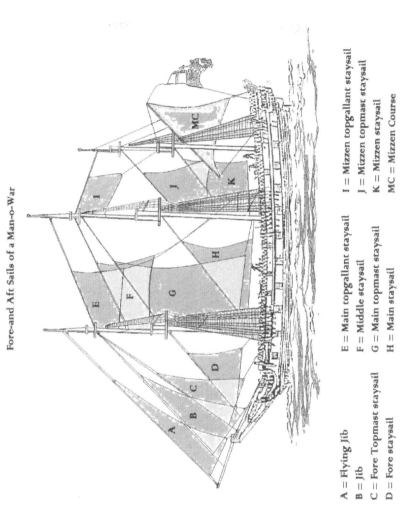

Fore-and Aft Sails of a Man-o-War

A = Flying Jib
B = Jib
C = Fore Topmast staysail
D = Fore staysail

E = Main topgallant staysail
F = Middle staysail
G = Main topmast staysail
H = Main staysail

I = Mizzen topgallant staysail
J = Mizzen topmast staysail
K = Mizzen staysail
MC = Mizzen Course

British Navy Watch System (The bells)

(most commonly used in the Age of Sail)

The Navy day began at noon: Sights of the sun were taken by the Sailing Master and/ or officers and any navigation students (e.g. Midshipmen) using an astrolabe, the Davis quadrant (or the English quadrant), octant or sextant as such were invented in order to ascertain the sun's zenith (locally) and determine latitude. When this was done (cloud cover permitting), the one responsible so informed the Officer of the Watch, who then informed the captain. The captain gave the order to "Make it noon and turn the glass", and the order was transmitted to those who performed various parts of the daily ceremony: the hour-glass was turned, the ship's bell was rung 8 times to indicated the end of the forenoon watch, and the boatswain blew his whistle (pipe) to summon the ship's company to dinner.

One bell was rung for each half hour according to the time-keeping device, which was the hour-glass. Two bells were rung on the hour. At one-thirty p.pm. for example, it is 3 bells for the afternoon watch. A watch is 8 bells long (the two dog-watches in the afternoon, which allowed all the men to be fed more easily and rotated the watches for the next day, shared the full 8 bells until after the Spithead-Nore mutinies, when they each have only 4 each).

The basic schedule, which did change a bit for make-and-mend day (usually Thursday), Sunday for church, and for any other reason the captain might revise it (such as punishment day – often Saturday).

Bells	Time	
8	noon	**Afternoon watch** begins; hands piped to dinner End of Forenoon watch
2	1 p.m.	Dinner is over
4-8	hourly	Log heaved hourly
8	4 p.m.	**First Dog Watch** (2 hours long); off watch piped to supper
2, 4	5, 6 p.m.	**Last Dog Watch** begins at 4 bells; lights out & off watch to sleep
6, 8	7, 8 p.m.	**Evening Watch** begins
2-8	8 - midnight	**First Watch** begins at midnight; Sentinel's cry "all's well" at each bell
2-8	Midnight - 4	**Middle Watch** begins at 4:00 a.m.
2-7	4-7 a.m.	Hammocks piped up at 7:00 a.m.
8	8 a.m.	**Morning Watch**; hands piped to breakfast
2-8	8 a.m. – noon	**Forenoon Watch**

(Note: one more bell than indicated is rung for the half hour following)

British Money – pre-decimal (pre-1971)

Britain used a system of **pounds**, **shillings** and **pence**, with coins representing various quantities of each, as follows:

Pound: not a coin before 1817 (then as the gold 'sovereign') – paper <u>notes</u> in values of 1, 5, 10, etc. were used and represented 240 silver pennies (pence): <u>1 pound</u> (£1) = 20 shillings = 240 pence

1 guinea (coin, originally made from gold of the Guinea coast of Africa) = 21 shillings (1 pound + 1 shilling)

1 crown (coin) = 5 shillings = 1/4 pound

1 half-crown (coin) = 2 shillings and 6 pence (stopped in 1970)

1 florin (a beautiful medieval English silver coin) = 2 shillings

1 shilling (coin) = 12 pence (1s)

1 sixpence (silver coin; later called a **'tanner'**) = 6 pence

1 threepence or threp'ny bit = 3 pence (in some places called "thrupence")

1 penny (a copper coin) = one of the basic units (1d)

1 ha'penny (copper coin) = 1/2 penny (pronounced "hay-p-ny"; stopped in 1969)

1 farthing (lowest value coin, a 'fourth-thing') = 1/4 penny (stopped in 1956)

The Prize Sharing system

Shares are
1/8 to the flag officer
3/8 to the captain (for a private vessel)
1/8 each to commissioned, warrant and petty officers
¼ to the crew

Glossary

aft – The rear or stern of a ship. (the square end, as opposed to the pointy end, called the bow)

abaft – Behind or to the back of, as 'abaft the mainmast'.

beakhead - The small deck in the bow in front of the forecastle where the boom is mounted and where the crew's lavatories were (from whence followed the term 'head' to mean toilet).

bend – A sailing term meaning to attach the sails. When in place and ready to use they are 'bent'.

blocks - Pulleys.

boatswain – 'bo'sun': A highly skilled warrant officer in charge of deck and rigging operations (not sailing) and the supplies for all repairs. He assigns and oversees all deck work. The bo'sun likely had a private cabin and might eat in the gunroom with the commissioned officers. He would only stand watches on a small ship.

bow – The front of a boat or ship. (The 'pointy end', to which the bowsprit is attached.) The center wooden beam up the very front of it, to which hull planks are attached, is the 'stem'.

bower - A ships' two biggest anchors ('best-' and 'small-'), and their cables; carried at the bow.

bloody flux – A disease: dysentery. It is an intestinal disorder that might be caused by numerous infections, resulting in severe diarrhea with blood and mucus in the feces. The disease is accompanied by with fever and abdominal pain.

Blue Peter – A nickname for a signal flag, letter P (Square of blue with a white square inside it). It was flown in harbor to summon all ship's crew aboard for departure.

braces - Those ropes of the 'running rigging' that were used to turn the yards from perpendicular to a ship's keel to slanted – as needed for sailing closer to the wind. Square sails hang on the yards.

brail up – To raise the lower corners of a sail to cause it to stop drawing.

breastwork – (Not a navy thing): a land defense often being not much more than a berm of earth or rocks, possibly with sharpened stakes protruding from it, to give protection to soldiers behind.

broach - This disastrous event for a ship occurs when it turns sidewise to the waves in a storm, whether by human error or magnitude of weather. The next wave that strikes the ship on the side may capsize or flood it causing extreme damage and/or injury, and likely sinking.

cable – The anchor line. – OR - A measure of length = 200 yards.

capstan – A rotating machine with a vertical axle mounted through the deck. Above deck, men insert poles horizontally and walk in a circle to rotate it. Ropes (e.g. anchor cables) attached to it below decks are wound up on it to pull - to raise the anchor or sails to raise spars aloft.

careen – To set a boat on the beach at high tide. When the tide is out its bottom can be worked on.

catted / cathead – When something is tied to the cathead (e.g. – an anchor) it is 'catted'. The catheads are beams that protrude sideways from the sides of the ship at the bow and used for jobs like raising the anchors without them hitting the hull.

Cat-o-nine-tails – 'cat': A whip with many knotted ends used to serve out punishment (ordered by number of lashes). In the navy, it was kept in a red baize bag.

collops – Bacon fried with eggs.

complete (verb) - "To complete" a ship is to finish everything necessary before going to sea; provisions, arms, men, etc., as: '*HMS Swan* was completing at Plymouth'.

commodore – The officer in charge of a small group of ships (an admiral would command an entire fleet) He would almost always be a captain, and might be referred to by either word.

confused seas – A sea state in which wind-driven waves, often from distant storms, approach the ship from different directions simultaneously, usually making the motion very uncomfortable

coxswain – 'cox'n': The man in charge of a small boat: its captain. He orders the men who row or sail it; a petty officer who commands the captain's gig or barge.

crinkum-crankum - Fancy-work.

cracking on - An expression meaning to raise all possible sail and make haste.

farthing – ¼ penny (essentially a 'fourth-thing') – see table on English money.

fathom – A measure normally used for depth, equal to six feet.

fiddle – A raised strip of wood around a surface (e.g. table or desk) that keeps objects from falling off when the ship heels (tilts). A fancy desk might have custom fiddles for items like inkwells.

forecastle - Usually pronounced 'foc's'l'. It is the foreward section of a ship where the crews quarters were. In most larger ships it was a raised area forward, the top of which is the **foredeck**.

fother – To cover a hole in the hull below the waterline by tying a sail or other canvas over it.

'full and by' – A sailing condition when the ship is as close to the wind as she can get and the sails are drawing to the fullest. On a square-rigger this would require "bowlines", which are sheets (ropes) from the forward bottom corner of the sail to a point forward (i.e. toward the bow).

glass – A word used consistently for three very different things: a telescope, the ship's timing device, which was an hour-glass, and the barometer. As to timing, the [hour-] glass was reset to local time, if needed, at noon every day when sunsights were taken and the new navy day began. It was then turned every hour, at which time the log was heaved and, if in soundings – the lead line was employed. A 'half glass' is half an hour.

gratings – Rectangular wooden frames with criss-crossed wood strips that are used as hatch covers. (They must be covered with tarps if weather-proofing is needed.) Tipped up on end they were used as a place to tie a man for punishment: being lashed with a 'cat-o-nine-tails'.

gunwale – the top edge of a boat's side. In ships the hull might extend up above the top deck in the waist and effectively act as a solid railing.

HMS - "His Majesty's Ship". Note that *Swan* (Volume 2) is not referred to thus, because the acronym was not officially used in the British Navy before 1789.

head - (see "beakhead") The toilet on a ship.

heave / hove – To pull or push, as on a line. – OR - a ship can 'heave to', meaning adjust sails and rudder in a manner that causes to ship to stop forward motion and lie quietly in rough water. Hove is past tense, as 'the ship is hove to.' Also, come into view, as 'the man hove into view'.

holystone – A lump of soft sandstone used to scrub decks to ensure the hard oak is smooth with no splinters. The deck is then sluiced with seawater, resulting in an almost whitewashed appearance.

idler – A sailor who always works the "day watch". He would normally not stand night watch –e.g. Cook, carpenter, the boatswain and purser, sail maker and cooper and their mates.

Jonas – A person who brings bad luck aboard a superstitious ship.

hounds – Protrusions high on a mast onto which blocks are hung for the halyards used to raise the yards.

larboard – The left side of a ship, opposite of 'starboard'; (now replaced by the term 'port').

lay aft – A command meaning: "Go to the back of the ship," or "Go find the captain on the quarterdeck or in his cabin" or "Go find the officer of the watch," or similar.

league – 3 statute miles (as opposed to the much shorter distance of a cable, about 200 yards).

lead – (or lead-line): A short lead cylinder into the bottom of which a lump of tallow was set. It is affixed to the end of a line knotted at fathoms and tossed over the side (heaved) to measure depth. The tallow picks up evidence of the bottom – shell, sand, pebbles, etc. as an aid to knowing where the ship is. Two different lengths of line were used: one of about 25 fathoms for shallow areas (in soundings) and one of about 100 fathoms for deeper.

lugger – A smaller ship equipped with lug sails. Lug sails are set on booms that are not symmetrical to the mast and may be turned and tightened in a manner that allows these built-for-speed boats to outrun and out-point any square-rigger. Not surprisingly, they were popular with pirates.

mizzen – The aft-most (rearmost) mast in a sailing ship, and its sails (e.g. Mizzen course)

money system, English – see appendix

ordinary – In addition to its normal meaning, a ship 'in ordinary' is out of service; "mothballed". Also, a rating (rank) of seaman which is below 'able seaman' but above 'landsman' or 'waister'

poop – The upper aft deck of a ship under / beneath the mizzen sails.

priddy – To organize and clean or shine up, as in "priddy the decks".

pusser – The spoken version of the warrant officer's title "Purser". This man is the ships' accountant and normally responsible for purchasing supplies. (See also – "slops").

reave – To lace a rope though pulleys for whatever its function.

sheet / sheet home – Lines (ropes) to the bottom corners of a sail to control it / Sail pulled fully tight & cleated (or belayed).

shilling – A coin of old English money = 12 pennies, or pence. (See English money table)

shot garland – a tube of canvass hung by each cannon to hold its ammunition (cannon balls)

skylarking – The game of "follow me if you can" as played by the young boys aboard tall-rigged ships. They would fearlessly climb and swing from rope to rope & mast to mast.

slime draught – medical term possibly peculiar to the navy at the time: some undefined potion to help the patient with sleep or stool softening

slops – (i.e. "The pusser's slops"): Normally the term referred to ready-made clothes that were sold by the pusser to the ship's sailors, but could include other supplies such as soap or tobacco, but not alcohol. From the older English term sloppes, meaning trousers.

smoke it – An expression meaning to discover a ruse or to understand.

soundings – Depth measurements. A ship is "in soundings" if it is shallow enough that the depth can be measured (usually with the short lead line).

spar – Any of the wooden components of the rigging: masts & booms.

speak – To enable the captains of ships at sea to converse via speaking trumpets, each ship would let its sails loose to stop and "speak" the other. They did not say 'speak to', just 'speak'.

splice – A place where rope is joined to itself to repair it, extend it, or make a loop.

splice the main brace – Although this expression literally means to repair the rope used to rotate the main yard, its true meaning is to reward the entire crew by serving out an extra tot of rum.

starter / to start – A short piece of rope with a knotted end (makeshift whip) or a riding crop used to jolt a man into action. On many ships, used very frequently by the petty officers.

stem – See 'bow'. Front vertical beam of the hull (Leading to the modern expression 'stem to stern').

stern – The aft (back) end of a boat.

starboard – The right side of a ship (facing forward). The opposite of 'larboard' (now 'port').

stroke oar – A person, not a thing: the oarsman in a small boat who controls the pace of rowing; the little boat's 'captain'.

stuns'l – Spoken form of **studdingsails**. (See sail illustration.)

supernumerary – An unofficial extra; a passenger, like a lieutenant being carried to his ship.

taffrail – The stern rail of the stern-most deck (the poop deck or quarterdeck, depending on the ship's construction).

top hamper – The standing rigging & spars above the primary masts: topmasts and above.

truck – The very top of a mast, often being a decoration such as a painted ball above a block (pulley) that could be used to raise signal flags.

van – The front group of a line of ships or convoy, followed by the 'center' and the 'rear'.

waist – The center (top deck) of a ship; the area of deck between the quarterdeck and forecastle.

waisters – Men who normally work in the waist at unskilled jobs; mostly hauling on the lines – sheets, halyards, braces, etc. Usually landsmen; untrained workers.

weather gage – In fighting sailing ships, the advantageous position of being upwind, from which the one with the weather gage can fall down on his enemy in any direction he chooses.

yards (yardarms) – Horizontal spars of a square-rigger's rigging. They are attached to the masts with hoops that permit them to be rotated and raised or lowered for positioning the sails. The sails hang on the yards and are reefed or furled onto them.

Printed in Great Britain
by Amazon